Praise for the Midnight Breed series by LARA ADRIAN

BOUND TO DARKNESS

"While most series would have ended or run out of steam, the Midnight Breed series seems to have picked up steam. Lara Adrian has managed to keep the series fresh by adding new characters . . . without having to say goodbye to the original ones that made the series so popular to begin with. Bound to Darkness has all the passion, danger and unique appeal of the original ten books but also stands on its own as a turning point in the entire series with new pieces to a larger puzzle, new friends and old enemies."

—*Adria's Romance Reviews*

"Lara Adrian always manages to write great love stories, not only emotional but action packed. I love every aspect of (Bound to Darkness). I also enjoyed how we get a glimpse into the life of the other characters we have come to love. There is always something sexy and erotic in all of Adrian's books, making her one of my top 5 paranormal authors."

—*Reading Diva*

CRAVE THE NIGHT

"Nothing beats good writing and that is what ultimately makes Lara Adrian stand out amongst her peers.... Crave the Night is stunning in its flawless execution. Lara Adrian has the rare ability to lure readers right into her books, taking them on a ride they will never forget."

—*Under the Covers*

"...Steamy and intense. This installment is sure to delight established fans and will also be accessible to new readers."

—*Publishers Weekly*

Praise for LARA ADRIAN

"Adrian has a gift for drawing her readers deeper and deeper into the amazing world she creates."

—Fresh Fiction

"With an Adrian novel, readers are assured of plenty of dangerous thrills and passionate chills."

—RT Book Reviews

"Nothing beats good writing and that is what ultimately makes Lara Adrian stand out amongst her peers . . . Adrian doesn't hold back with the intensity or the passion."

—Under the Covers

"Adrian has a style of writing that creates these worlds that are so realistic and believable . . . the characters are so rich and layered . . . the love stories are captivating and often gut-wrenching . . . edge of your seat stuff!"

—Scandalicious Book Reviews

"Adrian compels readers to get hooked on her storylines."

—Romance Reviews Today

Praise for Lara Adrian's books

"Adrian's strikingly original Midnight Breed series delivers an abundance of nail-biting suspenseful chills, red-hot sexy thrills, an intricately built world, and realistically complicated and conflicted protagonists, whose happily-ever-after ending proves to be all the sweeter after what they endure to get there."

—Booklist (starred review)

"(The Midnight Breed is) a well-written, action-packed series that is just getting better with age."

—Fiction Vixen

Look for these titles in the *New York Times*
and #1 international bestselling

Midnight Breed series

. . . and more to come!

Hunter Legacy Series

Born of Darkness
Hour of Darkness *(forthcoming)*

Other books by Lara Adrian

Contemporary Romance

100 Series
For 100 Days
For 100 Nights
For 100 Reasons

Historical Romance

Dragon Chalice Series
Heart of the Hunter
Heart of the Flame
Heart of the Dove

Warrior Trilogy
White Lion's Lady
Black Lion's Bride
Lady of Valor

Lord of Vengeance

BORN OF DARKNESS

A Hunter Legacy Novel

NEW YORK TIMES BESTSELLING AUTHOR

LARA ADRIAN

ISBN: 1939193222
ISBN-13: 978-1939193223

BORN OF DARKNESS
© 2018 by Lara Adrian, LLC
Cover design © 2017 by CrocoDesigns

www.LaraAdrian.com

Available in ebook and trade paperback. Unabridged audiobook edition forthcoming.

BORN OF DARKNESS

CHAPTER 1

The Mojave Desert stretched in endless directions under the inky night sky. This was no-man's land, nothing but acres of bleak terrain bristling with forbidding vegetation and all manner of sharp-toothed nocturnal predators who prowled the dark, searching for prey.

As dangerous as the Mojave's wild inhabitants were, there was no hunter more lethal than the Breed male currently speeding along the empty ribbon of pavement behind the wheel of an ancient Chevy pickup truck.

Tonight, though, Asher hadn't gone out to hunt for himself. He'd left the old ranch some thirty-odd miles out in the desert on a mission to pick up animal feed and household supplies. Not his favorite thing to do, making the trek into civilization at the Nevada state line, but it was an obligation he'd eventually taken on as a favor to the aged human who'd given him shelter a decade and a half ago. Ned Freeman had accepted him with few questions asked and no apparent fear or disdain for who—and what—Asher was, or where he'd come from before ending up on the old man's parcel of desert land.

Since Ned's passing last year, the modest homestead and its assortment of animals had no one else to look after them, so Asher had stayed. And why not? He didn't have anywhere pressing to be. No one waiting for him somewhere else. As a laboratory-spawned assassin, he'd been born and raised for a solitary life. It was all he knew or wanted, even now.

Driving Ned's truck along the uneven, winding road that cut a path down the middle of the Mojave Preserve as far as the eye could see, Asher took cold comfort in the vast emptiness of the land that had become his home. The two-hour errand that began around eight tonight had turned into five after the truck blew a tire on the way out. The old spare Ned had stowed behind the seats in the cab wasn't in much better shape, he had discovered, which had meant hoofing his ass to the 24-hour gas station at the highway for a patch and some air.

It was a relief to be heading back to the ranch after hours among the crush and noise of humankind. People made him twitchy, and not only because the sight of him put most mortals on edge. At six-foot-six, weighing two-hundred-seventy pounds on a lean day, and most of his skin marked with tattoo-like *dermaglyphs* that announced him as one of the purest of the Breed, he didn't exactly blend in.

It had been twenty years since the Breed was outed to the humans sharing this planet with them, but relations were still tenuous at best. Fortunately, those problems belonged to others among his kind. Asher was glad to leave the political fire-fighting and heroics to the warriors of the Order and their commanders stationed in major cities around the world. As for himself? He'd done enough killing, and he had never been anything close to a hero.

Settled back in the driver's seat with the window rolled down to let in the cool night air, he stared ahead at the narrow, pot-holed stretch of asphalt illuminated by the dim yellow headlights of the rumbling pickup. A coyote howled off in the distance, a song that was quickly picked up by others who joined in a haunting chorus.

Asher respected these hunters. He'd had to kill one when multiple attempts to warn it off Ned's chickens had failed, but he'd taken no pleasure in it. Not that killing was ever a pleasure.

Do your duty, boy.

The low, menacing command slithered through his mind. His old Master's voice, the Breed madman who had created Asher and scores of others like him in his lab. On a snarl, Asher snuffed the reminder of Dragos and his hellish Hunter program. Reaching for the knob on the truck's old radio he cranked up the only station it got without static to full blast.

No point in traveling down memory lane. His was nothing but a field of landmines waiting to blow. Instead, he let the noise of a morose country song drown out the equally unpleasant noise in his head while he focused on the road in front of him.

He was only fifteen minutes from the ranch when his headlights sparked a glint in the distance roughly a mile up the road. A sleek black luxury sedan, pulled off the pavement about fifty yards onto the hard-packed sand of the desert.

Asher's nostrils flared as a sense of unrest rolled over him. Not many people had business this far off I-15, and nothing good tended to result when they ventured out into that bramble-choked sand cemetery. This deep into the darkened desert, and at this late hour, you either stopped here deliberately or under duress.

Over time, he'd seen enough of both to know.

His thoughts flashed to a night some twelve years ago, when he'd stumbled across a fellow Breed male—a former Hunter, like him—in this remote part of the desert. The male's name was Scythe, and he'd dragged himself out to the Mojave to die in the sun after losing a woman he loved and her young son. It was Ned who'd insisted they bring Scythe back to the ranch and help him heal if they could. But it was Asher who'd ultimately refused to let the other male give up. He'd kicked Scythe's ass through weeks of recuperation, until his Hunter brother was finally well enough to leave.

Not that one good deed could ever make up for all the wrong Asher had done in his life. Wouldn't even make a dent, in fact. But he was glad that Scythe had lived through it and although they hadn't kept in touch much, Asher had heard the male had since taken a Breedmate and was living a good life in Italy somewhere.

He had a feeling whatever was going on near the parked black sedan wasn't going to end nearly as well.

Not his business.

Not his problem, either.

Asher scowled and turned off the music, silencing the raspy-voiced crooner who was lamenting about the woman he didn't know how badly he wanted until she was gone. Almost against his own will, his foot eased off the gas pedal as he studied the large car up ahead.

It looked empty, though for how long he couldn't be sure. No visible tire issues, no scent of smoke or other outward signs of vehicle trouble. Which meant the real trouble was taking place somewhere among the spindly Joshua trees and cactus patches in the desert off to the right.

The old truck's headlights were dim as it was, but Asher doused them completely and rolled to a quiet stop several yards behind the sedan. He killed the engine and shoved open the rusted-out door.

The instant his boots touched the ground he knew with cold certainty that something was wrong.

It was quiet. Unnaturally quiet. No bugs scuttling over the sand, no scorpions clicking over rocks, no bat's wings beating heavy in the night.

He tipped his head back and scented the air.

People.

Three men, two apparently bathed in competing, cloying colognes, the other reeking from a recent meal laden with garlic. By the stench of it, the guy must have enjoyed a large garlic pizza with garlic crust, chased with a garlic smoothie.

Voices sounded in the distance, bulky shapes moving against the black silhouettes of the scrubby trees and spiked vegetation. The trio of olfactory offenders were shoving another person ahead of them in the dark. The sound of something hard and metallic connecting with the soft flesh and bone of a skull was punctuated by a sharp, pained yelp and the abrupt shuffle of feet stumbling and a body going down on the sand.

"Get up!" The barked command was low, but reached Asher's ears like a gunshot.

Another voice answered, this one pitched several octaves higher and talking fast, the words indiscernible even to his heightened hearing. But he didn't need to hear what was being said. The anxiety pulsing in the night air was unmistakable. As was the menace of the three men who had no idea they weren't the only killers in the immediate area.

"You heard him. Get the fuck on your feet and keep moving," ordered the second man, his garlic breath wafting on the light breeze along with his sadistic chuckle. "Unless you want us to plant your skinny ass right here. The boss don't care how this goes down, only that you never come back."

The soft cry came again, followed by a thready plea for mercy that made Asher's jaw clench.

Fuck.

Old memories roared up on him like a black wave, too swift and powerful for him to hold at bay. A chorus of similar begging cries filled his ears, his senses overwhelmed by the vivid, merciless battering of all the sins he'd witnessed in his past.

And those he had perpetrated.

Unwanted reminders of what he once was were bad enough, but teamed with his unique Breed ability to experience anyone else's painful memories in full sensory detail and total recall with the briefest touch made Asher's preference for solitude a necessity as much as it was a way of life.

What he damned well didn't need was to get involved with whatever was going on between Garlic Breath and his heavily perfumed partners and the scrawny teen who'd evidently irritated someone enough to order these men to drag the kid out here to certain death.

But that didn't keep Asher's feet from moving beneath him, stalking straight toward the trouble.

"Problem, gentlemen?"

"What the fuck!" One of the Cheap Cologne brothers swiveled around on his polished shoes, his dark suit jacket flapping open to reveal the empty holster strapped across his chest. The gun he was holding had bright red blood on it from when he'd evidently pistol-whipped the dark-haired kid in the oversized hoodie and loose jeans. Now the thug didn't seem so tough. His weapon wobbled in his hand as his gaze lifted, then lifted some more, to meet Asher's narrowed glare. "Where the hell did you come fr—"

The blurt died in the back of his gaping mouth when he looked at Asher—really looked at him—taking note of the unearthly glow of his irises and the sharp points of his fangs, which had erupted from his gums in response to the fury now streaking through his veins.

"Oh, shit." The goon staggered back on his heels, dropping his weapon on a choked scream. He took off at a dead run, scrambling blindly into the desert while his patchouli-drenched comrade made a fast break for the vehicle. Asher barely glanced up to follow either human's retreating form. The vapor trail they left in their wake was like an unseen tether that would lead him to both of the men no matter how fast or far they tried to run.

Garlic Breath wasn't as smart as his companions. "Fucking bloodsucker," he snarled.

He had one hand on the kid's small shoulder, possibly the only thing keeping the limp and beaten youth upright. The kid's head drooped low, a face with delicate Asian features all but concealed by longish, blood-matted hair.

Garlic Breath shoved his silent captive to the ground with one hand, his attention—and his weapon—fixed on Asher now. The semiautomatic pistol clutched in his ham-sized fist didn't shake at all. "Eat lead, you Breed asshole!"

On a roar, he pulled the trigger in rapid fire, three close-range shots aimed at Asher's chest. All but the first one missed. And while that single round to the right of Asher's sternum wouldn't slow him down, much less kill him, it did piss him off.

Before Garlic Breath could squeeze off the rest of his magazine, Asher reached out and crushed the barrel of the gun as if it were made of foil.

"You were saying?"

Shocked eyes went wide, staring up into Asher's bleak face. The goon couldn't answer even if he tried. Asher had the man's throat in his fist. He crushed the fragile windpipe with one idle flex of his fingers. On a garlic-soaked gurgle, the human exhaled for the last time before his limp body fell to the desert floor like the rubbish it was.

Asher turned an assessing eye on the youth who lay prone and eerily still in the nearby bramble. He resisted the impulse to reach out and feel for a heartbeat, instead listening to the quiet, shallow breaths and watching as the slender spine and rib cage moved nearly imperceptibly beneath the baggy sweatshirt.

The kid was alive. At least that counted for something.

Meanwhile, he had two other problems to contend with.

Calmly, without a speck of feeling, he retrieved the bloodied pistol from the sand where Cheap Cologne Number One had dropped it and fired a single shot into the darkened desert. The gunfire echoed, then the fleeing coward hit the ground several yards away, dead on his feet.

Asher turned to find the last of the three men at the shoulder of the road, scrambling to get inside the black sedan. Another bullet could have easily stopped him, too, but Asher's former line of work balked at such crude methods.

He told himself it was that cold part of him that propelled him into motion, and not the gut-kick he'd felt when he heard the battered, defenseless kid pleading for mercy that was never going to come.

"Where you think you're going?"

Asher's deep, unfazed voice made the last of the cowards jump so hard it might have been mistaken for an epileptic convulsion. Trapped between the opened driver's side door and Asher's massive presence now, Cheap Cologne Number Two pivoted clumsily, hands held up in front of him.

"Oh, God! Wait a second, all right? Wait!" The man spoke in a rush, eyes darting as he edged further into the car, as if some instinctive part of him that couldn't accept his imminent demise held out hopes of making it behind the wheel before Asher ended him.

Cute.

The thug licked his fleshy lips, sweat sheening his oily brow as he seemed to consider his few, and dwindling, options.

"Look, I don't want any trouble from you, uh... sir. I just wanna be on my way back to Vegas and outta your hair." He tried to smile, but his lips didn't seem to be communicating with his brain. His mouth trembled and his big teeth started to chatter. "Please... you gotta let me go. I swear, you won't ever see me again after tonight."

Asher had no doubt about that. Briefly, he considered letting the coward continue to bargain and plead. Not for his own enjoyment, but so he could find out who these three fuck-knuckles worked for. But that was a slippery slope, one he didn't want to slide down. Didn't matter who these dead men worked for, or what the kid might have done to warrant such a cruel demise.

No, once he dealt with the last of this garbage, he'd find out where the kid belonged and ensure he got there safely. After that, it would be up to the kid to take care of his own neck. Asher would cocoon himself back at the ranch with his work and the animals and have a clear conscience. Clear being a relative term.

Regardless, there was no need to dig any deeper or insinuate himself any further into this situation than he already had.

But Cheap Cologne kept talking. "Okay, okay... I think I get it now. This is your turf and we're trespassing out here. Right, big fella? So, how can I fix this? You want cash? I can get you cash."

"I don't want your money."

The growled reply made the human's face blanch. His hand crept up near his throat, where his Adam's apple bobbed on his hard swallow.

"I don't want your blood, either."

Relief escaped the human on a gusting breath. He glanced over his shoulder, back toward the moonlit desert, then he said something really stupid. "You want the girl?"

Asher scowled, only now realizing the obvious. "The kid is a female?"

He nodded. "She's yours, if you want her. I won't tell a soul. Just let me go, and you can do whatever you want with the bitch." A note of confidence stole over the human's face. He even managed to smile. "Take her. Then you and I can just... forget this."

Asher grunted, far from amused. "I never forget."

With lightning speed, he thrust his hands out and twisted the man's head until the spinal column snapped in two. With the corpse crumbled to the pavement, Asher walked around to the back of the sedan and took stock of his surroundings.

Three dead bodies and an unconscious young female in need of medical care.

Just fucking perfect.

To think a blown tire had been his biggest headache when he set out earlier tonight.

He'd been in the area for about fifteen years and managed to keep a low profile. Though if by chance law enforcement decided to roll through this section of desert before the coyotes and vultures got to the three dead men, he knew he'd be getting a visit. Just because no one bothered him didn't mean folks were unaware of his presence. Ned's ranch was one of only a handful of homesteads between Cima and Kelso, and while there were plenty of Breed living in Las Vegas proper, he would be first on the list of suspects due to proximity alone.

He feared no man, but the thought of being caged or collared, or having to kill those sworn to protect and serve didn't sit well with him. Especially when he'd done them a favor by eliminating some of the riffraff.

With one last glance toward the small form still lying on the sand where she collapsed a short while ago, Asher popped the trunk with a mental command and cursed when his suspicions were confirmed. There beside the spare tire and jack sat two rusty shovels, a tarp, and some electrical tape.

Grimly, he grasped one of the shovels and stalked back into the sand and bramble, figuring he'd check on the kid one more time before getting busy digging a grave for her would-be murderers.

When he reached the spot where the girl had fallen, Asher stopped in his tracks and blew out a low curse.

"What the hell?"

She was gone.

CHAPTER 2

Naomi stumbled more than ran, her feet moving so sluggishly she wondered if someone had tied the laces of her Vans together when she wasn't looking.

But it wasn't her shoes slowing her down. It was her head.

Damn, it hurt.

She'd spent the better part of her night being manhandled by those Vegas gangsters. Her skull had already been ringing from what she was sure was a concussion following the initial blow she'd sustained when they'd stuffed her in the trunk back at Casino Moda.

Now, her left temple was pounding like a drum, her senses foggy after the pistol-whipping that had been the crap icing on an already shitty predicament.

At first, when Leo Slater's henchmen had confronted her on the elevator at the casino, she'd been pissed at herself for getting caught, but it had never occurred to her that she wouldn't survive the night. Shocking how quickly things had escalated. Even when they took her straight down to the basement and out through the secret underground entrance to the garage, she was confident she'd squeak through somehow. But then Gordo, the big guy with the noxious breath, plowed his fist into her forehead and it was lights out.

She woke up as they were hauling her out of the trunk in the middle of the desert under a black sky. Not good.

But even then, she hadn't given up on herself. She was skilled at getting out of tight spaces and dangerous fixes. Hell, she'd survived so much in her twenty-six years that nine lives wouldn't have cut it. She was sure she'd been born with a dozen-plus. It was only the sight of the gangsters' guns and the tomblike silence of the Mojave's back forty that made her worry that her streak of seemingly endless luck had finally run out.

She'd always been wired for fight over flight, but she clued in pretty quick that her only hope of escape was to fake meekness and lull the three idiots into a sense of complacency as they marched her out onto the sand. All she had to do was play her role and bide her time until she had a chance to make a break on foot. It had been a good plan—her only plan, really—until Gordo's buddy got impatient and smashed the butt of his Beretta against her cheek.

The last thing she remembered was dropping to the ground and pleading for them to spare her. Some of that had been part of her game, but as her vision had begun to fill with stars and her skull became thick with cotton, she realized a moment of true fear.

Odds were damned good she was about to die.

Then *he* showed up.

Not some white knight riding in to save her, but a Breed male. Big. Grim. Lethal.

Possibly the only thing worse than eluding certain death at the hands of Slater's henchmen was the fact that she'd been spared by an even bigger threat to her existence.

She wasn't sure why the immense vampire had come to her rescue, but she wasn't about to stick around and find out. Whatever his reasons, she wasn't keen on offering up her carotid in payment.

Not to mention anything else the snarling immortal might have in mind.

So, she was back to Plan A.

Run and hide, then figure out a way to get back to Las Vegas in one piece.

If only her legs were on board with that plan. Every step over the hard, uneven sand seemed to require Herculean effort, like trudging through molasses. The night was as dark as pitch, but she was slowed even more by the fogging of her vision and the incessant drumbeat inside her battered skull. Nausea rolled over her, making her stagger.

"Suck it up, buttercup," she berated herself under her breath. "You've gotten through worse shit than this. Just keep moving. Keep pushing."

Buoyed by the self-directed pep talk, she put her head down and took another few steps… only to run into a massive wall that seemed to materialize out of the cool night air.

Except this wall was warm. Hot, even. And constructed of muscled flesh and immovable, solid strength. And this wall smelled good too. Dark spices mixed with clean soap and something less easy to define. She breathed the scent in and moaned in reflex at the vast improvement over anything else she'd been inhaling all night.

"There's no need to run." The deep voice jolted her mind back to cold reality.

Holy shit!

She leapt back, then pivoted around and bolted in the opposite direction with everything she was worth.

But there he was in front of her again, blocking any hope of escape.

She drew up short, huffing and sagging, on the verge of passing out.

"I said stop running, girl."

"Fuck you!"

She tried to dodge him, but his big body was faster. Unearthly so. "You realize you're only wasting what little energy you have left, don't you?"

Was he taunting her, or just stating the sad facts? Either way, she didn't like it.

She glanced up, forced to tilt her head so high in order to see his scowling face that the hood of her sweatshirt jacket fell back off her head.

Immediately, she wished she hadn't looked. It wasn't that he was ugly, as much as she wanted to pretend he was. Not quite handsome, but arrestingly masculine. Compelling on a primal level that made even her contused senses respond with unwanted appreciation.

His face was rugged and shadowed beneath the shaggy brown waves of his overgrown hair, as though Heaven's sculptor had taken a rough-hewn block of stone and chiseled away until he was almost done and then stopped. Hard planes, sharp angles, square chin.

She couldn't tell the color of the eyes that scrutinized her from below the chestnut slashes of his brows. Banked embers lit his irises, their heated glow leaving no question that he was something *other*.

As if the sharp, pearly white tips of his fangs weren't enough to remind her what she was dealing with here.

A cold, emotionless killer.

She'd seen him in action as she'd played possum and watched from under her lowered lashes while he dispatched Gordo and the other two thugs. He was ruthless. His methods swift and brutal, without hesitation. She'd made it a point to stay as far away from his kind as possible, but every species since Earth's creation had serious menaces like him. The kind of guy no one wanted to run into in a dark alley because you knew only one person was coming out and odds were it wouldn't be you.

And now, here she was, defenseless and alone with this enormous Breed male in the middle of the Mojave, the unmarked burial ground for countless hookers, runaways, and card cheats. Nowhere to run and no one to hear her screams, even if she could muster the juice to attempt either one.

She glanced up at him again, trying to judge his intentions. The rough-hewn face staring down at her was unreadable, but there was conflict in his eyes. As if standing there with her was the dead last place he wanted to be too.

"You're bleeding," she pointed out, her gaze flicking to his chest. "Gordo shot you."

He shrugged. "It's nothing. I am Breed. It will heal in a few hours."

"I know what you are."

She didn't mean for it to come out sounding like an accusation, but it was too late to call it back. To be fair, she hadn't met a man of any stripe, mortal or otherwise, that she could truly trust in all her twenty-six years. Well, except Michael. And he hardly counted because he'd been more like a brother to her since they were both orphaned kids running loose on the streets.

Shit. *Michael.*

He must be worried sick about her.

By now, her phone was probably blowing up with calls and messages from her best friend asking for her status. Not that she could answer even if she wanted to. Her phone was buried in a dumpster back at Moda, tossed there along with the fake student ID Leo Slater's hired help had taken from her in the moments before they stuffed her into trunk of the sedan.

"What's your name, girl?"

"Zoe," she replied, letting the lie fall off her tongue as easily as it had when the trio of goons came to escort her away from the casino floor. She had scores of AKAs, so many it was sometimes difficult to remember her true given name. The one her mother, Aiko, had given her on the day she was born. The one she hadn't heard spoken since she was eight years old.

Her unlikely savior grunted, studying her in unsettling silence for a long moment. "You don't seem like a stupid child, Zoe," he remarked. "So, what kind of trouble were you in with men like those three and their boss?"

She swallowed, trying to decide what would serve her best with this dangerous man who seemed to have fallen for her teenager disguise as readily as her original captors had. But this Breed male was no steakhead like Gordo and Company. His shrewd, glittering gaze was fixed unblinking on her, and she felt with a cold certainty in her marrow that he would know if she tried to feed him any more lies.

"I tried to steal something from them tonight. From a casino."

He grunted. "Money?"

She nodded, wincing at the resulting pain that small movement caused. "Yeah, I took a little bit of money from a slot machine that went on the fritz. They caught me before I could make it out the door with it."

His square chin lifted, then he gave a faint shake of his head. "Maybe you are stupid. Greed and bad choices are two of the main reasons people end up out here in the middle of the night."

She had no doubt he was right. And although she was giving him a small helping of honesty, she saw no reason to explain that the "little bit of money" she attempted to steal tonight was in the neighborhood of two grand, nor that the fact she'd even gotten close to that sizable amount of cash was because she'd managed to finesse one of the machines in a way only she could, then bribed another player a hundred bucks to collect her winnings for her and hand them over.

Instead of the gray-haired old lady from Kansas meeting her at the elevator with her payout as agreed, Naomi had been intercepted by Moda security.

She refused to call her motivation greed, but she supposed she had to cop to the fact that it had been a poor decision to take such a big risk. From here on out, she wouldn't rely on go-betweens when it came to collecting her takes at Slater's casino. She'd have to start getting more creative.

She rubbed absently at her wrists as she tried to think clearly.

Everything hurt. It had been a long day and an even longer night. Her brain was scrambled and she just wanted to go home, climb into her bed and lie down for an hour or ten. Even though some dim logic reminded her that a long sleep was just about the worst thing she could do for a concussion, she was so exhausted it was all she could do to remain upright. If she didn't get out of this desert soon and back on the road to Vegas, she was liable to collapse right where she stood.

With her brain fogging over and her legs growing weaker underneath her by the second, her capacity for clever plans and daring moves was fading fast. Along with her options. She had to rule out her original plan to run and seek shelter until she could hoof it or hitch her way back to the interstate. In her current condition, she'd never make it anywhere on foot.

Which meant she was not only in this Breed male's debt tonight, but at his mercy too. Since both fight and flight were off the table so long as he was looming over her, all she had to work with was her negotiation skills. And chutzpah.

She might as well grab onto both and roll the dice.

God, she liked it so much better when those dice were loaded in her favor first.

"Look, Mister, ah… what'd you say your name was?"

"I didn't." Those glimmering Breed eyes seemed to bore right through her. "I'm called Asher."

Unusual name, and strange way of putting it, too. But then nothing about this night had been normal, least of all this run-in with him.

"Okay, Asher." She nodded, reminded by the painful slog of her brain inside her skull that even small movements weren't a good idea right now. His scowl darkened when she wobbled under the wave of another round of nausea. "As I was saying, Asher, I really appreciate what you did for me here. And even if you're not concerned about that hole in your chest, I'm sorry you got shot trying to save my bacon. Right now, I just want to go home and take a nice hot bath, then sleep for a week. I'm sure you must have things you'd rather be doing tonight as well."

As she spoke, his gaze traveled her face in measured scrutiny. If the displeasure in his expression was anything to go by, he didn't seem to like what he saw. "You talk too much."

And he hardly spoke at all, not that it mattered. She couldn't read his stony face and unearthly stare any more than she could gauge his clipped, measured words and toneless growls. All she knew was he seemed as eager to be done with her as she was to put this entire evening in her rearview mirror.

"Okay," she announced, feeling almost cheerful. "So, I guess I'm going to be on my way now. Seeing as how Gordo and his friends won't be needing their car anymore, I'll just go find the keys and get on the road."

She forced a tight smile despite a blooming ache in her jaw, but he didn't smile back.

"You don't even look old enough to drive."

She scoffed. "I'm twenty-six."

"Like hell you are." Those blazing eyes roamed over her again, from head to toe this time. It was a short trip, considering she was only five-foot-two. She was also buried in layers of loose clothing that could have fitted

21

three of her inside.

"I'm not a girl," she murmured, indignation ripe in her voice. "Those goons only thought I was a kid because of how I'm dressed and because I told them I was underage. I thought that would be enough for them to turn me loose, but I thought wrong."

He hardly seemed pleased to hear it. "You're not a child?"

"I may be a foot-and-a-half shorter than you and about a hundred pounds soaking wet, but I'm a full-grown woman."

Probably not the smartest thing to tell a predator like the one now narrowing his gaze and cocking his head to study her more closely, but she blamed the reckless blurt on her mounting concussion. Besides, if this male wanted to assault her, her state of adulthood probably wouldn't matter and he'd already had ample time and opportunity to do his worst.

At least, that was the rationalization she clung to as she prayed for her only viable escape out of this mess.

Talons of pain closed over her throbbing skull, tightening their grip. She moaned before she could stop the pathetic sound from escaping her.

"You're hurt. That lump on your head needs medical attention."

"I know," she said, as much as it cost her to admit it. God, she hated feeling weak and helpless more than just about anything else in the world. She spent much of her childhood that way and had fought every single day to make sure she never felt that way again.

She heard his deep exhalation—and the curse that rode it. "The nearest hospital is in Henderson. You're in no shape to drive, let alone make it that far."

He was probably right. No, he was definitely right. A sudden rush of exhaustion flowed over her and she moaned, wearier than she could remember being in a very long time. Her head was starting to spin, her vision clouding over. Dammit, she was fading fast. Getting behind the wheel now would probably only finish what Leo Slater's thugs set out to do with her.

Still, what other choice did she have?

"Let's go," he stated flatly.

"Go?" She blinked up at him dully, watching that squared chin dip with his curt nod.

"To the hospital. I'll take you there."

Oh, shit. Was he serious? Get in a vehicle with him? Trust that he would actually do what he said and not detour somewhere else instead, or maybe decide to collect on her debt with a pint or two of her blood?

"No." Her reply shot out of her, no easy feat when her tongue was thickening inside the cotton dryness of her mouth. She took a step back from him and her vision swam. "I'll be fine," she murmured, her words slurring as she spoke. "I just... need a minute... to... rest and... catch my..."

She was conscious long enough to feel her knees start to buckle beneath her.

But if she hit the hard sand and bramble of the desert an instant later, she had no idea.

For the second time tonight, her world went suddenly, inescapably, dark.

CHAPTER 3

Asher held the unconscious woman in his arms and let his muttered curse fly on the night breeze.

She weighed next to nothing, even garbed in yards of shapeless fabric and denim. As displeased as he'd been to learn she was not only female but an adult woman besides, at least one small thing had gone in his favor tonight. The clothing spared his fingers from touching her bare skin. If he'd made that tactile connection, his mind would now be flooding with all the worst of her most agonizing memories.

He stared down at her drooped head and silken shoulder-length black hair, realizing only now how beautiful she actually was. To call her features delicate barely did her justice. Aside from the oversized, plain clothes she wore, she looked like a perfect porcelain doll, a petite, ebony-haired angel sleeping in his big arms.

Her almond-shaped eyes had been a stunning shade

of golden-brown before they fell closed. Now her lids shuttered her tilted, intelligent gaze, thick fringes of ink-black lashes floating against the milky smoothness of her face. The cupid's bow mouth that he doubted ever got much rest while she was awake was now slack, soft breaths gusting through parted lips that were far too sultry for his peace of mind.

"Zoe," he said, hoping the sound of her name might wake her.

She didn't so much as stir. And for what wasn't the first time, he wondered if that was even her name at all. The woman was a scrapper and a fighter, that much he could guess. Not to mention a thief, by her own admission. But she was also a fool if she thought she could run so far afoul of an obviously powerful casino boss that he had ordered her dead, then waltz right back to Vegas as if nothing happened.

Then again, not his damn problem.

Yet here he was, no further away from this whole unwelcome situation than he had been the moment he pulled Ned's truck off to the side of the road to take a look.

No, he was even deeper now—at least until he cleaned up the bodies and dropped his unwanted baggage off at the nearest hospital emergency room.

Whatever trouble she got into after that was none of his concern.

Asher carried her to the area where Gordo and his companions lay, carefully placing her on a clear patch of sand while he went to work finishing his clean-up job. Once the large hole was dug then filled with its three permanent occupants, he drove the sedan far enough into the desert bramble that it wouldn't be spotted from the road anytime soon. Then he went back to deal with the female.

He half-expected her to be gone again when he returned. Or maybe he hoped she would be.

But she was still where he left her, still snared in the unnatural sleep that was going to do her more harm than good if her concussion was as bad as he suspected it to be.

He crouched down beside her, trying not to linger on how soft and innocent she looked. Or how she was so pretty it almost hurt to look at her. How long had it been since he had a woman?

A month, he guessed. Hell, maybe two.

Too long by far, based on the primal stirring he felt as her sweet, warm scent invaded his senses, igniting a possessive need in him he didn't want to acknowledge. The urge to touch her was almost too much for him to resist.

The dark red blood currently drying in a thin rivulet at her temple wasn't helping matters either.

His fangs were already extended from his earlier battle rage. Now they throbbed in his gums for an entirely different reason.

"Zoe. Wake up." She lay unmoving, disturbingly still. He shook her shoulder, hardly able to feel the diminutive flesh and bone beneath the thick sweatshirt. "Zoe?"

"Uhhnn…" Her lids fluttered, but her eyes didn't open. And while her muscles twitched under his grasp as he continued to jostle her awake, she was only barely responding. "Tired…"

He frowned, having little experience with the sick or wounded. He'd been with Ned till the end of his mortal life, but the old man had made it easy by dying in his sleep. Judging by the woman's incapacity to remain awake or upright, he had a feeling if he didn't do something to get her conscious soon, she might never wake up either.

"I know you're tired, but you have to get up now."

She groaned in protest, burrowing her face deeper into her oversized hoodie. Her voice was thin and drowsy, her speech slurred. "Go 'way, Michael. Lemme shleep."

Michael?

Hearing her murmur the other man's name spiked something more than curiosity in him. Something deeper than irritation too. If she was accustomed to this other male waking her—this Michael—then where the hell was he right now? Shouldn't her life or death be that man's concern more than Asher's?

"Come on, Zoe," he said, more gruffly than intended. "On your feet now."

When she continued to lie there, he raked his fingers through his sweat-dampened hair and expelled a curse. Then he reached down and took her under the arms, lifting her drowsy body onto her feet.

If he hadn't held her up she would have sagged to the ground the instant he let go.

He could see this was going nowhere productive, so with one arm scooping her behind the knees he brought her back into the cradle of his arms and started heading for the old truck. As if the first time he'd held her against him like this hadn't been torment enough, now he felt every curve of her small body, each steady beat of her heart.

She wasn't his, but he'd have laid his life down for hers tonight. He knew that with a certainty that hammered like a war drum in his veins. Fortunately, there were few situations where his genetics and training might fail him, but the truth of what he'd been willing to do for this woman he didn't know and shouldn't give a damn about took him aback as he carried her to the truck.

If he didn't waste any more time, he could have her at the hospital in Henderson within the hour. Plenty of time to drop her at the door and make it back to the ranch well before sunrise, which was key for his own continued good health.

If he was lucky, maybe Zoe's head injury would erase all recollection of what happened out here tonight—including his intervention. God knew he wished he could forget it, but he doubted very much he would ever purge the memory of her pretty face and sherry-colored eyes from his thoughts. To say nothing of her brutal near-demise.

Shifting her slight weight in his arms, he opened the passenger door and gently set her inside the cab. She started to list sideways but he righted her, forced to climb in partway along with her just so he could reach around and fasten her seatbelt to hold her in place for the drive ahead.

It wasn't until that very moment that he spotted something else about her that he hadn't noticed before now and damned sure was never going to forget.

"Son of a bitch."

Beneath the stubborn curve of her chin, nearly obscured by sundry bruises, scrapes, and grime, was a small red birthmark he wouldn't mistake for anything else.

A curse exploded out of him, low and ripe, as he

stared at that singularly significant teardrop-and-crescent-moon symbol.

This female was a Breedmate.

Asher stared at her, fury mounting in him. That tiny mark changed everything. Because now that he'd seen it, this woman was no longer a problem he could simply roll into the nearest emergency room before speeding off to resume his life without looking back.

Women with this mark were rare. Precious. Cherished by his kind. Protected at all costs and with every last scrap of honor a Breed male possessed. Even a stone-cold killer like him respected that unwritten protocol.

But that didn't mean he had to like it.

"Fuck." Asher left her in the passenger seat and paced a tight circle on the dusty shoulder of the narrow two-lane while he tried to decide what to do about her now.

No choice but the obvious one. He had to take her back to the ranch with him.

And then he had some calls to make. Favors to ask of the only members of the Breed truly equipped to deal with a Breedmate on the wrong side of a powerful enemy who'd already made it clear that he wanted her dead.

Rounding the truck with determined strides, he climbed in behind the wheel and started the engine. It rumbled to life, vibrating like a low-level earthquake the way it always did for the first few minutes it was running. Not even that was enough to wake the injured Breedmate beside him on the wide bench seat.

Asher bit off another harsh curse and threw the truck into gear, roaring onto the deserted stretch of pavement.

He drove as fast as the old Chevy could handle, not slowing down until he pulled off the main road and hit the dirt lane that would eventually dump them in front of Ned's secluded homestead.

As he pulled up to the front of the place, the truck's yellow headlights glancing off the old house and its collection of paddocks and outbuildings, he couldn't help but try to view it through a stranger's eyes—her eyes. And it definitely wasn't much to look at. Not that he hadn't taken care of it while he'd been there.

He had, the way Ned liked things done. Which meant the plumbing worked great, the foundation and construction were both rock-solid, and the place was well-insulated against the cold that clutched the desert on long winter nights. Asher had installed good windows and doors over the years, and had, at Ned's insistence, added half a dozen solar panels to the roof to harness some of the energy off that relentless desert sunshine Asher took care to avoid.

He frowned as he noted the chipping white paint on the porch and the lack of any real landscaping or yard. The chicken coop was in good repair and wasn't sagging. And the pair of bony old horses—Trixie and Jubilee, after Ned's two sisters who had passed from smallpox when he was a toddler—had a paddock that Asher tended each night, making sure the barn was full of good, fresh hay and ample water.

But as far as charm? The old house and surroundings were decidedly lacking.

Not that he or Ned had ever needed charm.

And as far as Asher's unexpected guest was concerned, she wouldn't be staying long enough to suffer for any lack of luxury she might be accustomed to up in Vegas.

It was a safe place for her to lay her head until he could make necessary arrangements for her relocation. Because Breedmate or not, when those goons who'd been sent to make sure she stayed in the desert didn't show up for work tomorrow, their employer was going to want answers. And Asher could only guess that there would be hell to pay once the casino boss learned he'd lost his men and the little thief he'd planned to eliminate.

He leapt out of the truck, pocketing his keys as he crunched over the gravel around to the other side. She flinched when he unfastened her seatbelt and gathered her into his arms. Her head slumped against his shoulder, her voice a thready whisper. "We home yet, Michael?"

Asher ground his molars together at the reminder of the male she apparently depended on for comfort, in spite of the fact that *her Michael* had evidently left her to contend with Gordo and his friends on her own.

"You're safe now," he told her tightly as he pivoted to kick the door shut behind him.

A mournful howl from the other side of the screen door greeted him as he stepped onto the porch. Sam, Ned's aged yellow hound, peered at him from inside the house with pathetic big brown eyes. Asher shook his head slowly, confounded by the animal. Damned dog had him around day and night and generally paid him no mind unless he had food in his hands, but the second he left the ranch to run a quick errand, you'd think he'd left the poor mutt for the better part of a year.

With his elbow, Asher shoved open the door he never bothered to lock and stepped inside the dark house. Sam's face, already pretty sad-looking thanks to

Mother Nature, was even more pathetic as he regarded Asher and their new arrival with something close to disdain.

"Yeah, I know. I'm late and this doesn't look like your bag of kibble."

He felt like an idiot talking to the beast as if he were his roommate, but after Ned passed the place seemed too damned quiet without a bit of conversation now and then. Even if it was one-sided most of the time.

Sam yawned, then shook his head in a motion that sent his droopy ears and loose jowls flapping, then he loped behind as Asher dropped the truck's keys on the kitchen table and carried the Breedmate further inside.

Options for where to keep her for the night were as few as the accommodations were meager. There was the couch in the living room, but the relic was made of old, nubby fabric embellished by two long pieces of electrical tape that ran the length of the worn-out cushion. He knew from experience the thing was far from comfortable, and besides, half the time Sam had commandeered it for his bed.

The guest rooms, while plentiful between the two down the hall and the pair of long, roomy bunkhouses in a connected wing out back were empty but for some half-completed furniture projects Ned had given up on years before he lost his eyesight and assorted junk the old man had been hanging on to and Asher hadn't yet gotten around to purging.

Which meant the only viable place to offer was the master bedroom, his room since Ned had been gone.

No need to flick on the lamp switch. His vision was even more acute in the dark, and a blast of incandescent light might only cause more pain for the brain-injured woman in his care. He placed her on top of the thin blanket, making sure her head came down gently on the pillow.

Her contented sigh as she settled back onto the bed tugged at something rusty and unused deep inside him. Empathy and compassion had never been his strong suits, given his background. Spending a few years around Ned and the animals at the ranch had loosened him up a bit, but he was still a piss-poor choice when it came to looking after someone.

Too bad for this female, because for the time being—until he had arrangements in place for her safety and protection somewhere else—he was all she had.

His gaze strayed to the Breedmate mark under her chin. No wonder he'd missed it earlier. The darkening, fist-shaped bruise that rode her jaw line all but concealed the small birthmark now. He'd been murderous enough when he spotted the three big men beating a defenseless victim. To understand now that the intended was a Breedmate? Asher's rage rocketed through him as fresh as ever, and all-consuming.

As much as he wanted to assure himself that none of what happened tonight concerned him, there was a part of him that twitched with the urge to find the bastard who'd called for her death and deliver justice the way only someone like him could. He'd gone easy on the three gangsters. When he found their boss, he'd rip his fucking head off and make it into a hood ornament for Ned's old Chevy.

He had a feeling he would actually take pleasure in that killing. And he'd do it bare-handed, skin-on-skin, because he was sure that man's terror and agony would be a memory he'd relish reliving over and over.

Heavy mouth-breathing behind him clued him in that Sam was parked inside the bedroom. He turned toward the dog and found Sam's large head tilted in curiosity at the woman in Asher's bed. His brown eyes seemed to hold a note of surprise as much as they seemed to question.

Asher's mouth quirked in an unwilling smile. "If that's meant to be a commentary on how long it's been since we've had female company at the house, I'm well aware of the answer. Never."

Sam whined in response, high-pitched and pleading.

Asher grunted. "Yeah, she's pretty, but don't get attached. She's not staying."

Whether he was talking to the hound or to himself, he wasn't sure. Either way, after seeing to it that she was comfortable and well enough to make it through the night, his first priority would be getting on the phone to arrange for a new, better place for her to recuperate. Preferably as far away from Vegas—and him—as possible.

Rounding up the dog, the two of them headed out of the room. After letting Sam out to the yard to do his business, Asher hit Ned's old medicine cabinet in the hallway bathroom and riffled through the stale contents. A box of over-the-counter pain relievers hadn't been opened since the time of Ned's passing. They expired a month ago, but they were better than nothing.

Armed with the pills, a glass of water, and a compress he filled with ice from the kitchen, he returned to the bedroom.

As he suspected, she was still out cold. Her face was pale around her cheeks and mouth. So pale that for a moment he wondered if he'd underestimated the seriousness of her injuries. He'd only witnessed the tail end of her ordeal at the hands of her assailants. The large knot on her head was a big concern, but she could be suffering from broken bones or worse for all he knew.

Scowling, he set the glass and other items on the nightstand, then took a seat on the edge of mattress to take a closer look at her. She had so many scrapes and contusions, it was hard to decide where to start.

He resisted the urge to feel her bare forehead and check for fever, focusing instead on her breathing. It was soft and slow, but unlabored. As gently as possible, he laid the cold compress against her bruised cheek and temple, using a spare pillow to keep it in place while he let his gaze travel the length of her clothed body.

The only way to know if she had wounds he wasn't seeing was to touch her.

He was fairly certain based on how determinedly she'd run earlier that her body was largely unharmed, but adrenaline was a tricky thing. He'd seen pain in her eyes at various points tonight and he wanted to be sure the tough little scrapper wasn't in worse shape than he already feared.

Starting at her ankles, he slid his hands gently over her denim-clad legs, moving slowly upward and concentrating on the lines of the bones as he went. She was small, but leanly muscled and athletic. He'd expected her to be scrawny based on her petite frame, but as his hands and fingers moved over her hips and other hidden curves concealed beneath her clothing, he was tormented with a barrage of mental imaginings of what she might actually look like without the oversized garments intended to disguise the woman inside.

Bad idea, letting his mind take the wheel down that

road.

But he was already picturing her in his head. Already wondering how soft her impossibly perfect skin would feel under his fingertips, under his mouth . . . under his naked and thrusting body.

Fuck.

He gritted his teeth and forced the fantasy out of his mind. Best he forgo the rest of his examination of her. If she had broken bones or other problems, he'd just have to wait until she was conscious and could tell him what was wrong. Right now, all he needed was for her to open those warm sherry eyes and sit up to take the pain medicine he brought for her.

"Zoe, can you hear me?" She moaned quietly in response, her brows pinching in a frown. "Open your eyes for me. It's time to wake up."

When her head started to thrash on the pillow, he reached for the dislodged compress. At the same moment her face swiveled toward him again, landing her cheek against his open palm.

The skin-on-skin connection shot through him like a bolt of lightning.

Her eyelids flipped open as if she might have felt the power of it too.

For one instant—an instant that seemed to last an eternity—their gazes locked and held. She murmured something in her raspy, sleep-thickened voice but Asher was beyond hearing it. Ripped from his spot on the edge of the bed with her, he was hurtled into another place and time, his mind snagged on a painful memory.

Her memory.

Steeped in the sights and sounds and emotions of the moment, he was living it all through her senses. Through one of the rawest experiences of her young life. And she was sobbing. Choking on little girl tears as she sat in the middle of a squalid one-room apartment clutching a stuffed pink teddy bear to her chest.

"Mama, please, don't go! Why can't you stay home with me tonight?"

An elegant young Japanese woman dressed in a red silk dress and high, thin-heeled sandals came out of the open bathroom and squatted low until they were eye to eye. She was beautiful, her delicate oval face framed in a long curtain of shiny black hair. Smoky dark brown eyes dominated her features, and tonight her lips were slicked with scarlet color so glossy it looked like glass.

"Now, Narumi, didn't you promise Mommy no tears tonight?" She smiled, but it didn't reach her gaze. "You know how hard I work. Doesn't Mommy deserve to go out and have some fun with other grownups once in a while?"

A sigh and a hesitant nod. "I guess so. But I don't like your new friend. He hurt your face last time."

The pretty smile faltered. One slender hand came up to the ghost of a bruise that lingered beneath her left eye, not quite erased by the makeup that covered it. Mommy wore a new ring on her finger since it happened. The deep red gemstone glittered as she dabbed tenderly at her cheek.

"Don't you worry about Mommy, okay? I'm a big girl, I know what I'm doing. I can take care of myself, all right? And so can you, pumpkin. Now, be good for me and get dressed for bed. I promise I'll be home before you wake up in the morning."

"No, you won't." A soft recrimination, uttered on a raw, aching throat.

A sigh was her only response. She leaned in and her red lips felt cool and sticky against her daughter's brow. Then she stood up and smoothed out her dress, pausing to take one last look in the mirror before she glided to the chipped and aged door.

"I love you, sweetheart."

She scurried out, the sound of her high heels clicking on the apartment building's steel stairwell as her terrified little daughter moved to the window and peered through tattered drapes at the large black limousine that idled below, praying that the bad man inside wouldn't hurt her mommy again.

Asher's hissed curse punctuated the silence of the bedroom. The adult version of that sobbing, frightened child had since drifted back into her slumber. He was glad for that now, relieved to be freed from her gaze as he drew his hand away from her face and stood up.

His heart was hammering as painfully as hers had been. Sorrow and anger clogged his throat, along with the fear and loneliness this child had apparently lived with on regular basis.

It was almost too much for him to bear. How she'd managed to cope with the force of those powerful emotions at her tender age he had no idea.

He stepped away from the bed, watching her sleep. He would come back to wake her and give her the pain meds and water. Right now, he needed air.

He needed space to breathe for a few minutes, at least until the overwhelming blast of Zoe's emotions—or, rather, Narumi's—had a chance to subside.

CHAPTER 4

Naomi woke to someone at her bedside repeatedly washing her outstretched hand with a warm, wet cloth.

One that tickled and smelled strongly of Alpo.

Peeling one eyelid open, she waited for the banging in her skull to kick up again like it had been doing all night, but there was no pounding ache. No muffled cotton-head feeling or dizzying wave of nausea. That was a relief. The worst of the storm that had been raging in her cranium after the blows she'd suffered from Slater's goons had finally passed.

Her vision was clear now. And it was suddenly filled with the panting mush-mouth and inquisitive big brown eyes of a giant yellow hound nosing into her face from the side of the bed.

"Well, hello there." She frowned, swallowing on a dry mouth. "Who are you, the hospital comfort animal?"

The thick tail started thumping enthusiastically in response, a soft whine building as the beast attempted to get closer to her, practically crawling up on the bed.

"That's Sam," a deep voice answered, disembodied thanks to the massive dog blocking her view of anything else in the room.

But she knew that low growl. She'd been hearing it in her dreams most of the night, nagging her to open her eyes at least half a dozen times, bossing her like a drill sergeant when all she'd wanted to do was sleep for days.

Asher. She remembered his unusual name. Against her will, she remembered his ruggedly handsome face, too, the chiseled cheeks and strong jaw that made her pulse speed a little faster in her veins.

What the hell was he doing at the hospital with her?

And then it hit her—she wasn't in a hospital emergency room bed. She was in a bedroom of a small house. One that evidently belonged to the lethal Breed male who'd turned Gordo and his two buddies into buzzard bait.

She'd been sleeping in the big vampire's bed.

"Oh, my God." She scuttled back against the headboard, drawing her knees up to her chest. The abrupt movements combined with her mounting alarm made her temples throb, but she had bigger problems at the moment than a bump on the head. She glared at him over the grinning, drooling face of the hellhound who'd now managed to get all four paws up on the bed.

"What have you done to me?" Frantically, she felt her neck to make sure it was still intact. It was. And now, both he and the big dog were staring at her as if she'd lost her mind. "You said you were going to take me to the hospital last night."

He stepped further into the room, holding a steaming mug in his hands. "Yes, I did."

"You lied to me." Did that actually surprise her? She knew better than to put her trust in any man, so what had she done? Put her faith—and her life—in the hands of a proven killer. A fucking vampire, for crissake. "I'm out of here."

She whipped her legs over the other side of the bed and pushed to her feet. Not good. The wooziness was back again, not as awful as it had been out in the desert before she had apparently passed out for the night, but enough to knock her back onto her behind on the mattress.

"You're not going anywhere," he stated calmly. "And I haven't done anything to you, except make sure you were comfortable and that your head injury didn't worsen overnight."

"I'll bet." She scoffed, too outraged to worry about making him angry. "Is that what you tell all of the hapless women you capture and drag out here to your lair?"

"My lair?" Chestnut brows quirked, he glanced around the sparsely furnished room with its hand-hewn four-poster bed and chunky nightstands. Adjacent to the foot of the king-size bed stood a chest of drawers topped with an old television set that would have been an antique a decade ago.

Not exactly a Gothic house of horrors, but what did she know about the Breed? Most reasonable people had given up on the antiquated view of vampires in the two decades his kind had been living in the open among humans.

And her experience with members of the Breed wasn't much. Purely by choice.

She preferred to keep it that way, especially after witnessing Asher's deadly skills last night.

Right now, the only thing she needed to do was find the nearest exit.

She tried to stand up again, but the enormous hound had belly crawled up next to her and flopped his big head in her lap. She sighed, finding it hard to resist the pleading eyes that stared up at her, begging for her touch. Begrudgingly, she scratched him behind the floppy ears and under his jowly chin.

She felt Asher's eyes on her from the other side of the room. "You like dogs?"

"Of course, I do. What kind of monster doesn't like dogs?" She glanced over her shoulder at him and found him scowling. "He belongs to you?"

He gave a faint shake of his head. "He's Ned's dog."

"Who's Ned?"

"A friend. He died last year and left me this ranch."

Naomi tilted her head at him. "Then I hate to break it to you, Asher, but Sam's your dog now."

Cobalt blue. That was the color of Asher's eyes. She hadn't been sure last night in the desert. It had been too dark, and his gaze had been too hot, lit up like amber coals from the moment he arrived on scene to take care of the men who'd hurt her.

He watched as she continued to stroke and pat the blissed-out dog. Those deep blue eyes reached inside her somehow, feeling oddly familiar after everything that happened last night. His gaze felt intense, far too intimate.

"I think you just made a friend for life," he said, the corner of his broad mouth tugging in a wry smile. And it was a nice smile too. Transformed the hard angles and stern lines in a way that made her stomach flip like it did on an amusement park ride.

She immediately stilled her hand, folding her arms across the front of her bed-rumpled hoodie. Dammit, she did not want to warm up to this male—this dangerous stranger. Nor his dog, for that matter.

"Do you have a phone I could borrow?"

Asher's smile vanished. "What for?"

"I need to call someone and get a ride out of here. You said it yourself last night, I need to see a doctor."

He shook his head. "You'll be fine. The concussion could've been worse. What you need right now is rest and nourishment."

He held the mug out to her. Watery yellow broth with pale noodles and tiny flecks of carrot and diced, anemic white meat swam nearly to the brim.

"What's this?"

"Breakfast. I know from living with Ned that humans are in the habit of eating in the morning. Unfortunately, all that's left in the cabinets are some of his old staples. I found a can of soup that wasn't going to expire for another few weeks. I don't expect it will give you botulism."

Gee, after a rave review like that, how could she refuse? But his deadpan offer of canned chicken noodle for breakfast was in earnest. He had actually cooked something out of consideration for her, even care, if his solemn expression were any indication.

Still, she had places to go. People to reassure that she wasn't lying in the middle of the Mojave with a bullet in her head. Poor Michael was probably out of his mind with worry now that it was morning and she still hadn't returned home or checked in to let him know she was okay.

God forbid he get so concerned he would call in a missing person's report.

The last thing either of them needed was to invite the police to start sniffing around.

That thought only renewed her need to get out of there and back to Las Vegas as soon as possible.

Gently pushing away Asher's offered mug of soup, she shook her head. "Thank you for the thought, but I'm really not hungry."

She dislodged Sam's snoring bulk from her lap and forced herself to stand. Not so bad this time. She just had to take things easy.

"So, about that phone," she said to Asher. "I've got someone waiting to hear from me and I really should be going before he sends a search party. He tends to worry when I'm out of touch for an hour, let alone all night."

Asher's face darkened the longer she rambled. "Sit down. You should rest some more. It's too soon for you to be on your feet."

"No, it's not." She spread her arms as if to show him how much better she felt, even did a little jig despite the woozy feeling that followed. "See? Ninety-nine percent back to normal."

"I said sit down, Narumi."

She went stock-still, every muscle in her body seizing up, every cell clanging with shock at the sound of that name on his tongue.

Her oldest name. The one she had refused to use since her mother's death when Naomi was eight years old.

"What did you just call me?"

He set the mug of soup down on the nightstand.

"That's your name, isn't it? Not Zoe. Narumi."

"No." Her head shook side to side. "No, that's not my name. But you're right, it's not Zoe, either. My name is Naomi. I haven't used that other one for a long time. I don't like to hear it. In fact, only one person other than my mother even knows that name, and it sure as hell shouldn't be you."

"You're talking about Michael?"

As if the first bout of shock wasn't staggering enough, now this? "How do you know so much about me? What the hell is going on here?"

"You talk in your sleep, for one thing," he replied calmly. "Which isn't surprising considering how much you talk when you're awake." At her small scowl, he went on. "You mentioned your man's name several times while I was tending you overnight. And in your daze before you lost consciousness out in the desert."

Part of her felt compelled to correct him about Michael being "her man" but that was just one more fact about her life that was none of his business. It was the other insight he seemed to have that troubled her the most.

"How do you know my given name? Do you . . . did you know my mother?"

"No."

"Do you know Leo Slater?"

His brow creased even deeper. "No. I do not know him, either, but I am familiar with his name."

"Everyone in a two hundred mile radius of Las Vegas knows his name," she bit back icily.

"Yes," he agreed, holding her in a suspicious, narrowing gaze. "Is he the casino boss you attempted to steal from last night?"

He must have taken her silence for the confirmation it was. A curse hissed out of him and he scoured his hand over the whisker-darkened grizzle of his jaw. "What does Leo Slater have to do with your mother?"

"Nothing. Forget I brought either of them up."

His answering chuckle was grim. "You ask too much, Naomi."

She hiked up her chin. "Tell me how you know my other name. I think you owe me that much, don't you?"

For a moment, she wasn't sure he'd respond. He seemed lost in his own thoughts, pacing a tight track on the other side of the bed from her while Sam slept like the dead between them.

"Every one of the Breed is born with an extrasensory or other preternatural ability unique to them," he explained. She nodded, not entirely ignorant of a few of the basics of their species, much as she wished to be. "My gift—though I use the term loosely—is the ability to experience full sensory recall of another person's memories when I touch someone. Only the most painful ones. The traumas. The moments of darkest fear or agony. The memories never fade. Once I feel them, they never leave me again."

"I'm sorry, Asher. I don't… I can only guess what that must be like for you." Naomi stared at him, losing a bit of her grasp on the anger and indignation she felt just a moment ago. She couldn't imagine anything so awful. Being cursed to bear someone else's worst experiences and never be able to escape them.

Which meant he now knew some of her pain too.

"You touched me last night?"

"Not intentionally. I'm careful." His lips pressed together, then he exhaled another harsh curse. "Last night when I came in to give you water and pain pills, you grew agitated. You were tossing your head on the pillow and I... reached for you. For a moment, I touched your face."

She blinked at him, recalling as in a dream all of the times he came in to check on her, to gently rouse her and make sure she was okay and not in any discomfort.

"What did you see?" God, she hated how small her voice sounded, how weak and afraid.

"You were young, I'm guessing four or five. Your mother was with you in a studio apartment. She was wearing a red silk dress, getting ready to leave on a date with someone waiting in a limousine outside."

Naomi's breath leaked out of her on a sharp sigh. "I remember that night. It wasn't the first, or the last. But I remember the red dress."

"You begged her not to go," Asher went on, his deep voice quiet, sober. "You didn't like her new boyfriend because he was abusing her. Even at your young age, you recognized that. And you were crying. You were afraid for her, and terrified to be left alone."

Naomi felt those emotions gathering in the back of her throat now. She remembered everything about that moment. She remembered thinking that one night her mother was never going to come back.

And then one night, finally, she didn't.

She inhaled, pushing the memory down before it made her feel any weaker for how she had failed to protect her beautiful mother. The only person who had ever cared for her, loved her. At least until Michael came along and gave her the sibling she never had. During their shared time on the streets as orphans hustling tourists and scraping to get by however they could, they had cobbled together an unconventional little family of misfits.

And none of the people she loved would ever need to scrape or hustle again as long as Naomi had something to say about it.

Which meant she really needed to get her ass back to Vegas, and soon.

Smoothing her rumpled clothing and hair, she came around her side of the bed, edging toward the open door. She wasn't going to kid herself that she could outrun Asher, but she hoped by showing him that she was steady on her feet he might be inclined to grant her that phone call.

She cleared her throat. "I guess this is the part where I say thanks a lot or sorry for the memories, then get on my way. Unfortunately, Gordo trashed my cell along with my ID back at the casino, so do you have a land line out here, or maybe a satellite phone?"

She took a step nearer to the threshold, and suddenly the bedroom door slammed shut all on its own. "Holy shit."

She whirled to find Asher still standing several feet behind her, his face unreadable. But those deep blue pools were sober and determined. "We need to talk, Naomi."

"I thought we just did." She swallowed, but kept her facade of flippant confidence firmly in place. "This was fun, Asher, but I've got people waiting for me to come home, so I'll thank you to let me go now."

He didn't budge. "You have a mark under your chin, Naomi."

"I've got marks all over me, thanks to Gordo and his asshole buddies," she scoffed, pretending she didn't understand in spite of the alarm that was building inside her.

But Asher wasn't playing her game. No, the Breed male was as deadly serious as she'd seen him thus far. "I'm talking about the symbol. The teardrop-and-crescent-moon. I'm talking about the fact that you're a Breedmate."

She shook her head as if she could refute both the birthmark and what it meant.

"You're a Breedmate," he insisted. "One of a small number of women on this planet who are something more than mortal. Something more than simply human."

Naomi swallowed hard. She had been twelve years old before she learned that the unusual red birthmark she bore had separated her from other girls. She'd simply counted herself lucky that she never got sick—not even a sniffle—and that she'd been born naturally strong and athletic.

It wasn't until she was in foster care for the third or fourth time that she met another girl who had the same symbol somewhere on her body. Jessamine's mark was on her belly, hiding in a field of freckles that sprinkled most of the pretty red-haired girl's fair skin.

Jessie knew things Naomi didn't. Things her mother had whispered about the Breed and what women with the Breedmate mark meant to them. How only Breedmates could bear vampire offspring, and only after a mutual blood bonding with a Breed male, a connection that would link the mated couple in both body, heart, and emotions for as long as they lived. Which, as a mated pair, meant something close to eternity.

And, like the Breed, Breedmates had unique talents

and abilities all their own too. Jessie could conjure storms and other weather at her will. Naomi's talent wasn't nearly as awe-inspiring, but it had proven useful to her over time.

Most recently, last night at Leo Slater's casino.

But it wasn't going to help her deal with the formidable Breed male studying her intensely from an arm's length away.

"You are a Breedmate, Naomi. And as a Breed male, that means I am honor-bound to protect you. At least until you're somewhere safe with people who will help you stay that way."

"Honor-bound to protect me?" She barked an uneasy laugh. "Well, if that's all this is about, then no worries. I hereby release you from that obligation. So, we're done here."

"It's not that simple."

"Yes, Asher. It is." As she loaded up her arguments in the hopes of persuading him to let her go, the rest of what he said started sinking in. "Wait a second. What do you mean, until I'm somewhere with people who can help me stay safe? What people?"

"The Order."

"What?" She gaped at him, torn between outrage and disbelief. "The Order, meaning that group of warriors who are the most lethal and dangerous-to-know Breed males walking this good Earth since... well, I guess since you stepped foot on it?"

A grim smile tugged at the corner of his mouth. "They were here first, actually. Hundreds of years before I was created. And the Breed as a species has been walking this planet for much longer than that. Thousands of years."

"Whatever," she shot back, incensed and not a little nervous. "I don't need a history lesson. What I need is for you to let me go, Asher. Right. Fucking. Now."

With her rising voice, Sam sat up on the bed and cocked his head at her. She scowled at the dog and his obstinate owner.

"It's too late," Asher informed her evenly. "I've already alerted the Order of the situation through an old friend of mine who's in contact with them. Someone will be getting in touch with me soon to make further arrangements for your transport to a Darkhaven safe house."

Holy shit, he was dead serious. He had every intention of steamrolling her into his twisted notion of protection, no matter what she said or wanted.

"No. This is nuts. You're nuts if you think you can just lock me up in this room and hold me captive until what? Until you or your friends from the Order ship me off to someplace I don't know and don't want to be?" She crossed her arms, fuming now. "We have a word for that, you know. It's called abduction."

He took a step toward her, then another, until less than a foot separated them in the small room that seemed to be shrinking before her eyes the closer Asher came to her. His big body radiated heat and that spicy, delicious scent that had clung to the blanket and sheet on the bed and drove her mad most of the night.

"I have a life of my own, Asher. I have people I care about waiting for me in Vegas. I want to go back to them. I want to go right now."

He slowly shook his head, the first signs of remorse edging into his determined blue stare. "I'm sorry, Naomi. What you want isn't possible now. Not when you and I both know there is a powerful man in that city who wants you dead. I cannot send you back there to get killed."

"I can handle myself."

"That may be so," he said, almost gently now. "But you are too precious to take that risk."

Did he mean too precious to the Breed, or something else? The way he was looking at her, she couldn't be sure. His low, tender voice made her veins run hot, loosening something deep inside her. Something soft and yearning.

She backed away from him, needing the space in order to breathe. "I want to talk to Michael. I need to see him, Asher. You can't keep me away from the only family I have!"

Anger and frustration swelled inside her, bringing a sting to the backs of her eyes. Tears welled, but she refused to let them fall—not even in an attempt to sway his sympathy. Assuming the monstrous vampire had any to speak of. Instead, she stared up at him mutinously.

The sight of her rising emotions only seemed to harden his handsome face. He exhaled a heavy sigh. "You can get in touch with your Michael or anyone else you like… once you're in the Order's hands and out of mine. Then you'll be their problem to deal with."

Without another word, he stepped around her and stalked to the bedroom door. "Sam," he growled, his pointed finger a command for the dog to leave the room with him.

Naomi looked at him in disbelief, shocked that this was really happening. "Where are you going?"

He didn't give her an answer. "I expect the Order will be in contact anytime now. With any luck, you'll be on your way out of here come nightfall."

He walked out, closing the door behind him.

Naomi listened to the metallic snick of the tumbler as he locked her inside. She bit her lip, hopeful as his long strides and Sam's clicking paws retreated down the hallway.

Then she swiped impatiently at the tears that spilled onto her cheeks now that she was alone. And she smiled, feeling a small spark of hope kindle to life in her breast.

Out of here come nightfall?

Fat chance. She'd be out of here within the hour—or die trying.

CHAPTER 5

"Stop looking at me like that."

Sam lay on the floor of Ned's furniture workshop, his chin resting on his outstretched front paws while his sad brown eyes stared up at Asher in silent judgment.

For the past twenty minutes since he left Naomi locked inside the bedroom at the other end of the rambling house, Asher had been weathering Sam's disapproval—and his own self-directed disgust. On a muttered curse, he picked up a detail chisel to refine some of the scrollwork on the piece of furniture he'd been trying to perfect for the better part of a year now.

The handcrafted headboard, once it was finished, would replace the old one in the master bedroom. Not that he didn't appreciate Ned's craftsmanship. Hell, before the old man became blind a few years ago and could no longer enjoy his favorite art form, he'd taught

Asher everything he knew about coaxing beauty and function from even the most ordinary slab of wood. Ned's furniture was sturdy and comfortable, much like the man, and although Asher appreciated his friend's work, it was just that the bedroom didn't feel like his so long as Ned's belongings dominated the space.

Asher hadn't been in any big hurry to make the transition, but he enjoyed having something productive to do with his hands, especially during the long stretches of daylight out in the desert.

And now, when it was all he could do not to think about the female being held against her wishes and her will in the other part of the house.

"You really think I wanted to lock her up like a damned prisoner?" he asked Sam, chipping carefully into one of the complicated flourishes he was carving into the headboard. "You think I don't know what a fucking violation that is, taking away someone's freedom?"

He knew better than most. For nearly the first half of his life, he'd been enslaved in a place he didn't want to be, his life belonging to someone else. Dragos's assassin program, the Hunter program, had been a brutal, cold existence. One Asher had endured from birth to early manhood, along with a number of other Breed males unfortunate enough to have been created in that sadistic madman's lab.

Asher and the others like him—all of them half-brothers by blood and eternal brethren by the shared hell of their experience—had been kept enslaved by a shackle not even the strongest first-generation Breed male could break. There were times Asher could still feel the cold polymer of his ultraviolet-powered collar fastened around his neck.

There were moments when he still woke up bathed in icy sweat after nightmares—vivid, full-sensory memories—of what those UV collars could do to someone exploded with brutal clarity in his mind.

The Hunters' enslavement had been so complete, none of them even had names. Every boy, teen, and man in the program was referred to simply as what he was— a Hunter. Just one of the many ways Dragos ensured none of them ever felt whole. They were property. Tools and instruments, not feeling beings. They were nothing more than lethal weapons to be called upon—or destroyed—at their master's whim.

The names they called themselves came later, after the survivors escaped the lab and had to learn to make their own way out in the world beyond their collars and cages.

Asher blew out a harsh sigh, shaking off the talons of his past before they could drag him any deeper.

Sam was still staring at him expectantly, as though measuring Asher's character by how long it was going to take him before he got up and let their beautiful hostage free.

Or maybe the judgment was coming from inside Asher's own conscience.

At least Naomi's captivity would be temporary. It couldn't be more than a few hours until the Order stepped in to take better control of the situation. Then she would have her freedom again, though not back in Las Vegas for a while. Not until and unless the warriors deemed it was safe for her to return, which likely meant after Leo Slater and any other enemies she may have made had time enough to forget her.

Asher wished it would only be a matter of time

before he was able to forget the female. Putting Naomi out of his mind would have been impossible even before he touched her and absorbed her painful memory of her childhood.

He couldn't deny his attraction to her. With her dark, delicate outward beauty she was the loveliest woman he'd ever laid eyes on. But combined with her fiery, tenacious personality and quick intellect, not to mention her core of indefatigable inner strength, he'd be a goner if he had to spend more than a handful of hours in her company.

None of that made him feel like less of a bastard for the boorish way he'd handled things with her today.

He glanced at Sam and shook his head. "Go ahead and say it. I'm an asshole."

The dog yawned and flopped onto his side to nap, having apparently given up on Asher's sense of honor.

Asher grunted. "I guess that makes two us."

Probably three, counting Naomi.

Given her tenacity and obvious courage, he'd expected to hear some protest or other sounds of rebellion coming from the bedroom at the other end of the house. But she'd been utterly quiet back there, almost resigned to everything he'd told her. He hadn't hoped for her distress, but he hated to think the fight had gone out of her that easily.

And there was a part of him that wondered if her apparent capitulation was anything but....

His phone buzzed on the workbench beside him. The display showed no number, but when he spoke with Scythe in Italy a few hours ago, the male told him to expect a call from one of the Order's leaders in the area.

"Asher, this is Kade," said the deep voice on the

other end of the line. "I head up the Order's command center in Lake Tahoe. I understand you've got a situation on your hands."

"You could say that." He gave the Order commander a run-down of everything that had happened in the desert last night, culminating with Asher's discovery of Naomi's Breedmate mark and his decision to bring her to his place.

"You did the right thing," Kade assured him. "If this female's put herself in the crosshairs of a son of a bitch like Leo Slater, there may be no place far enough for her to run. Slater's not someone to fuck with. If the rumors are true, there's hardly a square mile of desert surrounding Vegas that doesn't contain at least a dozen graves filled with someone who either got in the way of his temper or his profits."

Asher's veins tightened to hear the Order warrior confirm what he already dreaded. "Naomi's got both strikes against her after trying to steal from his casino last night."

"Why'd she do it? She had to know if she failed, Slater was going to come after her with guns blazing. How much money is worth that kind of risk?"

"I don't know," Asher replied. "But I don't think this is the first time she's attempted something like this."

"How so?"

"She was wearing a disguise, a damn good one too. She looked like a teenage boy when I first saw her. I never would've guessed she was a female, let alone a full-grown woman. If she'd been able to make off with whatever she attempted to steal from Slater's casino, all she'd have to do is ditch the disguise and make her getaway. They'd be looking for school-age punks, not a beautiful woman with the face of an angel."

"Face of an angel, eh?" Kade replied, a hint of amusement in his deep voice.

Asher cursed himself for the slip. His opinion of Naomi's beauty had no relevance to the conversation. And if he didn't already know that Kade was blood-bonded to his own beautiful woman, his Breedmate Alexandra, Asher might have found even less humor in the warrior's intrigued response.

"Does Naomi know she's a Breedmate?"

He considered her less-than-enthused reaction, and her lack of surprise when he tried to explain what her birthmark meant. "She knows."

Kade made an approving noise. "Has she been told you're bringing the Order in to provide protection and a safe house for her?"

"Yes."

"How did that go over?"

Asher grunted, a non-answer that no doubt expressed more than words could. "There is a man," he told the warrior. "A human, I'm guessing. He's in Las Vegas. He's... important to her."

"A lover?"

Asher's molars clenched involuntarily. "I don't know. Possibly."

"Okay. We'll sort everything out with her once we have Naomi in hand," Kade said. "We're still a good six hours from sundown, but I'll send a team out to your place ASAP. In the meantime, just keep her calm and comfortable..."

The Tahoe area commander was still talking, but Asher's ears were suddenly tuned to another sound. Sam heard it too. His droopy ears perked, he lifted his head and glanced at Asher in question as the unmistakable rumble of Ned's old Chevy roared to life outside.

"Holy hell."

"Something wrong?" Kade asked.

Asher's feet were already moving, the phone still held to his ear. In a flash of movement, he was standing in the main living area of the house. The door to the master bedroom stood ajar. So did the door leading out to the porch.

"The pick-up plan's going to have to wait," he muttered to the other Breed male. "I've got a problem over here."

"Something happen with the woman?" Kade's voice held a grave edge. "Is Naomi all right?"

Asher scoffed under his breath. "Yeah, she's fine. She's stealing my damn truck. I'll be in touch."

He ended the call, daylight blasting in from the yard. The noontime desert sun scorched his eyes, and that unforgiving ultraviolet light drove him back in spite of the fury that all but spurred him to charge out and drag the foolish woman back inside. But he was too late to reach her.

With one arm raised to shield his face, he peered out at the yard and driveway.

Ned's truck was already halfway to the desert road, bouncing over potholes and kicking up clouds of yellow dust as Naomi made her escape under the cover of broad daylight.

CHAPTER 6

"Holy shit, Nay, what the hell happened to you? I've been blowing up your phone for the past twelve hours."

Michael rolled his wheelchair back to make room for her to enter the small 1950s bungalow located in a residential neighborhood northeast of the Strip. As she stepped inside, he peered around her, frowning when he spotted the unfamiliar pickup truck in the short driveway.

"Where'd you get the jalopy? Or do I even want to know?"

"Probably not." She closed the door behind her and unzipped her hoodie as she walked past him, peeling away the bulk of her ill-fitting clothes until all she wore was a black tank top and baggy jeans. The house was quiet for eleven A.M., especially considering there were five kids currently living there at last count. "Everyone still asleep?"

"Yeah." Michael gave her his typical mother-hen look. "We all had a long night, mainly because I was rattling around until sometime after four o'clock. You know they can sense when something's wrong or either of us is upset."

She bent and dropped a chaste kiss to the top of his sandy blond hair. "I know. I'm sorry I made you worry."

Michael's small home had been an unofficial safe house for street kids since he'd bought it five years ago, using the bulk of the insurance settlement he was awarded two years after being hit by a drunk driver who'd plowed through a crosswalk on Flamingo Road. The depression he'd suffered over his inability to ever walk again had taken him to some dark places. It hadn't helped that his long-term boyfriend had abruptly decided Michael's months-long hospitalization was a good time for them to "take a break and see other people".

Naomi's friend had lost so much so suddenly, but it was the dream of helping other kids like him—kids like Naomi and him both—who'd been dealt shitty hands in the life lottery and had no family of their own that pulled Michael through and gave him new purpose.

It had given her purpose too. Seeing him through the year of intense therapies, all of the ups and downs that followed his accident and the long road to recovery, had galvanized their friendship and their commitment to the kids they wanted to help.

They'd been roomies ever since. In addition to the bedroom with its pair of twin beds that she and Michael shared like brother and sister, two other rooms had been outfitted with bunkbeds and space for six kids each, eight if they had to make do for the short-term. One room was reserved for boys, the other for girls.

The house wasn't a palace by any stretch, but it was comfortable and it was home. And when the city's shelters and flophouses were full, it meant a safe place for any kid under eighteen to lay their heads and get three squares with no fear of judgment or payback.

Anything was better than ending up a ward of the state. Naomi knew that firsthand. A system that expected kids who'd already had their trust dragged over broken glass a thousand times before to put that same trust in a bunch of bureaucrats who didn't know them, and didn't give a shit about them, aside from checking off their little forms and passing the buck to the next person in line? It wasn't any wonder most kids slipped through the cracks or became so desperate for a sense of normalcy they'd accept even the most dubious offer of kindness from anyone who gave them a second glance.

If she and Michael had anything to say about it, no kid would ever feel they had nowhere to go or no one to trust.

This dream of theirs, as humble as it was, meant everything to her. More than that, it was the one good thing she'd done with her life that she knew would have made her mother proud.

But there was no question she'd pushed the limits last night and it almost cost her life.

It would have, if not for Asher.

God. Asher.

Talk about dubious offers of kindness. His had come with strings attached, too, evidently. Or, rather, a locked cage.

She flopped down on the living room sectional and let out a groan, clutching her skull.

"Good lord, look at you." Michael parked his wheelchair in front of her. Although his round face was pinched with worry, even anger, he kept his voice at nearly a whisper. "You've got bruises all over you, Nay. What the fuck happened last night after you texted that you were in the clear and on your way home?"

"Everything kind of went to hell at that point," she admitted, then relayed the highlights of how she'd been intercepted by Casino Moda security and knocked out cold for a ride down the I-15 to the middle of the Mojave. "They dragged me out of the car and walked me out onto the sand at gunpoint."

Michael sucked in a breath. "Sweet Jesus, Joseph, and Mary." Slapping a hand to his chest, he closed his eyes for a long moment, then exhaled slowly. When he looked at her again, his hazel gaze was filled with a mix of horror and relief. "Okay. You're obviously alive, so chalk one up to your uncanny ability to land on your feet no matter the predicament. But dammit, Naomi. This shit is getting serious. You know Leo Slater doesn't mess around."

"I know." She knew that better than most people. And last night she'd gotten a pretty hefty reminder. "But like you said, I'm obviously alive."

He frowned. "Right. And *how* exactly did you manage that?"

"I had some... help."

"Unless you're going to tell me that a unit of Special Forces soldiers dropped from the sky to save you from three of Slater's henchmen—three heavily armed henchmen—then I can't even imagine what kind of help it took to get you out of this fix, Nay. And that doesn't do anything to explain the rusted-out heap that's parked in the driveway."

She smirked in spite of the gravity of what happened to her—both last night in the desert and this morning at Asher's house. Michael always had the ability to diffuse even the worst situation and make her feel that everything was going to be all right.

"It wasn't a Special Forces unit, and nobody dropped from the sky to save me." She glanced at him, knowing he was going to find the actual truth even harder to swallow. "It was a massive Breed male. He drove up in that old pickup truck and calmly took out all three of Slater's goons in about a minute flat."

"A Breed male?" Michael gaped at her. "Please don't tell me you ended up being a vampire's midnight snack on top of everything else last night."

She shook her head, then winced at the dull throb of her temples. "Asher didn't bite me. He said he was going to bring me to the hospital, but instead, after I passed out from a concussion, he took me home with him and looked after me all night. It wasn't until this morning when I woke up that things really got weird, ending with me locked in his bedroom."

Michael choked on his gasp. "*That's* when things started to get weird? Go on, then. I'm all ears."

"He saw my birthmark."

"You mean your Breedmate mark," her friend corrected helpfully.

She scowled. "Don't call me that. It's only a birthmark, unless I wake up one day and decide I want to have little vampire babies or something. Which I won't, and I don't."

Michael shrugged. "That mark is also the only reason you managed to escape from inside a locked room, am I right? That handy little Breedmate talent of yours for manipulating metal gears and magnetics. That same one you've been using to finesse jackpots out of casino slots and roulette wheels for about as long as I've known you." He chuckled. "Is that how you hijacked your Good Samaritan's truck out there too?"

"I didn't *finesse* the truck," she muttered. "I didn't have to, because I found the keys left on the kitchen table."

Which didn't excuse the fact that she stole Asher's truck. Stealing money from Leo Slater was one thing she'd never apologize for, but she couldn't deny the pang of guilt she carried knowing she'd taken something from Asher when all he'd done was help her.

"As for being a Good Samaritan," she added, "I wouldn't go that far, Michael. Good Samaritans return lost wallets without taking any of the cash. Good Samaritans walk old ladies across busy streets, and volunteer at food banks. They don't murder three gangsters in cold blood over a woman they don't even know. They don't insist that they're honor-bound to protect someone just because of some silly birthmark, then proceed to make arrangements to ship said person off to a vampire safe house God knows where like I'm a piece of furniture or a prized sow."

"He did all that?"

She nodded tightly. "He told the Order about me, for fuck's sake. If I hadn't split, later tonight I'd be dealing with not only Asher but any number of Order warriors intent on guarding my life because of some antiquated moral code."

"Your badass Breed hero knows the Order?"

Naomi shot him a flat stare. "You don't have to act so impressed with him, you know."

"He saved your life, darling. Of course, I'm impressed. And I'm damned grateful to him."

Naomi smiled at her friend, warmed by his affection.

And she supposed if she slowed herself down and gave her outrage a minute to cool, there was a part of her that couldn't help being more than a little intrigued with Asher too. She had so many questions about him. So much she wanted to know, like how he'd met his friend Ned and what he'd been doing with his life before that time.

She had seen a hauntedness in his deep blue eyes. A pain she could not name. Maybe all she saw was the wounds of his unique gift—his curse to experience all the anguish and distress of whomever he touched. What must that be like for him, day in and day out? How did he cope with a lifetime full of such memories? She wanted to know, wanted to ask him all of these things and so much more.

Not the least of which being why, if he was so willing to protect her life, did he not already have a Breedmate of his own?

Michael reached over and gave her hand a gentle squeeze. "If I ever see this Asher of yours, I mean to thank him for saving my best friend."

"Asher's not my anything," she grumbled, getting up from the sofa. "And if I'm lucky I'll never have to see him again."

Michael's brows lifted. "Oh, sweet sister from another mister. He's a hottie with a body, isn't he?"

She wanted to laugh, but she was too busy fighting

off a sudden wash of heat. She could literally feel the blood rushing to her cheeks as an unwanted image of Asher's muscled bulk and ruggedly handsome face took form in her mind's eye.

He was more than hot. He was unearthly masculine and easily the most arousing man she'd ever seen. *Breed*, she corrected herself. She wasn't quite prepared to think of him as simply a man, let alone one she could be attracted to. Especially after he pulled that caveman routine on her this morning. Regardless of how noble his intentions might have been.

"I think the word you're looking for is psychotic," she said, and headed into the kitchen, desperate for some water—or maybe a stiff drink. "And anyway, it doesn't matter what I think about Asher. I've got bigger things to think about—namely my next move with Leo Slater."

Michael rolled into the room after her. All of his humor and teasing faded at the mention of Slater. "What are you talking about, your next move? Naomi, siphoning off some of Casino Moda's profits might have seemed like a hoot and a half when you first started this game of yours, but shit got serious last night. You almost got killed."

She filled a glass of water from the tap and downed it, then shrugged. "I landed on my feet."

"Barely. Have you seen yourself? You're full of scrapes and bruises." He hissed a quiet curse, shaking his head. "If not for the mercy of a stranger—a Breed male who by your own description could have just as easily turned on you last night—odds are you'd be lying under a pile of dirt somewhere in the Mojave right now."

"It's not about me. It's about justice, Michael. It's about making sure no kid who comes through our door ever has to be turned away because we're out of beds or out of food. It's about taking something from a powerful, corrupt asshole like Leo Slater and giving it to someone who really needs it. Someone who deserves it."

Michael let out a slow sigh. "No, Naomi. It's about your mother. It's about what Slater did to her. I know you want to do right for these kids, but this is about vengeance for you. And if you're not careful, you're going to end up just like your mom. Missing and presumed dead at Slater's hands."

It hurt, hearing him say that. Not because he was wrong, but because he knew her better than anyone ever had. As much as she wanted to provide for the kids growing up on the streets abandoned and terrified as she had after her mother's disappearance, she was also out for blood.

Leo Slater's blood.

Her plan had always been to milk him dry through a series of increasingly humiliating, unsolved heists. She already had a dozen wins under her belt, never mind last night's blunder. And now she had her eye on an even bigger prize—a combined jackpot that had been accumulating for months at Moda.

Naomi wanted to walk off with it all. She wanted Slater to be made a fool in front of his investors and high-roller clientele for his lack of security. Eventually, she wanted to destroy him.

Then, someday, once he was reduced to squalor and shame, all of his power stripped from him because of her, she wanted to confront him face-to-face and tell him it was she who took away everything he had—just as he had done to her.

Only then, after he knew what she'd done, she

wanted to be the one to drive a knife into his heart.

"You don't have to worry about me," she insisted to Michael. "I know what I'm doing. And I *am* careful."

"No, sweetheart. You're not." He shook his head soberly. "Not anymore, you aren't. This vendetta you have against him is making you reckless. You need to quit, Nay. I mean now."

"I can't do that, Michael. Not until I make this last score."

He was about to protest further, but the sound of shuffling feet on the linoleum in the hallway put an abrupt halt to their conversation. Twin boys, dark-haired and mocha-skinned, with lean bodies and rounded cherub faces that said they were barely into their teens, stepped cautiously into the kitchen. Naomi had never seen them before, and she saw their uncertainty when they caught sight of her too.

"Hi," she said, offering a friendly smile.

Michael pivoted his wheelchair to face them. "Hey there, guys. Sleep okay?"

His irritation with her faded instantly now that the kids were in the room. The boys offered wary nods, but kept glancing at Naomi. The slightly taller one laid a protective arm around his brother. His sharp, dark eyes took in her appearance, lingering on the bruises shadowing her face and chin.

"Who's she?"

They didn't ask about her injuries. Most of the street kids had wounds and scars of their own, and there seemed to be an unwritten code that prohibited uncomfortable questions.

"I'm Naomi," she said. "I hope we weren't talking too loud out here and woke you?"

The kids gave vague shakes of their heads.

Michael touched her shoulder and smiled at the twins. "Naomi lives here too. She's like a sister to me. Sometimes that means we argue like siblings." That got a smile out of the shorter of the two boys. Michael glanced up at her. "Nay, this is Max and Billy. I'm hoping they're going to stick around for some breakfast?" He raised a questioning brow toward Max, the taller one, who was clearly the boss.

The boy's slight weight shifted from foot to foot as his brother glanced at him hopefully. "Yeah," Max murmured. "I guess we could eat. Do you think we could take showers too? It's been a few days and..."

He trailed off, looking down at his threadbare kicks, shame rolling off him in waves. Naomi wanted nothing more than to drag him into her arms and tell him he mattered. To promise him it wouldn't always be this way. But she'd stood in those same tattered shoes and shaky trust enough times to know that nothing would send him running faster than a hug or a well-meaning lecture.

She folded her hands in front of her and gave the kids a warm, casual smile.

"You can use the shower in the master bathroom," she told them. "End of the hall. Towels are in the linen closet, second door down on your right. Help yourselves, then when you're done, be sure to squeegee the tile and hang your wet towels up to dry on the hook behind the door, all right?"

Strange as it seemed, while most middle-class teens rebelled against house rules and parental guidance, the kids that came through their makeshift shelter seemed to appreciate being given a few responsibilities. Maybe feeling that they were contributing something took away a bit of the embarrassment of needing—and accepting—someone's help. It also reminded them, albeit subtly, about the importance of showing respect and having self-discipline.

They didn't have a whole lot of rules here. Kids came and went of their own free will. And the promise not to pry or contact police, parents, or social services, kept more of them coming back—even, in some cases, staying until they were able to get on their feet.

In return, she and Michael had a strict "no violence, no drugs" rule, and each child was expected to clean up after themselves. They took anywhere from six to ten kids on a given day, which meant some nights there was a kid conked out on the sofa as well. If they had more space, they could not only provide longer term accommodations but also increase the number of kids they could help.

Which brought her thoughts right back to the huge jackpot ripe for the picking at Moda. One-point-three-million dollars and some change would not only mean land and a proper shelter for the kids, but would ensure the operation stayed viable for years to come. And besides, there was a lot of poetic justice in the notion of using Leo Slater's money to fund a charity for orphaned and neglected children.

She watched Max and Billy leave the kitchen to make their way back down the hall in search of towels.

"Kills me every time," she murmured softly to Michael, her heart aching in a way that she couldn't describe to anyone who'd never felt it. "Did they tell you anything?"

He shook his head and raked a hand through his short hair. "Nope. I'm guessing it's Dad who's the problem. Billy has a set fingerprints on his upper arm that he kept trying to hide by pulling down his sleeves. Big hand, wrapped all the way around and then some. And when I answered the door, they both looked relieved I was in a wheelchair. Probably figured they could outrun me if they had to."

The saddest part of it all wasn't that they'd likely felt that way. It was the fact that their survival depended on them holding that fear close to their hearts and never forgetting it. Often, it was the people offering help who were the ones with the potential to hurt them even more than the people they were running from.

That was the reality of living in the streets. Two young, fresh boys with pretty faces could make an industrious flesh peddler a lot of money. Once they were hooked on drugs, their lives were over and they'd be begging to stay.

Naomi shoved off the weight of her maudlin thoughts and focused back on Michael with a wry grin. "If they thought they could outrun you, they haven't seen you tearing down the Strip in that chair like you've got a rocket under your scrawny ass."

He chuckled. "Scrawny ass? You should talk."

She laughed, glad to be falling back into normal mode here at home. Their teasing was an integral part of the day to day. It had to be. If they couldn't find a way to compartmentalize and lighten the heavy load of watching these kids struggle, they'd both go mad.

She cuffed him lightly on the shoulder. "I'll do the eggs and bacon. You're on toast duty."

"Yes, boss." He wheeled over to the refrigerator and pulled out two loaves of bread while Naomi busied herself in the cabinets, getting the necessary pans and seasonings. "Don't think I'm going to forget where we left off before the boys showed up, Nay. My legs may not work anymore, but my brain is in tip-top shape. And I've got a plan."

She swiveled a narrowed look on him. "What kind of plan?"

With the kids well out of earshot, he lowered his voice to a conspiratorial whisper. "You want to hit Slater's casino again for the big score? Fine. We do it my way. And we do it tonight."

"What? After last night, are you crazy?" She shook her head. "I have to lay low for a while first. Give Slater a chance to get comfortable again."

"Nuh-uh," Michael said, that familiar old hustler's gleam lighting up his hazel eyes. "Think about it, Nay. Right now, he probably doesn't even know his guys are missing yet. He's probably sitting by the pool drinking a Bloody Mary getting jerked off by his masseuse, thinking everything is fine and dandy. Soon, though, probably after he's had a five-course lunch and another hand job, he's going to start making calls to his men and realize he's not getting calls back. He'll be annoyed, but he sure as fuck won't think one tiny woman could've taken on three of his armed goons, so he'll give it a little time. By late afternoon, he's going to start really wondering. He's going to start making calls to other, bigger goons to go and find them."

"You're right. Shit, you're absolutely right."

Once the black sedan was found wherever Asher must have ditched it, suspicions would rise. Initially she'd been nothing but another cheat in one of his many casinos, a gnat that needed to be smacked. He'd handed off the chore of dealing with her to his thugs, and to his mind, that was the end of it. But to realize she'd gotten away? Slater wouldn't like that one bit.

It would eat at him, make him feel weak. Especially that he'd been outsmarted by a woman. He'd pull the security tapes from that night and he'd be looking for her. He'd be turning the city inside out until he found her.

"You know the last place he'll be looking for you?" Michael asked.

She nodded. "Yeah. Right under his nose. But how am I going to do it?"

"We," Michael corrected.

"What? Don't be ridiculous."

"I'm not. Aside from your magic when it comes to machinery and magnetics, I taught you practically everything you know about the grift. Cards, dice, you name it. Hell, I even showed you how to cobble together a decent disguise and where to get the best fake IDs this side of the Mississippi."

"No, Michael." She balked, shaking her head at him. "No way. This gig is too important. It's too big. I don't want you anywhere near it."

"Why, because I'm in this chair?"

She reared back, feeling as though he'd slapped her. "That's a low blow. And not anywhere close to the truth. You know that, right?"

When he said nothing, she walked over and wrapped her arms around his shoulders. "You're all the family I have, Michael. I'd die before I let anything happen to you."

"The feeling is mutual, Nay. So, don't think you're going to change my mind." He stared up at her with a hard, determined gaze. "You're not going back to

Slater's casino without me."

Every instinct she had was telling her this was too dangerous, too much risk. Especially now that he wanted to add himself to the equation. If anything happened to her friend...

"I don't know, Michael. I've got a bad feeling about this. Maybe it is too soon. I mean, what if I get spotted? What if Slater's got his security detail watching for anyone matching my height and build? They'll never let me close to the machines, let alone walk out with that size of a purse."

Michael didn't seem persuaded, not one bit. As much as she was motivated by vengeance on Leo Slater, he was addicted to the thrill of the chase, the glitter of ill-gotten gains. He always had been, at least before the accident. She couldn't remember the last time she'd seen him so energized. Part of her loved seeing her friend get excited—truly excited—about something again.

But another part of her was terrified they were about to make an enormous mistake.

"I'll worry about the how," he told her. "You worry about breakfast, then you're going get some rest before we start putting our plan together for tonight's big score."

CHAPTER 7

The only thing Asher hated more than the Vegas Strip was the Vegas Strip on a Saturday night.

It was oceans of people, moving like a school of fish containing species of every size, color, and shape in existence. There were the brightly dressed, heavily made-up girls donned in sashes or sparkling tiaras that proclaimed them "bride-to-be" or "finally legal" toddling on heels they could barely maneuver sober, never mind after five drinks. The guys were no exception, carousing in packs to celebrate their last hurrah on the eve of their wedding, surrounded by the other bachelors determined to get them into trouble. The tourists with their Vegas hats and shirts emblazoned with the ubiquitous reminder that what happened in Vegas…

All of this raucous, carefree mass of humanity clogging the Strip stepped blindly around or over the many homeless men, women, and kids who peppered the sidewalks and alcoves on the path between one shining casino and another.

Asher lengthened his stride and veered out of the crowd, into Casino Moda with a sigh of relief. Sure, it was owned by a murderous mobster, but at least it was a little less frenetic than the street.

The space was cavernous with high, blindingly white walls and a ceiling that had to be a hundred feet up. The tasteful marble floors glowed under the light of a massive crystal chandelier dripping with intricate cut-glass shapes that shimmered and sparkled like diamonds.

If Leo Slater wanted his flagship casino to seem both exclusive and slightly intimidating, he'd succeeded. Most of the patrons who'd come to surrender their money to Slater's coffers were working-class folks lured inside by the fantasy of instant, easy riches to be had on the other side of the polished brass revolving doors. Others, the glossy few, were dressed richly in designer labels and clothing that conveyed an air of excess and the casual disregard of those looking for a good time and willing to burn wads of cash in exchange for a few hours of thrills at any one of Moda's beckoning tables or gleaming slot machines.

Asher strode inside wearing a black leather jacket over a black T-shirt and black jeans. Waving off the cocktail waitress who swooped in with eager eyes and a lace-up vest three sizes too small for her plastic-enhanced breasts, he moved into the crowd, taking mental pictures of everything around him. The endless field of musical, clacking slots. The location of the tables in relation to the security desk, the placement of the cameras. The faces of the pit bosses and dealers.

All of it.

And as he cataloged his surroundings, he searched every face for sherry-colored almond eyes and a cupid's bow mouth he felt certain he would know anywhere now. Of course, if Naomi was in the casino as Asher suspected, odds were she'd bear little resemblance to the beautiful woman he knew her to be. The androgynous getup she'd been hidden beneath last night was only one of her many disguises.

Asher scowled, stepping deeper into the throng.

After putting the Order on standby following Naomi's escape, he'd had the entire day to fume and berate himself for letting her slip away. He wasn't quite certain how she'd managed to open the lock from inside the bedroom but in the past hour he'd been in the city, from all he'd learned about Naomi Fallon, AKA Naomi Pierce, AKA Naomi Sato, AKA several other aliases, he had a feeling picking simplistic locks was only one of the tricks in her repertoire.

Well, he had a few tricks of his own. As a Hunter, he wasn't only skilled at cold assassinations, but he was also an expert tracker. He hadn't met a quarry yet that he hadn't been able to chase to ground.

That went double when he was very likely the only thing standing between Naomi's life and another date in the desert with some of Leo Slater's hired muscle. If they got their hands on her again, Asher had no doubt it would be on orders to not only end her but make an example out of her as well.

It was that thought that had racked him until the sun had finally crept below the horizon, freeing him to head out after her. He'd been pissed as hell that she stole Ned's old truck, but it had also been her mistake.

He hadn't had the heart to trade the decrepit pickup in on something new after Ned's death. The Chevy got him where he needed to go most of the time, and since it was the only vehicle he had, Asher didn't want to lose it. The truth was, he'd grown a bit sentimental about the rusty relic—rather like had about old Ned too. So a few months ago, after a couple of crackheads up at the state line broke in to snatch a twenty-dollar bill he'd carelessly left tucked into the cup holder, Asher had installed a GPS tracker under the hood.

Which is what he used to trace the truck to the driveway of a small house a couple of miles off the Strip.

He'd paid a visit to that address before coming to Moda, but the place was empty. Empty of people, that is.

He'd found plenty of other interesting things inside. There were bunk rooms in both spare rooms, the beds all neatly made but showing signs of recent occupation. Threadbare duffels and black garbage bags filled with kids' clothing took up space in both rooms, as if the children staying there either had only just arrived or were soon on their way out.

And there were other items of interest to him too. Particularly in the last bedroom at the end of the hallway—the one filled with Naomi's uniquely intoxicating scent and the soapy odor of a human male. Inside that room were two twin beds and a clear delineation between one side of the space and the other.

Which meant Naomi and Michael weren't living together as lovers, but platonically. If he wasn't mistaken, Michael was in a wheelchair long-term. There were ramps outside and the master bathroom was fitted with rails and a portable seat in the shower.

By all indications they were simply roommates.

Why that understanding had given him such a deep sense of relief, Asher still didn't want to know.

He thought back to the other items he discovered. The open shoebox on a bureau in Naomi's room filled with passports, driver's licenses, student IDs—all with some variation of her photo on them, all undoubtedly fake. There were numerous IDs belonging to one Michael Carson at the bottom of the box too. Between the two of them they must have had upwards of a dozen different aliases.

And on Naomi's side of the room he'd found a makeup table littered with tubes, kits, eye color pots, lip pencils, and countless other items. In her overstuffed closet had been a couple pairs of jeans and some T-shirts, but enough costumes, wigs, and disguises to outfit an entire theater troupe.

Asher felt no guilt for his tactics or his reconnaissance. He had one job right now, and that was to protect Naomi, not just from Leo Slater and his lackeys, but from herself as well. Asher's hunch that her theft from the casino last night hadn't been the first time only intensified with each further clue he traced to her.

And as he stood in the middle of Casino Moda, every predatory instinct he had told him that she was there, somewhere amid the swarm of drunken, boisterous patrons. He just needed to know where to look.

Even if Slater was already on to the fact that she'd gotten away and evaded the dirt nap he'd had planned for her, the arrogant bastard certainly wouldn't be looking for her under his own roof again. Only a damned fool would come and hit the same casino they'd gotten caught trying to nick the night before.

A fool or a brazen genius, Asher thought, scanning the large space for anyone who might remotely pass for the Breedmate.

For the next hour he strolled around the casino, stopping off at the cage to buy some chips to help him blend in with the crowd. He tossed a few at the Caribbean Stud table, absently eyeing his cards before taking another look around the room.

The slot machines.

Since that was where she'd mentioned being last night before everything went to hell with Slater's goons, it was as good a place as any to start looking for her now.

Twice, by the slot machines, he'd seen young women that could've passed for Naomi from behind. Gleaming raven hair and petite frames, but when they'd turned around, the resemblance ended.

He had to get her face out of his head—an almost impossible task since he'd thought of little else for all of the hours he was trapped inside waiting for dusk. Besides, she was clearly a pro when it came to disguises and blending in. She wouldn't look anything like herself tonight. He had to think outside the box. Think like Naomi.

Another half hour went by without a sign of her anywhere at or near the slot machines. To continue his covert search of the casino floor, he moved on to the Spanish Twenty-One table closest to the pit of roulette wheels. Sliding a pile of chips onto the betting circle, he let his gaze trail over the tables and the players gathered around them.

It wasn't until he caught sight of a little old woman across the floor from him, her back and shoulders hunched as if from the late stages of osteoporosis, that he stopped cold and stared.

Gray-haired and slow-moving, she wore a long dark skirt and a similarly bland tunic and flowy wrap that hung off her slight frame. He couldn't see her face. Not any part of it, as she was walking away from him toward the ladies' room along with a herd of chattering middle-aged women in matching bright pink baseball caps and team jackets emblazoned with embroidered dice on the back.

Asher stared so intensely that more than one of the cackling pink ladies turned uneasy looks over their shoulders, their most primal instincts sensing a predator hidden and watching within the throng. Not the little old woman, though. She kept walking, head down and shoulders up.

Asher felt a growl build from deep inside him. He would never mistake her scent. He picked it out from among the other heavier perfumes, spilled liquor, cigarette smoke, and countless stale smells that permeated the air of the crowded casino.

Just the tracest whiff of her warm skin beneath all of the clothing and artifice had all pistons firing inside him at once. Unbidden, carnal images of Naomi and him together blasted him in a rush. The two of them on his bed, him kneeling between her thighs, her head thrown back in ecstasy as he entered her.

His fangs throbbed in his gums and he sealed his lips together in a grim scowl to conceal them.

Not good.

He struggled to push down both the inappropriate thoughts and the sudden, persistent swelling of his cock.

The petite crone had disappeared around the corner into the restrooms and he swallowed hard past the grit in his throat, finally able to think straight again.

He told the dealer to put a marker on his spot and abandoned his cards to move in closer, until he was ten yards away from the restroom entrance. He took up a vantage point off to the side and waited, having half a mind to barge in after her. But the last thing he needed— the last thing either of them needed—was to create a scene. And there was the smallest chance that the old woman actually wasn't Naomi.

An infinitesimal chance at best.

If that wasn't her, he'd be damned. Hell, he probably was either way. He'd fed only a few days ago, but just the sight of the female had made him wild with the need to have her under his mouth. To close his teeth and fangs over that lean, silky neck and—

"Excuse me," a timid male voice murmured behind him after he'd been standing there for several minutes.

He wheeled around to find a ginger-haired human in his mid-twenties waiting awkwardly, a nervous smile pinned to his face.

Asher glared back at him silently, irritated at having been interrupted.

"You're, um… you're standing in front of the ATM," the other man murmured, his voice climbing an octave as he stared up at Asher, looking close to pissing himself.

Asher snarled and moved out of the way.

He turned back to the restroom as the pink ladies and a few other women who'd also been inside the restroom filed back out to the casino. No sign of Naomi, though. Impatient, he stepped far enough behind a large decorative column that the majority of his bulk was out of sight. Best case, he'd be able to intercept her without her bolting or bringing down the whole house with a scream or a struggle once she saw him there.

But he'd take her either way. He wasn't leaving Vegas without her safely in hand.

As he stood in wait, another few minutes went by. Followed by a few more. Foot traffic in and out of the ladies' room continued in a steady stream, but Naomi was nowhere to be seen.

Son of a bitch.

She'd ghosted him.

He wasn't sure if it had been pure luck that she'd slipped out of the bathroom in those few seconds he'd been in conversation with the other man, or if she'd somehow sensed him at her heels and successfully dodged him. All he knew in his gut was that Naomi was not that bathroom anymore.

He bit back a string of curses, if only barely.

She couldn't run far. Not this time. He'd found her once—or at least he thought he had—and he'd find her again. She was cagey and clever, but he was relentless. And if he had to tear the whole place apart tonight in order to save her from herself, he damned well would.

Because whether Naomi realized it or not, she was his.

To protect, he reminded himself sternly.

Even as a possessiveness unlike he'd ever felt spurred his body into motion across the casino floor.

CHAPTER 8

"Thanks for letting me have your jacket," Naomi told one of the club of five women she'd encountered in the ladies' room. She'd gone in behind them, feeling uneasy and jittery, as though Moda's eye in the sky was following her every move inside the casino. Or worse, as if someone stationed somewhere on the floor had her trained in his sights.

Naomi couldn't get into one of the restroom stalls fast enough. Heart racing, palms moist with anxiety, she'd stripped out of her gray wig and costuming inside the handicap stall and stuffed the whole kit and caboodle into the trash bin before coming out in the jeans and T-shirt she'd worn beneath. No one paid her any mind as she discreetly stepped to a vacant sink to splash soap and water on her face to erase the old-age makeup.

The "Diamond Divas Dice Club" stood in front of the mirrors, refreshing their perfume and primping while they chattered about which casino restaurant buffet to hit for the best early bird dinner. Drying her face with paper towels, Naomi offered her opinion to break the ice, then had smoothly begun a soft-sell negotiation with one of the ladies about buying her jacket as a good luck charm.

Wearing the Opium- and cigarette-scented jacket embroidered with the name "Gladys" on the front, Naomi had kept her head low as she strolled out of the restroom with the women a minute or two later as if she were part of their tight, conveniently concealing, pack.

"I really appreciate it," she told the squat, dark-haired gambler as the Divas paused with her on the casino's midway. "I think this is going to bring me some great luck."

"I hope so, honey." Gladys grinned as she patted her glittery pink fanny pack. "Best luck I had so far tonight was selling it to you for a cool hundred bucks."

Naomi smiled. "Enjoy your dinner, ladies."

Once the group headed off toward the seafood buffet she recommended, she turned the jacket inside out and slipped back into it. Now that she was on the floor again, she didn't want to attract undue attention with a neon pink billboard on her back.

She glanced at her burner phone to check the time. Shit. She was two minutes off schedule. Michael would be nervous because of that, but they had their signals all worked out hours before they arrived separately at Moda tonight. There would be no communication between them about the job until after they were both back home again. Being seen talking on their phones or passing any kind of hand signals across the floor to each other would not only put the night's plan at risk, but their lives.

Naomi glanced around warily, still feeling a niggle of unease even though she could find no evidence to back it up. Probably just paranoia because of what happened last night. Besides, there was still time to abort if either one of them felt they should. A quick glance through the crowd showed Michael paused to watch the roulette tables. He was clapping along with the gathered spectators, his pre-arranged signal that everything was a go on his end.

Naomi steeled herself and moved through the packed rows of slot machines, making a beeline for the bar to order a drink as agreed. Martini with three olives if she was ready to roll; Bloody Mary if she felt they should can the plan and clear out ASAP.

With her martini in hand, she walked back over to the slots and began feeding quarters into an empty machine four seats in from the aisle. She hadn't chosen that particular section by chance. At the head of her row, situated so that its tall illuminated jackpot sign faced the midway crowds and flashed for all eyes to see, stood Moda's biggest-paying machine.

The one with the one-point-three-million-dollar prize just waiting to be had.

Naomi casually moved from one machine to the next, progressing to the dollar slot sitting directly beside the sleek, towering Monte Carlo Fortune Bonanza, which was currently being monopolized by a bored-looking platinum-blonde piece of arm candy who was waiting for her sugar daddy to wrap up at the blackjack table across the way.

Naomi slid a twenty-dollar bill into her machine and pulled the lever. Like most of the people around her, she squealed with excitement when she hit for any amount of money and rubbed the glass as if she could will the most coveted symbols to appear.

The only difference between her and all the other poor saps around her losing their paychecks was that she actually could finesse the machine to do her bidding.

When she'd lost about half her money, she glanced over and saw Michael slowly making his way over to her.

Go time.

The blonde put another hundred into the Monte Carlo machine and yanked on the handle. Naomi's anxiety climbed with every second the woman remained in the seat. When she was about to surrender her third big bill, Naomi leaned over to her.

"Wanna tip for upping your odds with the big money machines?" At her neighbor's intrigued nod, she said, "Don't pull the lever to spin the wheel. Use the button instead."

As she confided the nonsensical advice, Naomi reached over and touched the red button. Not to push it, but just to let her fingertip rest lightly on the machine.

It was enough.

The woman sat back and pushed the button. She lost the round. Shrugging, she tried again, then again. "So much for your tip," she muttered, flouncing off in a huff.

Mission accomplished.

Michael rolled up only a few seconds later.

They didn't speak to each other, barely even acknowledged the other's presence at all. Naomi went back to her machine as Michael got situated next to her.

"How're the martinis at this dump?" he asked nonchalantly, the way any gambler might in order to strike up conversation with an attractive fellow player.

"They're kind of strong," she said with a rehearsed

giggle. A careless movement of her hand sent her glass toppling onto the carpeted floor. She hopped down to retrieve it, casually taking the opportunity to brush her hand over the side of the Monte Carlo Fortune Bonanza's sleek metal casing. She shrugged at Michael. "I guess that means I'm cut off now."

He chuckled, perfectly casual, smiling as she stepped around him with her empty glass. Her pulse was hammering, but she kept her bland expression fixed on her face.

"Take care," she told him, already edging away from the area.

"Thanks." He slipped a hundred-dollar bill into the machine and tapped the maximum bet button. "You too."

She turned her back to him, hands fisted loosely at her sides as she began walking.

And then she prayed like hell that they weren't making a colossal mistake.

CHAPTER 9

A woman's scream rang out somewhere in the casino.

Asher froze where he stood. He'd nearly completed his search of the roulette wheel tables and several pits of slot machines in the massive game area with no sign of Naomi. That high-pitched shriek sent a surge of adrenaline—and cold dread—coursing into his veins.

Holy fuck.

Don't let it be her.

But then another shout went up, followed by dozens more and the sudden cacophony of cheering voices, bells and sirens, and applause. Over in another section of the slots near the casino's main throughway, a ridiculously tall machine with a digital sign flashing an equally ridiculous name had evidently just paid out a mega-jackpot totaling more than a million dollars.

Nearly everyone in the place paused to look toward

the area where a crowd was swiftly gathering around the winner. Asher headed that way, too, craning to see who was at the center of the excited throng. He fully expected it to be Naomi—or her disguised likeness—as he neared the periphery of the cheering spectators.

But it wasn't her seated in front of the machine.

As Moda management and security officers moved in to greet the night's big winner, Asher realized it was a man. Sandy hair and a friendly, round face that lit with surprise and stammering elation as he pivoted around in his wheelchair to accept everyone's congratulations.

"I can't believe it!" he exclaimed, looking every bit the shocked and beaming new millionaire. "This is incredible! I won!"

Son of a bitch.

Michael Carson.

Naomi's friend hadn't just lucked into the biggest jackpot payout in the place. He had help. The kind of help only Naomi could provide.

Which meant she had to be close.

In one, single mental snapshot, Asher took it all in. Michael seeming on the verge of actual tears in his wheelchair. The one-point-three-million-dollar jackpot sign flashing. The casino employee rushing forward with a wide smile and a pile of papers for the winner to sign.

And there, at the periphery of the expanding crowd, an angel's face crowned in glossy black hair. No longer garbed as a crone, Naomi had shed all of her disguise and was now observing the chaos with a bemused smile on her face as she stepped back to make room for more people who pushed in. And she kept stepping back, slowly melting away like a shadow.

Not so fast, Asher thought, staring right at her.

She glimpsed him in that same moment, her sherry-colored gaze colliding with his amber-flecked furious one.

Her mouth dropped open in sudden, silent dread.

Then she pivoted and slipped out of sight, her petite size hiding her among the tight herds of casino patrons.

Asher dove into the crowd, cutting through with single-minded purpose. In the distance, he saw her round the corner up near the glass shaft of the soaring, central private elevator. For an instant, he lost sight of her.

"Fuck," he snarled under his breath.

Using the full speed of his Breed genetics, he flashed across the casino floor, nothing but cool air breezing through the clusters of slow-moving, mostly inebriated casino patrons on his way toward the elevator. None of the humans' senses were keen enough to track him, but there was one pair of eyes that found him and locked on with laser intensity.

A big Breed male wearing a dark suit, a wireless earpiece, and a Moda security badge on his hip stepped out of the elevator at the same moment Asher was rushing after Naomi at preternatural speed.

Icy silver eyes narrowed beneath the thick espresso-brown slashes of the male's brows. Asher knew him—or, rather, he used to know him. Back when they both were nameless boys, yoked and collared under Dragos's brutal Hunter program.

There was no kinship between them, then or now. Asher hadn't come away from the lab with many friends. Or any, for that matter. In the two decades since he and this male had escaped the program, their paths hadn't crossed until this moment.

Seeing a fellow former assassin now, here, and obviously employed by none other than Leo Slater made the killer in Asher tense for a fight. To the death, if necessary.

They squared off in silent challenge, Asher calculating a dozen lethal ways to open his attack while the other male's scowl deepened in suspicion.

"What are you doing here, *Asher?*" He leaned heavily on the moniker, scorn in every syllable. "Wouldn't have guessed you for the gambling type."

"I could ask you the same thing." He glanced at the shiny brass nametag pinned to the Hunter's jacket lapel. "*Cain*, is it?"

The male grunted, those shrewd eyes gleaming like the sharpened edge of a polished blade. By now four other members of Moda's security team had joined Cain outside the elevator bank. The men, humans all of them, looked to him and Asher in question.

"Everything all right, sir?" one of them asked Cain.

He gave a terse nod. "Get out on the floor. Make sure we're secure. I'll be right behind you."

As the unit fanned out to do his bidding, Cain's gaze swept the immediate area—including the path Naomi had taken only moments ago—before his attention swung back to Asher.

"Problem, brother?"

Cain's mouth drew tight at the growled endearment. "You'd better hope there isn't. Or I'll be right behind you, too, *brother.*"

Asher smiled a cold smile, then gave Slater's head of security a bump of his shoulder as he brushed past him without another word.

Everything animal inside him seethed at the threat

this killer posed—not so much to him, but to Naomi. And, now, even to her friend Michael.

Asher exited the casino, inhaling the night air as he headed out to the bright lights of the Strip. She wasn't hard to trace now. Two blocks up the sidewalk, she was rushing to the curb with her arm out, trying to hail a taxi.

She yelped as he hooked one arm around her midsection and hauled her away from the street.

"Keep walking and don't pull away from me or turn around unless you want to call more attention to us both." With his hand at the small of her back, he steered her alongside him and began walking briskly toward the garage where he'd earlier parked the truck.

Too smart to make a scene on the street, she fell into step beside him as instructed, her body trembling under his palm. "How the hell did you find me? And what do you think you're doing?"

"Saving your pretty neck for the second time," he muttered. "Come on."

Although he would hardly call her cooperative, she kept quiet the rest of the walk to the pickup truck. He put her in the passenger side, then went around and climbed behind the wheel.

She shot him an irritated glance as he started up the truck. "Since I see you had no trouble retrieving this heap from where I left it this morning, I guess that means you know where to drop me off."

"I'm not dropping you off anywhere."

"You most certainly are." She balked, pivoting to face him. "Take me home, Asher. Right now."

"I am. To my home."

"What? No! Dammit, let me out of this truck right now."

"Out of the question." When she lunged for the door handle beside her, he reached across the seat and closed his fingers over her hand. "If I let you go, you're going to end up dead."

"Didn't we already have this conversation? I told you I don't want your so-called protection. I just want you to leave me alone."

"I can't do that, Naomi. Especially not after the stunt you and Michael just pulled."

Her face blanched, but her stubborn chin went up a notch. "I have no idea what you're talking about."

He scoffed. "Really? I'm betting you've got about one-point-three-million ideas what I'm talking about."

She fell silent for a long moment. "Michael won that jackpot, not me. There's no reason for anyone at the casino to suspect a thing."

"Not unless they have a reason to study the casino security video and notice that an elderly woman hobbled into the ladies' room a few minutes before the big win, but never came out."

Naomi swallowed. "I felt like I was being watched. It was only you?"

"You'd better hope it was only me." He bit off a curse, infuriated by her brazenness—by her recklessness that seemed to border on suicidal. "For fuck's sake, Naomi. You have to know what it means to cross a man like Leo Slater. Are you deliberately trying to get yourself killed?"

"No."

"Then why, damn it? What the fuck are you trying to accomplish?"

"You wouldn't understand."

"Try me," he growled, taking hold of her slender

shoulders. He was vibrating with the force of his anger—and his worry for her. He felt his eyes burning with sparks as he glowered at her within the confines of the truck's cab. God help him, he wanted to shake her.

He wanted to drive his fist through the dashboard and rail at her for how close she'd come to danger. Danger she couldn't even begin to fathom, now that he knew Slater had a former Hunter on his payroll.

"Tell me why you're so hell-bent on this casino. On this man."

"He owes me. Let's just leave it at that."

"No. We're not leaving at that." He gripped her tighter. "You're not a stupid female, Naomi. In fact, you've proven yourself to be clever as hell. Except when it comes to Slater."

A chill swept over him as he relived the anguish and fear and helplessness of an innocent child who'd witnessed the brutality of life, the ugliness of it, much too young. There was a part of him—a part he kept buried deep down inside—who understood some of that too.

Asher searched her pained gaze, his hands still holding onto her. The connection renewed the memory he'd read from her before, but he didn't let go, unable—or perhaps unwilling—to release her. "It was Slater who hurt your mother, wasn't it?"

"Hurt her?" She spoke in a tight, but quiet voice. "He killed her, Asher. I can't prove it, but I know he did. The police have called the case unsolved. Just another woman who vanished off the face of the Earth after Leo Slater got tired of beating and using her."

"She went missing?"

"When I was eight years old. She left me alone for

the weekend and… never came back." Naomi swallowed, her eyes welling. "I kept waiting. I kept hoping, even after child protective services came to our apartment and took me away with them a couple of months later."

Asher exhaled a curse that boiled up from the pits of his soul. Her anger was one thing. He could've handled that in stride and been fine. In the short time he'd known her, anger and combativeness were the emotions she'd worn the most. Along with stubborn, unflagging determination.

No, those emotions she kept right up front for all to see.

It was the single tear rolling down her cheek that made his heart ache.

And the next one and the next after that. Her sadness over her mother ripped him clean in half.

He had no skill when it came to giving comfort or saying the right things. He'd been bred to deny any softness, any emotion that might make him a weaker instrument when it came to dealing death. Not even his time looking after Ned had smoothed all of his rough edges.

But he wanted to give Naomi comfort. He wanted to let her know that her pain was his now. That he would not only protect her, but do whatever was necessary to ensure Leo Slater never had the chance to hurt her or anyone else again.

Wordlessly, he moved his hands from her shoulders to the sides of her beautiful face, cradling her gently in his palms. She didn't resist him. Her gaze stayed locked on his as he smoothed his thumbs over the tears that now coursed down her face in steady streams.

And when he drew her toward him, her lips fell open on a quiet exhalation, a sound that was far from a sob. Asher brushed his mouth over hers, shocked at the current that roared through him at that first tender contact. He wasn't prepared for how sharply he craved her.

He wasn't prepared for how deeply this female was impacting his life. He didn't have room for the trouble she was bringing into his solitary world. And he sure as hell wasn't prepared to deal with all of the feelings she'd been stoking inside him from the moment their eyes first met.

He drew away from her on a low groan and a murmured apology that he didn't actually mean.

"Buckle up," he ordered her gruffly. "It's not safe for you in this city. And we've wasted too much time already."

She sank back against the seat in silence and drew the seatbelt across her body. When she was secured, Asher threw the truck into gear and sped out of the garage with renewed determination.

He would protect Naomi, with his arm and his life. As slim as his honor was, he couldn't live with himself if he allowed anything to happen to her.

And now, on top of that obligation, he would call in the debt Leo Slater owed her if it was the last thing he ever did.

As soon as he'd ensured Naomi was out of Slater's reach, that son of a bitch would be going down.

CHAPTER 10

He didn't say two words to her for the duration of the drive out of Vegas.

She told herself she was relieved to have his brooding silence beside her, especially since her lips were still burning from the heat of his kiss. It had been so unexpected, his tenderness coming right on the heels of his obvious frustration with her.

Had he kissed her out of desire? God knew she'd been entertaining some unbidden, purely sexual thoughts and urges where Asher was concerned. As angry as she wanted to be, and was, with the overbearing Breed male, she could hardly deny her awareness of him nor her body's all-too-eager response. Any woman with eyes in her head and warm red blood in her veins would find it impossible to describe Asher as anything less than panty-meltingly hot.

But that didn't mean the attraction was mutual. In

the instant before he'd covered her mouth with his, he seemed so angry she half-expected him to punch something—possibly even her. That is, until her eyes started leaking and those pathetically broken sobs started falling from her mouth before she could hold them back.

Humiliation flamed her cheeks, adding to the fire already settled there in the wake of his kiss.

How utterly embarrassing to have broken down in front of him like that. Tears, for fuck's sake. She never cried over her mother, least of all in the presence of someone else. Not even Michael knew how deeply the loss had truly wounded her. Now, she'd gone and blubbered in front of Asher like the heartbroken, abandoned eight-year-old girl she'd been all that time ago.

For all she knew, he might have done it simply to shut her up. Or, even worse, out of pity.

But his burning kiss hadn't tasted like either of those impulses. Not that she had been fit to judge. By the time his strong hands had closed around her shoulders, then cradled her face, she'd been too far gone to question anything but the intensity of her need to sink against him in surrender.

At the moment, all she wanted was to get as far away from him as possible and try to put the whole unsettling idea out of her mind.

As Asher turned off the starlit desert road and onto the bumpy dirt lane that led to the old ranch, Naomi hung suspended between the thrill of having bilked Leo Slater out of one of his millions and the concern she had for Michael in these next crucial hours following his big "win" at the casino.

By now, all of the casino paperwork would have

been signed, the check issued and in his hands, ready to be deposited in his bank account. But what if something had gone wrong?

What if it had all gone to hell after she fled Moda with Asher on her heels?

Naomi reached into her jeans pocket and pulled out her new burner phone to check for messages from Michael. No word at all yet. Dammit. Although they'd agreed he would text once he was in the clear and felt it was safe to make contact, her fingers itched with the need to check in with him.

She'd barely tapped the screen with the first letter when the device suddenly leapt out of her fingers and into Asher's right hand.

"What the hell?" She gaped at him, reminded of just how little she understood about him or his kind. "What do you think you're doing?"

"You have your little talents; I have mine." He dropped the phone between his parted thighs as he maneuvered the truck over the potholes and valleys of the rambling driveway. When they were parked in front of the house, he killed the engine and gave her a grim look. "If you care about your friend, the best thing you can do for him is keep your distance for a while."

She knew he was right, but it went against her grain to let any man—particularly this one—boss her and tell her what she could or could not do. "Fine, you made your point. I'll take my phone back now."

She held out her hand but he ignored it. Taking the keys and the burner in one hand, he got out of the truck and stalked around to open her door before she had the chance. "Let's get inside. It's not a good idea to linger out here longer than we need to."

His tone was grim, and sounded far from enthused at the notion of having her at his place for a second time. She nearly reminded him that the only reason she had been there at all was because of his insistence that she would be dead without him.

Begrudgingly, she climbed out of the truck and walked with him onto the porch where Sam's panting mouth and eager whining greeted them on the other side of the screen door. In spite of everything else that was upsetting and out of control in her life, the sight of the dancing, wiggling hound made a smile break across her face. At least someone was pleased with this unwanted arrangement.

"Hey, you," she said, dropping onto her haunches and giving Sam's swiveling rear and thick shoulders a good rub as soon as she stepped inside the dimly lit house. She laughed as the big dog turned excited circles in front of her and showered her chin in wet licks. "Oh, yes, such a good boy! Your dog's a nut, Asher. I mean, look at him. His whole body wags when I touch him."

Asher was looking, but not at Sam. When she glanced up from her squat in front of him, still petting and scratching the deliriously happy hound, she found Asher's eyes fixed on her. Those dark blue pools smoldered, tiny sparks crackling in their depths.

Snared in the intensity of his unblinking study of her, all the heat she'd felt during and after Asher's kiss swamped her all over again.

He made a strange sound in the back of his throat. Not quite a growl, but a deep vibration that seemed to call to something wild inside her veins. Her pulse kicked, throbbing in the side of her neck and lower, a heavy throb that made her legs go a little weak beneath her.

When he finally spoke, she saw the gleaming tips of his fangs. "I'll go turn on some more lights for you."

He disappeared into the dark of the house, moving silently, with the stealth of a ghost. Or something far more dangerous than that.

As soon as Sam heard him in the kitchen, his floppy ears perked and he trotted off ahead of Naomi. She followed, feeling suddenly awkward and uncomfortable in Asher's home. It wasn't as if she belonged there. And she felt pretty certain Asher was regretting her presence too.

"You know, if it's just a matter of laying low for a while, I do have other places I can go. I can get a new fake ID and change my appearance again."

He flicked on the light over the kitchen table and sent a scowl in her direction. "What are you talking about?"

"I don't think you really want me here any more than I want to be here."

"What difference does that make?"

She shrugged as if none of this was any big deal to her. "I'm just saying I have other options. I know plenty of other people I can call for help if I—"

"No one else can help you, Naomi. Only me now."

He looked so certain, so gravely serious, even she was tempted to believe that. She crossed her arms over her chest to stifle the shiver that swept over her. "Not even the Order?"

His jaw tensed as he studied her. "I can get word to them right now, if you prefer. There's a command center near Tahoe. They can probably have someone here to retrieve you in a couple of hours."

"No." She shook her head, cursing herself for even

bringing up his earlier threat to pack her up and ship her off to the Order without her consent. "I'll stay."

At least for now. She told herself it was a reasonable enough plan, at least until she got the all-clear from Michael. The farther they stayed apart for the time being, the safer it would be for both of them. Once the jackpot check from Casino Moda was in his bank account, their lives could resume.

She could handle a day or so here at the ranch with Sam and his domineering vampire housemate.

It was the thought of staying overnight that gave her more than a little pause.

"You will take the master bedroom," Asher informed her tersely. "I don't need the bed. Besides, I'll be on watch twenty-four-seven now."

She scoffed, leaning her hip against the counter as he turned on more lights. "On watch to make sure I don't finesse the lock and escape again?"

He pinned her with a sober stare. "I can make sure you stay inside, but I'm more concerned about keeping anyone else from getting in."

The gravity of his voice took her aback. He was more than concerned. He was grim with a certainty that shook her. "Who do you think will be looking for me? Slater?" She lifted her shoulder, considering. "He doesn't know I'm the one who's been repeatedly hitting his casinos this past year. I take care to always look different, never like myself. And last night was the first time I ever got caught."

Asher's face looked thunderous with building disbelief—and fury. "How many times have you crossed him?"

"I don't know. Ten or twelve, I suppose."

"Christ." His mouth pressed flat. "Using your Breedmate gift—what do you call it, *finessing*?"

She nodded. "With a touch, I can manipulate metals and magnetics. Simple gears, machinery. Locks."

He grunted. "And casino slot machines."

"Sometimes I hit the roulette tables too. For variety. All I have to do is rest my hands on the casing in order to make the connection with the moving parts and bend them to my will."

"For how much, Naomi?" His brows furrowed deeper, his big body radiating a heat she could feel all the way on the other side of the kitchen. "Holy hell. How much have you already taken from him?"

"Before tonight?" She licked her lips, her mouth going dry under the blazing force of Asher's stare. "A couple hundred grand. It's how Michael and I have kept the shelter open at his house. Without the money, those kids—"

"Damn it, woman."

His snarled interruption cut her off sharply. He stormed up to her, his face a mask of rage. And something else too. Was it . . . fear? He looked as if he wanted to take hold of her and shake her until her teeth rattled. Either that or kiss her again, although if he did that, she knew there would be no tenderness in it now. It would be punishing, brutal in a way that shouldn't have made her heart race the way it did now.

But he didn't take hold of her. He raked a hand over his hair, then glanced at the windows and sliders that looked out over the property outside. Nothing but endless blackness on the other side of the glass, yet when Asher's gaze swung back to her, it was bleak with dread.

Suddenly his cryptic statement that no one but him

could help her now—not even the powerful warriors of the Order—came rushing back to her like a chill wind.

"What is it?" she asked him. "Something happened tonight back at the casino. You know something, don't you? Asher, what aren't you telling me?"

"I ran into Slater's chief of security right after you took off. His name is Cain. He's Breed, Naomi. Worse than that. He's a trained assassin."

"Oh, shit." Her head felt light, as though all of the blood had drained away. "An assassin. Are you... are you sure?"

He said nothing, merely offered a grim nod. Of course, he was sure. No wonder he was acting as if she were one step from her grave all night. She probably was.

"He doesn't know you're with me," Asher told her. "As far as I can tell, he doesn't know anything about you. If he did, you never would've made it out of the casino tonight. You're safe for now. With me."

His calm reassurance helped take the edge off her fear—a little. She had no reason to doubt anything Asher told her, not even this. But he couldn't protect her forever.

Nor was he offering that.

"Oh, God," she murmured. "I have to warn Michael."

"No, Naomi." Asher shook his head. "The surest way to help your friend is to keep your distance now. Is there any reason for Slater to think the two of you were together on this?"

"No. We've never done a job together, and there's nothing to link us together inside or out of the casino."

"The house you share—"

"Is in Michael's name only. I don't even use the

address on any of my IDs." At his nod, she went on. "We arrived at the casino separately tonight, him about forty minutes before I got there. Once we were inside, we didn't talk or signal that we knew each other."

"But you did touch the machine to ensure he claimed the prize?"

She nodded. "We had it all rehearsed. The only change was my disguise. Before tonight, I've never been inside the casino without disguising myself. And I only ditched my old lady cover after I thought I'd been made somehow."

Asher cursed low under his breath. "You took off your disguise because of me. Because I was shadowing you. I'm sorry, Naomi."

"Not your fault." She barely resisted the urge to reach out and touch the tightly clenched fist that now rested on the counter near her. "All the mistakes I've made have been my own. I only hope the ones I made tonight don't end up hurting Michael. I'm not going to be able to relax until I hear from him that he's okay."

Asher gave her a vague nod. "You've had a long day. It's only going to get longer. Go on back and get settled while I put out some food for the animals."

She hadn't realized how exhausted she was until he mentioned it. Her neck was stiff from stress, her body aching and tense. Her eyes burned from remnants of her hastily scrubbed-off makeup and facial prosthetics adhesive.

"Would it be all right if I use your shower?"

He gestured over her shoulder, toward the hallway leading to his bedroom. "Halfway down the hall on the left."

"Thank you," she murmured. She started walking

that way, then paused to regard him over her shoulder. "I mean that, Asher. Thank you. For everything you're doing for me."

He merely stared at her, silent as he watched her leave.

CHAPTER 11

Asher grabbed a large bag of dog food from one of the cabinets and set it on the counter, trying to ignore to the sound of the water running through the old pipes of the house.

It wasn't easy. The plumbing rattled and groaned, which was normally just a mild annoyance on any other day. Combined with the knowledge that Naomi was standing naked under the warm spray just a short walk down the hall from him, the shower noise seem to go on forever.

And with that awareness came a lot of vivid images he couldn't seem to banish from his mind. Images of her black hair sleek and wet against her milky neck and shoulders, her petite body lathered with suds and slick under her moving hands.

He could practically feel her soft skin beneath his own hands, and as he imagined spreading her leanly muscled thighs to delve between them, first with his fingers, then with the full length of his cock, he shuddered with the rush of need that rolled over him.

"Christ." He raked a hand over his clenched jaw, his fangs aching and extended, filling his mouth.

Kissing her had been about the worst thing he could have done—for her sake and his own. Because now he knew what her sweet, lush little mouth tasted like and it had only made him hungry for more. Hungry to know how sweet the rest of her would taste under his lips and tongue. Or under the sharp press of his fangs.

If it was only lust driving him, he might have been able to deal with it. He hadn't fucked in a while, but he knew plenty of places he could go between here and Las Vegas to scratch that sort of itch. He doubted another woman's body would be enough to slake what he was feeling for Naomi. She stirred more than physical curiosity or need in him. She stirred more than simple blood hunger too.

She piqued his interest in ways no other female had ever before. More than just sexy and smart, she was resilient and strong too. Tough and tenacious as hell, despite her diminutive size. He respected that more than he cared to admit. But along with the steel spine she so obviously possessed came stubbornness the likes of which he'd only seen in a mirror.

No doubt about it, the woman was going to be trouble for him.

Already was, since his threat to dump her on the Order was an empty one now. No, after tonight, she was his to protect. If Slater or Cain or anyone else had ideas about harming her, they were going to have to come through him first.

He felt a thump against the back of his leg and glanced down at Sam's expectant stare and impatiently wagging tail.

Asher grunted. "Sure, now you're my buddy, eh, old boy? So long as our pretty visitor isn't in the room or if I've got your food in my hands."

Sam led him eagerly to his empty bowl, nudging his big head down to start eating even before Asher finished pouring the kibble. As the hound munched enthusiastically, Asher patted his short golden fur and the thicker hair at the back of the dog's neck.

Unbidden, a memory swept over him—one of his own—from around the time that he had first arrived at Ned's place after drifting aimlessly across the States following his release from Dragos's control.

They'd been sitting in this very kitchen, Ned eating a bowl of beef stew at the small table that still sat in front of the window overlooking the back of the property. It was dark and Sam was in need of a run.

"I'll take him," Asher had offered. *"You sit and finish your meal."*

Ned had given him a nod of thanks and continued eating. "Put his collar and leash on him before you let him out. That damn coyote's been prowling around again and I don't want Sam thinking he oughta go after it and try to drive it off. That pup's got more attitude than sense sometimes. Kinda like a couple other people around here."

Asher remembered smiling at the quip as he'd turned to grab the dog's woven nylon collar with its jangling tags. As soon as his fingers had closed around the cool, unbreakable material, his whole body had gone cold.

As if he were rooted in ice, he couldn't move. Couldn't think. Couldn't hear anything but the rush of his own blood pounding in his head. He'd been unable to breathe, feeling the ghost of another collar clamped tight around his own neck.

It was the sensation of Ned's leathery brown hand on his arm that shook Asher out of his stupor. It grounded him, pulled him back from a dark ledge. But in that moment, Asher had seen insanity just over the horizon. So close, he could almost touch it.

"No collar," he'd ground out, his voice wooden and distant.

Ned had squeezed his arm gently and nodded. *"All right, son. No collar, then."*

They never spoke of it again, and while Ned knew the basics of Asher's past—a consideration he felt he owed the old man in exchange for his willingness to share his home with someone so different from him— Ned didn't know about Asher's origins as a Hunter. He didn't know any of the hideous things Asher had been made to do while his neck was ringed with the collar he never dreamed he'd escape.

Ned never pried, never judged. Instead, he'd tried to convince Asher—unsuccessfully—that sooner or later he would need to leave the ranch and go find a family of his own. He didn't realize Asher's freedom only stretched as far as his legs could carry him. He would never be free of his memories. Nor of his sins.

A soft sound jolted him back to the here and now.

Naomi cleared her throat behind him, bringing with her the fresh scent of warm, clean skin and damp, shampooed hair. Her pink cheeks and shiny black hair sent an ache through him that he could hardly curb.

But no more than the long white T-shirt she wore. *His shirt.*

He scowled, all he could do to bite back the sudden

surge of his fangs and the heat that prickled his skin from head to toe. His erection was instant, and he knew he had to be glowering at her just from the agony of his arousal.

"I, um, hope you don't mind. My clothes smelled like smoke from the casino and I couldn't stand to put them on once I was clean. I found this T-shirt on top of the dresser with some other folded laundry."

His blood rushed out of his head and went south as he realized she was practically naked beneath it. Her breasts were small and high, with little need for a bra, not that she seemed to be wearing one. The cotton held no real shape on her small frame, but it was so thin he could just make out the dusky peaks of her nipples and the hint of her lavender-colored panties beneath it.

Holy fuck.

"It's fine," he snarled, pivoting if only to keep her from seeing the hot coals of his eyes. His *glyphs* were writhing with dark colors, all in response to the desire he felt for this female. When he spoke again, his voice was like gravel and thick from the crowding presence of his fangs. "We can head out tomorrow night to get you some clothes. We'll need groceries, too. I hope you're not hungry, since anything I have here is left over from when Ned was alive. Which means it's somewhere between inedible and radioactive."

She laughed. "I'm not hungry, but if I get there I'm sure I can figure something out."

"You'll have to, because I don't cook, either."

"Oh, I don't know about that. As I recall, you make a mean can of chicken noodle."

He felt her warmth behind him as she stepped further into the kitchen and went over to pet Sam, who was licking his newly emptied bowl. Her feet were bare, and he found himself staring, fixated on the peachy polish and the delicate silver band that circled one of her perfect little toes.

"Michael texted me while I was in the shower," she said, sounding more than relieved. "He says everything went off without a hitch. He's home, and he's got the check. He's going to bring it to the bank on Monday morning. It should clear in a few days, and it looks like Slater has no idea what hit him."

Asher hoped she was right about that, but his gut told him she and Michael were far from in the clear with Slater. They might never be safe again. Not if he ever got wise to their scam.

Dread over that eventuality cooled some of the heat he was feeling for the Breedmate who'd not only upended his solitary existence but lit it on fire. He wanted her, no question about that, but what he wanted most was her safety.

"What did you tell Michael? You didn't mention that you were out here with me, did you?"

"No." She drifted over to him, leaning against the counter. "I just told him I was someplace safe and that I thought it best to stay away for a while. I don't want him to have information Slater or anyone else could use against him if things get sticky. The more plausible deniability he has these next few days especially, the safer he'll be."

Asher nodded, studying her worried expression. "You and Michael are pretty close, I gather."

"He's like a brother to me. We've been family to each other for the past eighteen years, since we were both eight years old."

Eight years old. Asher exhaled a sigh. "Since you lost your mother."

"Michael and I met later that same year. My mom had been missing for a couple of months by the time child protective services came around to the apartment and took me in as a ward of the state. I bounced through a few group homes and foster situations that year, but nothing stuck. I guess I made sure of that. I kept running away, rebelling even more every time they tried to discipline me. I was, as most everyone put it, difficult."

Asher felt the corner of his mouth tug in a wry smile. It didn't take much to imagine a younger version of Naomi, headstrong and angry and independent, balking at the slightest attempts to break or contain her. Here she was, half his size even full-grown yet she'd had more courage as a child than he'd had even as a teen and a young man.

"Where did you finally end up?"

"On the street," she answered flatly, shrugging. "It was better than anything the state had in mind for me. At least the predators were easier to spot. I'd rather take my chances with the addicts and scumbags living on the street than the monsters who live in nice houses and smile at you as they invite you inside but don't show their claws until you've finally decided to trust them."

"Is that what happened to you?"

"A few times. But I trust my gut more than I ever trust anyone else, so I always managed to get out of there before the worst could happen." She glanced at him then, her soft sherry gaze bleak. "Michael had it much worse than me. He had a proper family once, the loving parents, the big house and a dog, the whole white picket fence Utopia. But then on his eighth birthday, he made the mistake of confiding in his mom that he thought he was gay. She told Michael's dad and instead of having cake and ice cream, his father beat the living shit out of him. It was so bad, Michael had to get his jaw wired shut."

"Christ," Asher muttered. His gut churned the way it always did whenever he heard about children being mistreated, and he struggled to find words of comfort.

Naomi swallowed audibly, emotion thick in her voice. "His parents told the doctors and the social worker who came to the hospital that he got in a fight at school. Michael didn't deny it. He never told anyone the truth. As soon as he was sent home to recuperate, he split and never looked back. We ran into each other later that year. I spotted him trying to lift a wallet off a tourist outside a fast food place. He got caught and the guy's shout drove him away. I saw where Michael ran to, so after I finessed twenty bucks out of an ATM, I bought a couple of burgers and drinks and brought them to him. We ate together inside a drainage pipe near the highway, and we've hardly been apart since."

Asher studied her, marveling at her fortitude. He even admired her little streak of larceny, considering she'd used it as means of survival and kindness, rather than for her own gain. Even her hits on Slater's casinos seemed to be done as a means of providing for others more than herself. The problem was her motivation. She wouldn't be the first person to lose their life because of an insatiable vengeance.

"How does Michael feel about you taking so many chances when it comes to Leo Slater?"

"He doesn't like it," she admitted. "He's been begging me to let it go for a long time."

"Smart man. I like him already."

She slanted him a sardonic look. "Anyway, I promised him this last job would be it for me. No more stealing from Slater. We have what need to keep the shelter going for a while, so I'm done with that now."

Asher narrowed his scrutiny of her, sensing there were things she wasn't saying. Things she hadn't promised Michael. "You're done taking money from Slater, but you're not finished with him yet. Are you."

Not a question, but a flat realization.

"I told you, Asher. I have a debt to collect from him. For my mother, for what he did to her and believes he got away with all this time. All the beatings and other abuse she suffered. And, finally, her death."

"How can you be certain he killed her? People disappear, Naomi. Even mothers sometimes walk away and leave everything behind."

"Not her." She shook her head, resolute. "The only thing we had was each other. That is, until Slater came along. He dazzled her with fancy cars and clothing, with promises of a better life—for both of us. But all he did was use her up. He destroyed her, first with the beatings, then with drugs. By the time she disappeared, she was only a husk of the woman my mom had been before she met him."

"And you want vengeance."

"That's right," she whispered, nodding. "I want to make him suffer. I want to ruin him, and then make sure he understands that it was me all along. I want to make him pay for all the things he's done, things that can't be excused or ignored just by greasing someone's palm or through any of his threats."

Asher grunted. "It's understandable, Naomi. I can't

tell you I wouldn't want the same things if I were you. But you have to realize even if you get your revenge on Slater, the odds of you walking away with your life are slim. Less than slim."

She shook her head, quietly dismissive. "I don't care what happens to me."

"That's where you and I differ, then. I do care what happens to you."

As he stared at her, Naomi's expression softened at those words. It only lasted for an instant. She exhaled and gave him a flippant roll of her eyes. "Right. Because I have a mark under my chin?"

"Yes," he answered solemnly. "Because you are a Breedmate."

But there was something more he was feeling too. Something he wasn't prepared to acknowledge, let alone express. When he thought about keeping Naomi safe, everything lethal and violent in him seemed to take on a deeper meaning.

He felt protective.

Possessive.

Those foreign emotions swamped him, along with the desire he'd barely been able to bring to heel since that reckless kiss back in the city. He couldn't keep his gaze from roaming over her again now, her scent and the vibration of her pulse so near to him driving him mad with need.

She must have sensed it—the low throb that seemed to charge the air between them. The kitchen felt too cramped, too warm. Electric with all of the things Naomi awakened in him.

She swallowed, but didn't move an inch.

"Anyway," she said, "the only things that matter to

me now are Michael and the kids we're trying to help. They're my family now. I would do anything for them."

"They're lucky to have you."

"What about you, Asher?" At first, he wasn't sure what she was asking. His brows knit in question and she tilted her head at him. "Do you have a family? A bunch of scowling, overbearing brothers like you somewhere out there?"

"I have no family," he answered tonelessly. That much was true, at least.

"What about Ned? Seeing as he left you his ranch and his dog, you and he must've been close."

Asher didn't know how to answer that. He'd never considered himself close to anyone. It wasn't how he was raised. Quite the opposite, in fact. But he had felt gratitude for the kind old widower who opened his home to a stranger, a drifter he had every reason to fear.

But Ned hadn't been afraid. He'd treated Asher like a person, not a monster. He'd treated him like an equal, not a servant or a tool. He gave Asher his respect. More than that, he'd given him his trust.

"We were... friends." The word felt odd on his tongue because he'd never used it to describe anyone before. "It seems strange here without him sometimes."

Naomi smiled gently, reaching over to lay her hand atop his. "I'm sorry you lost your friend, Asher."

The tender sentiment left a pang inside him that felt as unsettling to him as his admission that he missed the old man. Evidently, being around Naomi was a minefield of revelations. Not the least of which being how badly he wanted to take hold of her and feel her body against his.

He wanted to kiss her again, and if she continued to

touch him and talk softly about feelings, he was going to go mad. He pulled away from her and stalked over to put Sam's kibble back in the cabinet.

Behind him, she let go of a sigh. "Do you mind if I get a glass of water?"

"Help yourself. You won't find me to be much of a host."

She made an acknowledging noise then padded over to the cupboards and foraged for a glass. She filled it at the sink, then paused in front of the refrigerator to study the collection of curling, yellowed photographs that had been permanently stuck to the metal surface with magnets and old tape long before Asher had arrived on the scene.

"Is that him?" she asked. "The African American man in several of these pictures?"

"Yes, that's Ned." Asher stowed the dog food and glanced at the array of faded images. "The woman he's seated next to on the porch in this photo was his wife, Ruth."

Naomi looked closer and turned a warm smile on him. "She's beautiful. Did you know her too?"

"No. She died six years before I came here."

In the picture was a smiling fifty-something Ned, taken before his short black curls had turned white and his deep brown eyes had gone cloudy and unseeing. He and his tawny-skinned, gentle-eyed wife were seated side-by-side in matching wood rocking chairs. Asher had never seen such contentment in a pair of faces before in his life.

He'd never known such love existed.

"Ned made those chairs himself," he said when the silence stretched between them. "He told me after Ruth died he put them in the barn out back and couldn't bear to look at them again because they reminded him of her and everything they lost."

"How sad." Naomi glanced at some of the other photos before turning a curious look on him. "How did you two meet, anyway?"

"One night about fifteen years ago, I ended up outside Vegas. Wasn't much for letting any grass grow under my feet, and I had no idea where I wanted to go next. All I knew at that moment was I'd gone too long without feeding. More than a week, which is further than any of my kind should push it. I ran more than fifty miles before I finally saw signs of civilization. And by that, I mean a rundown gas station and convenience store. Nobody around except an old piece of junk pickup truck sitting at one of the pumps."

"Ned's Chevy," Naomi said with a smile.

Asher nodded. "This old black man shuffled out of the place and went over to start pumping his gas. He knew what I wanted the instant he saw me. Christ, I had to be a sight. My vision was hazy with hunger, and my fangs felt like they were on fire in my mouth. I snarled something at him. I don't even know what I said. I expected him to run—or try to. I wasn't there to kill him, but the way my thirst was racking me, he had to know it was a possibility."

"What did Ned do?"

Asher let out a bemused exhalation. "He did the damnedest thing. He held out his arm to me. He let me feed, right there where we stood. It was the most generous thing anyone had ever done for me. When I'd taken what I needed, he patted me on the head and told me to get in the truck with him. He said I looked like I could use a shower and a place to wait out the coming daylight."

Naomi looked at him, silent and clearly moved. "Sounds like Ned was a very special person."

"Yeah," Asher said. "Best I've ever known."

"You said you never stayed long in any one place. Where were you before that night?"

He shrugged. "Around."

"Well, I guess it was awfully lucky for you that you found Ned. Then again, I've got a feeling he'd say he was the lucky one. Seems to me you both needed each other more than you realized."

"Maybe," he agreed, lost in the old memories, the parts of his life that he'd never shared with anyone before. And never wanted to share until now.

Naomi smiled. "I guess maybe you came around at just the right time for me too, Asher. If not for you stopping last night in the desert, I wouldn't be standing here." She smiled, her pretty lips tremulous. "I guess what I'm trying to say is, I owe you my life. I don't know how I'm ever going to repay that."

Against every discipline that had been seared into him from the time he was a boy, Asher reached out, the desire to touch her too strong to deny. He cupped her fragile face in his broad palm. Stroked his thumb over the skin that was as soft and creamy as satin.

He growled a curse, a wordless warning to himself to not let whatever was building between them slip any further out of his control. "You stay alive, Naomi. That's all the payback I need."

He expected her to pull away from his touch, but she didn't. She stood still, as frozen in place as he seemed to be. She turned her face further into his hand, her gaze darkening to the rich, warm color of whiskey.

No question, it was an invitation. One he didn't know how he had the strength to refuse.

"It's getting late," he uttered, his voice deep and rough. He withdrew his hand, shoving it into the front pocket of his jeans. "Like I said, the bedroom is yours. I have animals outside that need to be taken care of, but you'll be safe in here for a few minutes until I come back. I'll see you in the morning."

He didn't wait to hear her reply.

He couldn't. His sanity depended on putting immediate distance between her tempting mouth and body, and his threadbare will to resist her.

He stalked out the kitchen door on a hissed curse, his breath steaming in the chill desert night.

CHAPTER 12

Cain stared out the large UV-blocked window of his penthouse suite at Casino Moda, watching the sun rise over the coppery mountain range in the distance. A storm was rolling in, bringing dark, boiling clouds and fat droplets of rain that streaked down the smoky glass with rapidly increasing intensity.

It was rare to get this kind of torrential soaking, especially during the daytime, but when it came, he relished it. The change in the air. The gunmetal gray sky pressing low over the mountains in the distance while lightning cracked and thunder boomed. The power of it sent vibrations all the way into his bones.

In a world where he'd always felt so big and indomitable, he supposed storms like this gave him some perspective that there were a few things on this Earth that he couldn't control.

Not that he wanted that reminder at the current

moment.

Barefoot on the pale gray carpet and dressed in loose drawstring pants that hung low on his muscled physique, he stepped away from the glass and turned toward the desk in his study to glance at the open laptop screen again.

The face that stared back at him had been niggling him for the past twelve hours. He'd looked at the images from far away, had zoomed in to the point that he could make out every line on her face, but damn it.

He still wasn't certain.

With a grunt of frustration, he dropped into the leather chair and began scrolling once more through the videos he'd compiled.

It had started a few months ago at one of Leo Slater's small casinos downtown. The Gold Mine was one of Vegas's most aged casinos and it looked it. The old-timers that frequented the tired establishment wouldn't have had it any other way, though. Cain supposed there was a comfort in those wallpapered halls and worn red carpet, a familiarity that made its patrons feel at home in a way that the sleek, marbled gloss of Moda never could.

Never one to pass up the chance to close his fist around a buck no matter who it was coming from, Slater accommodated the blue-haired set, offering up nostalgic games served up by uniformed, old-fashioned dealers and hawking early bird specials like meatloaf with mashed potatoes or Yankee pot roast with all the fixings night after night. The Gold Mine would have been more aptly named a bronze mine when it came to profits, and it would never truly compete with Moda in terms of income.

On the other hand, it also wasn't susceptible to the

whims of the jet-set, who no doubt would eventually bail on Moda and crown a new hotspot, leaving all that chrome and lacquer to tarnish and dry up. Boom to bust was a way of life on the Strip, but part of Cain's job as head of security for Slater Enterprises was to ensure the boss's financial interests stayed flush as long as possible.

The Gold Mine was Leo Slater's insurance policy against the fickle winds of fortune. So when the place had shown decreased profits in the slots and roulette pits every other quarter for the past year and half, Cain had taken notice.

At first glance, it hadn't seemed all that strange. But as he dug further, working through the cash flow with their analysts, he'd seen a subtle but strange pattern of medium to large scores that were out of proportion to the rest of the year. When he'd reviewed the year's prior books and found a similar, smaller pattern of losses on the machines, he only grew more suspicious.

All of which had led him to pull video surveillance on the days where unusually high payouts had occurred. There were dozens, and it had taken him days to go through them, even with his keen eye and heightened perception. Eventually, he'd sensed a pattern that couldn't yet be confirmed, but that he felt in his gut.

The same person was responsible for at least half a dozen of the wins. Maybe more.

Granted, she looked totally different each time. Sometimes she was taller, sometimes short. One day she was plump, two weeks later, as trim as a gymnast. Young, old, gray-haired and then platinum blonde. He even suspected she'd come in once or twice disguised as a man.

The only thing that never changed was the fact that

she was at least part Asian. There were literally millions of Asian people who came through the Gold Mine every year, so before he voiced his theory to Slater or the rest of his team and made a fool of himself, Cain wanted to be sure.

No one could disguise themselves that well without plastic surgery. Or without years of practice and execution.

But Cain had persisted, ordering the security teams at each casino to funnel video directly to him if there were any unusual scores. He'd even quietly checked with associates working for some of Slater's competitors on the Strip. No one else was seeing the repeated, apparently targeted, hits on their houses.

Which meant this mystery woman either had a beef with the boss or didn't have enough sense to realize the kind of trouble she was courting.

And from the looks of her—from the near surgical precision with which she disguised herself and the stealth with which she'd made off with easily a couple hundred thousand dollars over time—she wasn't lacking in the brains department. Nor balls.

So, that put him back to the only plausible motive.

For some reason, she had it out for Leo Slater.

And that meant, smart or not, she wasn't likely long for this world.

If Slater'd had his way the night before last, the woman would already be dead. She'd almost gone undetected, garbed in a hoodie and loose sweats, looking like any one of the many skater boys and other assorted punks who walked around the Strip with pants halfway down their asses and unkempt hair hanging into their faces. But then she'd hit a winning number on the slots—almost as if she couldn't help herself from trying another score. She'd evidently enlisted another gambler to collect her winnings for her, but by then it was already too late.

One of the pit bosses fingered her to some of Slater's meatheads on the floor and the word came down from the executive office to teach the little cheat a lesson. Cain had been pissed as hell to learn the boss had turned the girl over to Gordo and his two cohorts without bringing Cain in on the decision.

If Slater had known about the bread crumb trail Cain was chasing, no doubt he'd have been the first person called to deal with the situation. After all, the chief qualification on Cain's resume had been the sixteen years he'd spent as an assassin in the infamous Hunter program.

He'd expected his covert investigation of the mysterious thief to end abruptly the other night, but all he had was more questions. Especially after Gordo's company vehicle had been recovered three miles off the desert road with no trace of the girl or any of the three men sent to kill her in cold blood.

And then, there she was again last night.

Back at Moda, garbed in yet another clever disguise. At least, for a little while.

Cain played back the surveillance video from the casino's eye in the sky, fast-forwarding to the point where the crone with the humped shoulders made a beeline for the ladies' room and never came out again.

He knew that wasn't quite right. She had come out, but she'd ditched her prosthetics and costume and had apparently decided to hide in plain sight.

Cain didn't have to look far to find her.

He ran the feed captured near the Monte Carlo Fortune Bonanza machine, and there she was.

Damn, she a knockout too.

Petite, shoulder-length black hair, and a gorgeous face that looked as innocent as it was enticing. He knew she wasn't innocent, certainly not where Moda was concerned, but she hadn't done anything wrong last night either. He'd watched the video over and over last night and this morning, finding no reason to suspect her of anything more questionable than arriving at the casino in stage makeup and a disguise.

As for the big jackpot, that million-and-some-change had gone home with the man seated next to her, a single twenty-something paraplegic who'd wept tears of elation for nearly twenty minutes as casino management walked him through the paperwork and tax forms that preceded the presentation of his big check.

And still, Cain couldn't look away from his screen.

It didn't help that he kept circling back to the fact that Moda had another unusual guest last night. None other than a fellow former Hunter.

Asher.

He paused and flipped through the rest of the night's feed until he landed on the one captured from the other side of the casino, near the entrance. There was no disguising that massive bastard. He moved through the crowd with determined strides. A man on a mission.

No. Correction: A Hunter in search of his quarry.

What the fuck was that son of a bitch doing here? What was he looking for?

Cain let the video roll, keeping the focus trained on the Breed male and barely able to stifle his growl. He wasn't the only Hunter with no love for Asher. Hell, the male had earned every last ounce of scorn that came his way.

As the surveillance footage continued, he saw the moment Asher locked on his target. Those dark blue eyes narrowed with laser focus, Asher had cut through the thick crowd on the casino floor, his long strides carrying him in the direction of... the ladies' restroom.

Holy shit.

It was the woman. That's who he was looking for.

He watched the feed for a couple of minutes, his veins pounding with certainty as Asher took up a position just outside the restrooms and waited.

Were they working together?

And if not, what the fuck did he want with Leo Slater's persistent little thief?

Cain closed his laptop on an incredulous curse.

He didn't know what Asher was up to, but he was damned well going to find out.

CHAPTER 13

The rain had started sometime before dawn. Naomi knew because she'd been awake most of the night.

She had plenty of reason for tossing and turning until daybreak. Keyed up after the big hit on Moda. Concern for Michael and the wellbeing of the kids staying at the house. Dread over the fact that if Slater got wise to her, he could retaliate not only with his security team made up of homicidal human goons but a Breed male besides.

A trained assassin, according to Asher.

And then there was him. *Asher.*

Of all the thoughts that continued to plague her mind, it was being under the same roof with Asher that made sleep next to impossible.

It hadn't helped that the bedding and the T-shirt she slept in all smelled like him. Every time she closed her eyes, her head filled with images of him. His angled, rugged face and deep cobalt eyes. His square jaw and broad, lushly shaped mouth. Now that she knew what that mouth felt like on hers, she was finding it hard to think of little else when she was near him. As comfortable as it had been talking with him in the kitchen last night, every time he met her gaze she felt certain he knew how badly she wanted to kiss him again.

Yeah, she was pretty sure he'd figured that out.

When she'd reached out to touch his hand and tell him she was sorry about Ned's death, he couldn't seem to get away from her fast enough.

And although he had taken her face in his hands after she'd all but thrown herself at him with that mostly innocent offer to pay him back for all he was doing for her, he had evidently thought better of kissing her a second time. The way he practically bolted from the house, it was a wonder he didn't knock out the screen door as he went.

Naomi heaved a sigh and got out of bed. She didn't know where he was, or where he'd been during the night. The house was quiet except for Sam, who was parked outside the bedroom door, sleeping in a lump on the faded runner. He lifted his head as she came out, showering her outstretched hand with licks and nuzzles.

"Good morning to you, too," she murmured, padding quietly to the bathroom.

On the vanity was a packaged toothbrush and a tube of toothpaste, evidently placed there for her sometime between her shower last night and daybreak. After cleaning up a bit and running damp fingers through her hair, she stepped back out to the hallway.

Sam led her into the empty kitchen and over to his equally empty bowl. "Are you trying to get me in trouble, or do you really need some breakfast?"

He tilted his head at her, eyes pleading and basically irresistible.

"All right, then. Breakfast it is." She retrieved his food and poured some into the bowl, then refreshed his water too.

She couldn't help wondering how things were going back home, picturing the happy chaos of kids setting the table and helping with eggs and pancakes—one of Michael's specialties. The urge to call and check in was nearly overwhelming. But they'd already risked enough with their texting last night. Once the casino check was in the bank, then she could think about resuming her life back in Vegas.

Which would mean leaving Asher to resume his without her.

Why that thought gave her a pang of regret, she surely did not want to know.

She pushed the feeling aside, and turned her focus toward more productive ideas. After foraging without success for coffee or a means to make some, she settled on tea that she found in one of the cabinets. With a steaming mug in her hands, she moved through the house, slowly taking it all in—the upholstered furniture and TV from another era, the framed photographs and whimsical knickknacks. The old sound system and the collection of music CDs, classic R&B sharing shelf space with country albums of all kinds spanning the last couple of decades. There were book cases filled with paperback novels, their spines bent, pages yellowed. And one the floor near a worn recliner sat a basket of crossword puzzles and Sudoku, most of them solved with pencil in the shaky scrawl of an aged hand.

She saw snapshots of Ned and Ruth's life in this

house everywhere she looked.

What she didn't see was evidence of Asher.

Fifteen years he'd lived with the old man who'd given him shelter in his home; almost another year of living here without Ned. Yet Asher still hadn't settled in. He could leave tomorrow and there would be no signs that he'd ever been here at all.

Naomi sipped her tea and drifted into the back wing of the rambling house. This part was an addition, and down the hallway were a couple of spare bedrooms—both unfurnished, as if plans for a growing family or visits from Ned and Ruth's friends and relatives had never materialized.

Farther down this same hall, she heard a muffled scraping sound coming from the room at the end. The rhythm of the movement was fluid, thoroughly focused.

She paused at the open doorway of what appeared to be a woodworking shop and simply watched Asher work for a moment.

His head was bent down, those silky chocolate-brown waves hanging over his forehead as he painstakingly sanded the edge of an elaborately carved wooden headboard. He was barefoot and bare-chested, wearing only a pair of loose, faded jeans.

She stood and stared, mesmerized by the tangle of *dermaglyphs* that traced all over his chest and torso, and down onto his muscled arms. The Breed skin markings were just a shade darker than the rest of him now, but she knew they were a barometer of his emotions. In the short time she'd known him, she had seen them change colors multiple times, usually in fury.

Finally, he glanced up. He scowled, which seemed to be his usual expression whenever she was around. "Is anything wrong?"

"No." She shrugged, lifting her mug. "I hope you don't mind that I made some tea."

"Of course, I don't mind." He waited as if expecting her to leave then. Or hoping, maybe.

Naomi stepped into the room, glancing at the collection of pieces stored there. Hand-crafted chairs. Handsome side tables. A pair of bookcases. Even a tall armoire. Plenty of beautiful things to outfit most of the house. And all of it was expertly made, nothing less than a work of art.

She couldn't resist walking over for a closer look. "These are some amazing pieces. Why did Ned keep them all back here?"

"A few of them are his," Asher replied, his tone unreadable. "The rest are mine."

She swung an incredulous look at him. "Yours, as in you made them?"

He gave a vague nod. "Ned taught me the craft, before he lost his sight and the use of his hands. At first, I only helped him finish the things he had to abandon. After a while, I found working with my hands was a good way to occupy my mind, especially when I'm cooped up inside during the daytime."

She glanced at the headboard with its flourishes and interlocking swirls of inlaid wood. A pattern that was echoed on Asher's skin. "You're really good at this. You should move some of these pieces into the other rooms of the house. The side tables would work really great in the living room instead of the old ones in there now. If you want, I could show you how I'd arrange them."

He was staring at her as if she had just offered to shave his head. "I don't spend much time in the living room and I have no use for any of these things in here. It's just Sam and me in the house, and we don't need much."

"Have you ever thought of selling what you make, then?" She set her mug on a workbench so she could run her hand over the satiny curve of one of the chairs. "It seems like a shame to let beautiful things gather dust when someone could enjoy them."

"I have no interest in selling them, either." He put his sanding block down, aggravated and curt now. His gaze swept her from head to toe, displeasure in his tense expression. "You're still wearing my shirt. There's a small laundry room off the kitchen if you want to wash your clothes."

She offered a smile that went unreturned. "Thanks, I'll do that. I never could stand the smell of smoke. My mom used to bring it home with her every night she was at the casino with Slater."

Asher grunted. "As soon as the sun's down we'll drive up to the state line for food and supplies. You can pick up some extra clothes too. In the meantime, why don't you go find something to do. Read one of Ruth's books, or finish one of Ned's crosswords."

"Are you serious?" She folded her arms, frowning as he went back to work on the headboard as if she were already gone. His gruff tone and dismissive attitude chafed the first time she found herself in this house, but being on the receiving end of it now—especially after their kiss—stung her more deeply than she was prepared for. "Are you trying to get rid of me?"

He glared up at her. "I can't do that until I'm sure Slater is dealt with. And more than likely, Cain as well."

Her mouth flattened tightly, but only in an effort to

keep the pain out of her voice. "If I wasn't worried that I might put Michael or the kids who count on us at risk by going home right now, I'd already be gone."

She pivoted to walk out, but two paces away from him she stopped. She couldn't take the emotional confusion, nor the foolishness she felt at having allowed herself to feel something for this man—this cold Breed male—who clearly couldn't wait to be rid of her from his life.

She swung back around, furious with herself as much as him.

"Why did you kiss me in the truck last night, Asher?"

His face hardened. "Does it matter? It was a mistake. One I won't let happen again."

His words made the air in her lungs evaporate, made her stomach feel like a rock inside her. He resumed his sanding as if he had no more to say. As if it were that easy for him to dismiss her, not only from the room but from his thoughts.

"A mistake," she said, nodding, knowing she should feel the same way about it, but couldn't. "Did you do it because I was crying? Because you felt sorry for me?" She sucked in a shallow breath, staring at his lowered head and the bulky muscles of his shoulders as he scraped the sanding block over the already smoothed edge of the headboard. "Did you do it out of fucking pity, Asher?"

His hand stilled abruptly. On a low growl, he dropped the sanding block and shoved the headboard away from him, vaulting to his feet. Naomi stepped back, instantly questioning her own sanity for provoking him. It was hard for her to remember sometimes what he was, what this dangerous Breed male could do to her.

At the moment, though, he was simply Asher, the man who was turning her life upside down with a desire she didn't want to feel. A longing that centered wholly on him, this dangerous, solitary man she wanted against everything sane and reasonable she knew.

She stood her ground as he prowled toward her, albeit with a slight tremble in her limbs.

His stare incinerated her, his eyes ablaze and glowing with hot amber light. The *glyphs* on his broad chest and powerful arms swirled and seethed with a riot of dark colors—indigo, wine, and gold. His jaw was rigid, but as he pulled a breath through his tight lips, she glimpsed the pointed tips of his fangs.

"Yes, Naomi," he said, his deep voice as rough as gravel. "When I kissed you, it was because you were crying."

She inhaled sharply, hating that it sounded so much like a catch in her throat. When she glanced away from his searing stare, he reached out. His large hand curved around the back of her neck, leaving her no choice but to look at him.

"I kissed you because your tears put an ache in me, too," he murmured. He shook his head, piercing her with those otherworldly eyes that seemed to hold even more torment than what she felt churning inside her. "And because as much as I knew it would be a mistake to taste your lips, not even that was enough to make me want you any less."

Before she could say a word, he lowered his head to hers and took her mouth again. Not the tender brush of his lips against hers like in the truck the other night, but deep and hungered and raw. His tongue invaded, scorching her from the inside with every fevered lick and thrust. He kissed her like he wanted to eat her alive.

Like he'd been starving to taste her again and now nothing would keep him from claiming all of her.

The desire that had been smoldering between them since she woke up for the first time in his bed, alive only because of him, now exploded into a heat neither of them seemed able to contain. Where their first kiss had been tentative and uncertain, this one left no doubt about what they both wanted—needed—from each other.

Asher put his hand under the long hem of the T-shirt she wore. He moaned against her mouth, his fingers stroking over the thin fabric of her panties.

"Seeing you in this last night was torture. Now I can't ever wear it again without picturing you in it like this." He cupped her sex, kneading the growing ache that bloomed there. "And then knowing you were in my shower, naked and wet... *fuck.*"

His caress grew more intense, his big hand spreading her legs wider, granting him better access to the drenched juncture between her thighs. She arched into his touch, clutching his shoulders as her head spun with pleasure. His fingers were hot as he swept aside her panties, then delved into her slick cleft. Sensation shot through her with each caress, each rhythmic plunge of his fingers into her quivering body.

"*This* is what I wanted to do," he uttered between heated kisses, trailing his mouth down onto her throat as he brought her to the brink of madness with his hand. "It took all I had not to walk down that short hallway and join you in there."

Naomi moaned, moving helplessly against his palm and fingers. *"Asher."*

"That's right," he growled. "Now, maybe you understand why I kissed you. And last night as you showered in the next room, what I wanted more than anything was to feel you slippery and wet under my fingers, and then I wanted to fuck you, Naomi. I wanted to push you against the tiles and drive into you until I no longer felt this damnable need to be inside you."

"Oh, God." She was panting from his wicked touch, on the verge of climaxing right where she stood. "I wouldn't have stopped you, Asher. I had all those same thoughts too. I wanted all those same things. It's what I pictured as I touched myself in there. Imagining it was you touching me, stroking me the way you are now."

He purred low in his throat and stared at her with fiery need. "Did you stand under the warm spray and come thinking about me, sweet little Narumi?"

The sound of her name—her real name—should have felt wrong, jarring even.

No one called her that now. She didn't permit it. But hearing her given name on Asher's lips, especially when he was looking at her as though she belonged to him and only him, untethered something deep inside her.

She felt freed.

She felt seen.

And she felt safe, truly safe, perhaps for the first time in her life.

"Yes," she sighed against his lips when he came back for another kiss. "I did come thinking about you. Then I spent the rest of the night alone in your bed, wondering if you'd come in and join me. Wishing you would."

He let out a rough curse, the sound punctuated by the rip of her panties being torn away. Asher pulled the T-shirt over her head, then ran his hands along every inch of her nakedness. His muscles bunched and flexed, his *glyphs* pulsing and alive with color and movement—like living art dancing on his golden skin.

She couldn't bear the impatience to feel all of him too.

Skimming her hands down the sides of his torso, she shivered at the pure strength of him. There was no doubt he was more than mortal, no question that he was the most lethal, powerful man she'd ever been close to. But he was also flesh and bone, all of it pulsing and formidable and hot beneath her questing fingers.

He moaned low in his throat when she reached into the loose waistband of his jeans and took hold of his cock. Her breath stopped for a moment as she realized his size. But any hesitation she knew was burned away in the next instant as he thrust in her grasp, hissing when she gripped him tighter and began to stroke his length.

"I want to see you," she whispered. "I need to feel all of you."

When she fumbled a bit, he took over, unfastening the button and zipper and shoving the denim down. Naomi stared, marveling at the beautiful *glyphs* that tracked around his lean hips and onto his groin, disappearing into the dark thatch at the root of his cock.

She took him in her hands again, admiring him now with her eyes and her touch. His response was a deep, unfurling growl.

"Am I the first Breed you've been with?"

"The only one." She didn't miss the way his eyes glowed brighter at that admission.

"What about human men?"

She shrugged. "A couple, I guess. But it's been so long, it might as well be forever." She held his fiery gaze, still stroking him and trying not to let her knees buckle beneath her as he explored her body too. She was so wet for him, so hungry to feel him inside her she could hardly stand the wanting. "I've never wanted anyone the way I want you, Asher."

His mouth curved in a sinful smile. "Good."

He sank down in front of her on his knees, one hand gripping her hip to brace her while he spread her open to him with the other and nestled his face against her sex. His mouth engulfed her, his tongue pressing wet and hot between her folds, then circling her clit with merciless strokes that had her seeing stars behind her closed eyelids.

He made wildly erotic, animal noises as he licked her tender flesh and fucked her with his tongue. He was an unstoppable force, a storm she threw herself into with total abandon.

"Oh, God," she gasped, shaking as he drove her toward the crest of an intense release. She came against his mouth, shuddering and panting, her veins feeling as white-hot and electric as streaks of lightning. "Asher!"

She was still spinning in that oblivion and wracked with the power of her climax as he tore away from her on a low snarl and lifted her off her feet.

"Wrap your legs around me," he ordered her, his voice an otherworldly rasp.

With her ankles hooked behind his back, he held her aloft, his strong hands positioned beneath her thighs as he guided her slowly, inch by impossible inch, onto the length of his shaft.

The fullness went beyond pleasure and into pain, a sweet, delicious ache as her small channel stretched to accommodate the full measure of him. It felt so good she nearly came just from the overwhelming sensation of completion.

Then he started to move.

Holding all of her weight in his hands as if she were a feather, he glided her up and down, thrusting impossibly deeper with each controlled stroke.

She rocked against him, needing more. Needing all he had to give her.

He groaned as she coaxed him into a harder tempo. "You're so small, Naomi. I don't want to hurt you."

"I'm tougher than I look, vampire."

He grinned, a devilish flash of enormous fangs. "So you are."

"So, don't stop, Asher." She kissed him hard, giving his lip a meaningful nip. "And don't be gentle."

"Ah, fuck." His gaze was an inferno now, his amber irises devouring the narrow slits of his pupils. On a coarse snarl, he tightened his grasp on her and drove in hard—once, twice, again and again.

Naomi moaned, a tremor building swiftly into a release she could neither slow down nor contain. Her pleasure exploded out of her on a scream.

And still Asher kept going, ungentle and wild, giving her just what she demanded of him.

He came with a roar that should have torn the roof off the house, his release a scalding, endless jet that only made his strokes slicker and more fevered. The friction was too much, her body too sensitive.

Another orgasm rushed up on her, leaving her shuddering and boneless in its wake.

"Oh, God." She panted against his shoulder as she struggled to catch her breath. "That was… incredible."

His answering chuckle was dark with promise. "Yes,

it was. But don't think I'm finished with you yet. We've got hours of daylight ahead, and now that I know what you like, I intend to make the most of them."

CHAPTER 14

Asher hadn't spent so much time in bed in all of the fifteen years he'd lived at the ranch combined. Although, to be accurate, he and Naomi hadn't contained themselves strictly to the bed. They'd made use of the bedroom rug, the chair, even the dresser.

And they'd found a lot of creative ways to enjoy other areas of the house as well.

He should have been satisfied, but all he could think about after they returned from their evening shopping trip at the state line was how quickly he might be able to get her naked and underneath him again.

It didn't help his nearly permanent erection that when he stepped into the house after taking care of the horses and chickens, Naomi was bent over in the kitchen, her pert little ass looking ripe for the taking in her curve-hugging jeans as she rummaged through the cabinets and pulled out a frying pan.

Soft music drifted in from the living room sound system. Not one of Ned's favorite country albums, but a soulful jazz number the old man used to listen to on the days when Ruth seemed to be on his mind more than usual. As Asher watched Naomi sway and hum to the sensual song, he didn't imagine he'd be able to hear it again without thinking of her.

She glanced over at him as he let the screen door quietly close. Her slow smile as their eyes connected made his cock twitch behind his zipper.

"I'm making a chicken breast to put on some salad," she said, placing the pan on the stovetop. "Does that sound all right to you?"

"Make whatever you like. The kitchen is yours."

"Okay." She walked to the refrigerator and pulled out some of the fresh produce they bought, setting it on the counter next to the sink where he was now washing and drying his hands. "What's it like not being able to eat actual food?"

He shrugged, leaning against the counter as she rinsed the lettuce and shook off the water. "Your definition of food and mine are different, that's all."

"So, you've never even tasted fresh fruit or a perfectly seared steak? Or really good chocolate?"

"No. I could taste human food if I wanted, but only a bite or two. Breed digestive systems aren't equipped for crude nourishment like that."

Her gaze drifted to his mouth. "Only blood?"

"Yes. And only fresh blood, taken from a living vein."

She swallowed, and as her delicate throat worked he was suddenly very aware of the fact that it had been a few days since he last fed—too many, especially for a

Gen One like him. Later generations could push their bodies upward of a week, but not the purest of the Breed.

Yet as thirsty as he was, the idea of taking a basic *Homo sapiens* carotid held even less appeal than usual. Not when Naomi was standing in front of him.

"Why haven't you tried to take my vein, Asher?"

He ground his teeth together at her innocent question. She was off-limits for a lot of reasons, not the least of which being the fact that she was a Breedmate. He reached out and touched the small birthmark below her chin. "Because of this."

One sip of her blood would nourish him the way human blood never could, but it would also bind him to her like an unbreakable chain. For as long as either of them lived, he would feel her in his own veins, in his senses. And if she drank from him, there would be no other male for her, either. The blood bond was not only sacred between a Breed male and his woman, but eternal.

She deserved someone better. Someone worthy of her.

So, why did he feel such a profound yearning to pierce her tender skin regardless of all that?

He cleared his throat, his mouth suddenly as parched as the Mojave outside.

"Better get cooking," he muttered. "If Sam wakes up in the other room and smells chicken on the stove, you may have to fight him for your dinner."

She laughed softly. "Okay. No dinner for you, but you're sure you don't want anything?"

"I didn't say that." He prowled toward her, unable to resist the need to be close to her. "I definitely see something I want."

His arms circled her from behind and he stepped in close, groaning at the feel of her pressed against the front of his body. As small as she was compared to his immense size, he'd never felt anything more perfect than the soft warmth of her body leaning into his hardness. He moved his hips against her backside, his arousal on the verge of agony just to be near her.

She tipped her head back and sighed, slowly rocking to the music within the cage of his arms. "I've always loved this old song."

He grunted. "I've never appreciated it more than right now."

Her mouth curved as she gazed up at him from under the thick fringes of her lashes. "Dance with me." She turned inside the circle of his loose embrace, until they were facing each other with no space between them. She moved fluidly, rotating her hips as she looped her arms around his neck and held his heated gaze. "You're so stiff, Asher."

"I'm not much of a dancer."

"That's not what I meant." Rising up on her toes, she pulled his head down to her and slanted her mouth over his.

Her kiss exploded through his senses like gasoline thrown on a raging fire. He smoothed his hands down onto her rounded behind, squeezing her and drawing her up tight against his arousal. He wanted to be inside her, fused together with her. He would be, if not for the damnable barriers of their clothing.

"Whose brilliant idea was it to let you get dressed?" he snarled through fevered kisses. "Starting now, I only want to see you in my T-shirt or nothing at all."

She smiled up at him. "Sounds like a plan to me."

He kissed her again. "If you like that, just wait until you hear my other plans."

"Maybe I should've picked up some energy drinks," she said, sighing when he slipped his hands under her shirt and snapped the hooks on her bra. "Your Breed stamina's going to kill me."

"Are you complaining?"

"Not even close." She yelped in surprise as he lifted her off the floor and set her atop the counter. Her hands caressed his back, then tangled in his hair as he palmed her knees and spread her legs wide. He moved into the V of her thighs and caught her possessively around the back of her neck, crushing her mouth in a bruising, heated joining of their lips and tongues.

He didn't know how long they'd been kissing before his senses prickled with a niggling unease. He heard a sound outside—so faint he might have imagined it.

But he hadn't; it was real. His Breed hearing was too acute to be mistaken.

Someone was outside the house, somewhere in the dark.

"What is it?" Naomi asked when he paused to listen closer, his hand still curved around her nape. "Asher?"

He put his index finger against her wet, parted lips. Her almond eyes went wide and anxious. Pulling her down off the counter, he set her on her feet and whispered into her ear. "Go to the bedroom and lock the door. Take Sam in with you."

"Asher, what's—"

"Do it, Naomi." One of the horses whinnied in the paddock, a nervous sound that drew her attention toward the blackness on the other side of the back door. Asher gently caught her chin and brought her gaze back to him. "It's probably nothing. The animals get spooked all the time. But I need to make sure, so do what I ask. Please."

She gave him a faint nod, then left the kitchen.

Only after he heard the bedroom door close did Asher move. He stalked out of the house bare-handed, knowing if they had an intruder—especially the one he suspected—his best weapon was himself.

As he neared the horses' paddock, a dark shape peeled away from the shadows.

"This certainly is a homey little spread you've got here, Asher." Cain's voice was devoid of emotion, impossible to read. "Never thought I'd find you playing house out here in buttfuck nowhere. Especially not with that thieving little female in there." He chuckled low under his breath. "Apparently, you're full of surprises lately."

"If you've got any desire to keep breathing, Cain, you should get off my land."

The former Hunter strode forward, his steps unrushed. "I didn't come here to do battle with you, Asher. Not this time, anyway. After all, we both know each other well enough to realize that if it comes to that, neither one of us would give—or receive—an ounce of mercy from the other."

Asher wasn't about to deny it. "Then why are you here?"

"Curiosity," he replied. "Not so much about you, but about her."

"She's none of your concern." A growl worked its way up Asher's throat before he could tamp it down. "If you touch her, make no mistake, Cain. I will kill you."

The dark-haired assassin smirked and shook his

head, silver eyes glinting. "I don't have to touch her. She's a dead woman already, considering she's so hell-bent on screwing with Leo Slater."

Asher leapt at him, his fangs punching out of his gums as he grabbed Cain by the throat. "Did he send you? That murdering motherfucker already sent three of his goons after her and I dealt with them. Tell me what you know, or you're next."

Cain grinned, but there was a note of uncertainty in his shrewd eyes. And dawning realization. "You care for her." He chortled then. "Don't tell me you're attached to the little thief. I could understand why you had your hands all over her just now, but this is something more."

Asher squeezed harder, then released his former comrade on a sharp curse.

Cain rubbed his throat absently. "What kind of game are you two playing here? What does a son of a bitch like you need with the kind of money she's been stealing from Slater's coffers for more than a year? Two-hundred grand doesn't just get swept under the rug and forgiven. Particularly with a man like Slater."

Holy hell. The steep figure shocked him, but he kept his expression schooled. And he hadn't missed the fact that Cain was saying nothing about Michael's win the other night.

"Slater's got no room for holding grudges," he replied. "If he takes a few hits on his coffers, he's more than earned them."

Cain shook his head. "What's the matter, you weren't lowlife enough before we escaped the program, now you're a common thief too?"

He didn't deny it. As long as Naomi was in Cain's crosshairs, Asher wasn't about to take the target off himself. Not even to give the other male the truth. "You're one to judge, considering who you work for. You're taking Slater's money. The only difference is you're doing it with blood on your hands."

Now, Cain's face hardened. "We've both got blood on our hands, Asher, and it's never going to wash off. But at least I never killed my own brethren."

"We killed whoever Dragos ordered us to kill."

Cain shook his head. "You know damned well there's a difference between you and me."

"Then prove it. Walk away, and don't come back."

"I can't do that. Slater pays me to take care of his interests. And nothing interests him more than his money. He's going to want it back," Cain added. "If he finds out it's been her repeatedly hitting him, there won't be any stopping him. And he won't send a bunch of clowns after her the way he did the other night."

The newsflash that Cain just let slip took Asher aback. Slater didn't know it was Naomi gunning for him? All of her disguises, her patient strikes spread out over time as she methodically separated Slater from a couple hundred-thousand dollars.

To say nothing of the million-and-change that Michael walked away with last night with her help.

And Slater didn't know.

But Cain did, and that was equally dangerous—if not more so.

"Why did she do it?" the Hunter asked. "I've reviewed hours of surveillance footage. I've seen her operate. I know she's clever and ballsy as hell. So, why keep provoking Slater? Tell me that much."

As much as Asher needed an ally, he wasn't going to kid himself that he'd find one in Cain. Nor in any of his other Hunter comrades. They had all been sired off the same Ancient bloodline in Dragos's lab, but few of the former Hunters emerged from their enslavement with any bond of loyalty from their half-blooded brothers.

Least of all Asher.

He couldn't stake Naomi's life on the hope that Cain would give him that much consideration. But what other choice did he have?

"Slater killed her mother."

Cain hardly blinked. "He's killed a lot of people."

"Well, this time someone's come to collect on the debt."

"She's taken this shit too far. All she's doing is digging her own grave. At some point Slater's going to find out, and he's going to tell me to put her in it." At Asher's low growl, the other Hunter stared at him for a long moment, considering him in silence. "Slater's going to tell me to end her, and I'm going to do it because that's my job. I'm sure you can relate to that, right?"

The jab shouldn't have stung, but Asher had spent the better part of his life regretting everything he'd done at Dragos's command. He'd relived the depth and breadth of his sins time and again, thanks to the curse of his unique gift.

Cain's silver eyes narrowed. "The win last night at Moda—the big one on the slots. You were there with the woman. She didn't have anything to do with that take, did she?"

Asher feigned confusion and shook his head. "From what I recall, the winner was some guy in a wheelchair. So, unless she's one hell of a magician, I don't know how you came up with that idea."

Cain stared at him, menace in the sharp bones of his

face. "If it turns out either of you are working with this guy—Michael Carson—it's not going to end well for any of you."

"Is that a threat?"

"No," he scoffed. "Consider it a warning, although I don't know why you deserve one."

"I don't," Asher admitted. "But she does. She's a Breedmate, Cain."

A look of pure shock swept over the immense male. That revelation was the one thing powerful enough to stop even an ice-cold killer like him. Every Breed male, even the Hunters, knew their entire race owed their existence—and their future—to women bearing the teardrop-and-crescent-moon mark. Without Breedmates, there would be no more Breed. That alone made Naomi and the others like her more precious than any man's riches.

Still, Cain barked out a curse, looking more suspicious than ever. "This Breedmate. Is she yours, then?"

Asher wasn't sure how to answer that, so he settled on the truth. "Not in blood," he said. "But make no mistake, she *is* mine. And as long as I breathe, she is under my protection."

"Under your protection? A soulless bastard like you?" Cain raised his dark brows on a deep chuckle. "Then God help her if you're all she's got to count on."

Cain left him standing there in the dark, the stealth assassin fading into the night in much the same way he'd appeared.

It took Asher several minutes before he headed back into the house. Naomi met him with a relieved gasp when he opened the bedroom door and told her everything was okay.

"What happened?" she asked, seeking the shelter of his arms. "Was it... was someone outside?"

"It was nothing." He pressed a kiss to the top of her sleek black hair, hating himself for how easily the lie slipped off his tongue. "Probably just a coyote nosing around where it doesn't belong. Don't worry. If it comes back, I'll deal with it."

CHAPTER 15

He had insisted that everything was fine, but for the rest of the night Asher seemed distant, his attention remote. Naomi couldn't penetrate the shadows that shuttered his handsome, troubled face. Nor did he allow her to.

He deflected all of her questions and allayed her fears with reassurances that he would let nothing—and no one—ever get close enough to do her harm. He didn't have to say the words for her to know that Slater and the dangerous men who served him were foremost on his mind. Asher's concern was broadcast in his grim silence, and in the soldier-like way he prowled the house, an air of coiled readiness rolling off him in waves.

It was only when he took her to bed a few hours later that she felt him return to her completely. Naked beneath him as he brought them both to a staggering release, she had watched his dark blue eyes burn with desire for her and his *glyphs* dance with color on his gleaming skin. Feeling him move inside her, his powerful strokes obliterating everything except pleasure, there had been no room for doubts or worries about Slater and whatever might wait for her outside the shelter of Asher's arms.

He woke her in similar fashion that next morning.

With sleep still clinging to her and her body lax from a blissful exhaustion, Naomi moaned as she felt Asher's mouth kissing a warm path over her belly and then down onto her hip. His breath fanned hot against her sex as he nipped and teased her mound.

When his tongue cleaved into her seam and found her clit, she arched up on a hissed gasp of sensation. She opened her lazy lids, catching her bottom lip with her teeth as he began to kiss and suckle her in earnest.

"Asher," she whispered, already panting, melting for him all over again. "Wait. Let me clean up before you—"

"Lie back." His gaze smoldered as he glanced up at her. With one big hand splayed across her stomach, he used the other to hold her in place beneath his mouth. "I want you just like this. I like tasting myself on you and knowing this is all mine to enjoy."

He dipped his head back down to her as he spoke, lapping at her with unabashed carnality as he held her gaze. He caught the tight bud of her clit between his teeth and flicked his tongue over it, dizzying swirls that had her practically clawing at the sheets.

"Oh, God," she whispered, shuddering in response to every wicked stroke. "So good."

He groaned a low rumble of approval, rewarding her with another long, shameless lick into the cleft of her body. Flames danced along her skin as she arched into him. Had she ever felt so wanton before? She knew the answer, because she had never wanted any man the way she burned for him.

Her thoughts scattered as he continued to torment her with his tongue. "You're driving me mad, Asher."

His low chuckle vibrated against her tender flesh, but he showed her no mercy. Her orgasm shimmered at the edges of her consciousness, just out of reach. And he knew it, dammit. He knew exactly how to play her body and he was proving to be a master of control.

"Oh, fuck… let me come," she snarled at him, not caring how ravenous she sounded. It was too late to pretend she was anything less. When they were together like this, she had no defenses. She simply wanted him. Needed the pleasure only he was able to give her.

His fingers closed over her thighs and spread them wider, his hands as rough as his tongue was gentle.

She shivered as he pulled back and his warm breath washed over her.

"You're so beautiful here," he murmured, his voice an unearthly rasp. "Silky soft. Sweet and hot. Who needs food when I have you to feast on?"

Gone was the tentative teasing now, in its place pure hunger as he ate her alive, licking and sucking, sending pulsing waves of heat from her fingertips to her toes.

She moved her hips against his mouth with abandon, the ache in her belly spreading and growing, deepening into a need she couldn't contain.

"Please, Asher," she begged, catching his thick brown hair in her fists as shudders rippled through her core. She wanted to make it last, but the pleasure was as sharp as a knife now, and she was balanced precariously on the edge.

"You want to come, baby?" His low voice taunted her senses, his mouth still moving relentlessly over her inflamed flesh. His tongue dipped inside her and she groaned. "Come for me, Naomi. Give it to me now."

She couldn't hold back her release if she tried.

Her back bowed as he thrust two fingers deep into her body. The sudden invasion combined with the ecstasy of his clever tongue as he worked her clit in magical circles was more than she could withstand. Her climax built and swelled, until all she could do was cry out his name as she toppled from the precipice.

"Asher."

Blood rushed to her head and light exploded behind her closed eyelids at the tremors rocked through her in an endless wave of release. Her bones were liquid, her limbs weightless. Her nerve endings had become electrified, her senses shimmering like tiny diamonds behind her closed eyelids as she held him tight against her with one hand, riding the crest of her orgasm to the very end.

It should have wiped her out, the intensity of how hard and how often he'd made her come since that first time they'd been naked together. But being with Asher did something wild to her. It had unleashed a craving that only seemed to deepen every moment she was with him.

She wanted to chalk it up to the fact that she'd gone so long without physical intimacy or desire. Or maybe it was the newness of being with a man as attractive and powerfully sexual as Asher.

For all she knew, this insatiable desire might have been an elemental response from the part of her that wasn't quite mortal finally coming into contact with the part of him that was Breed.

But Naomi sensed a more profound connection than any of those things.

She was starting to care for him.

Impossible. They barely knew each other. This was all hot and thrilling and overwhelming because of the circumstances. Life and death. Danger at their heels. And the fact that he had stepped in to save her from it all like some dark knight she never dreamed might actually exist.

That's what made being with him feel so damned exciting. That was the reason she felt so totally, gut-churningly wild for him, even after they'd scratched that initial itch.

Except none of those things seemed to explain the raw ache that had opened up inside her since she'd met Asher. An ache that was only growing deeper and harder to ignore every time he touched her or grazed her skin with the sharp points of his fangs.

Try as she might, she couldn't dismiss the longing she had for something she'd been so certain all her life that she would never want.

The kind of bond she now knew she could only ever share with Asher.

God help her, she was astonished to acknowledge the very real possibility that she was falling in love with him.

"Hey," he said, his deep rasp a thick rumble as he moved up the length of her body. He gently tapped her temple. "Everything okay up here? Are you all right?"

She blinked, still reeling from the aftershocks of bliss and her own startling realization. "Yeah," she murmured, gazing up into molten eyes and the ruggedly beautiful face that never failed to steal her breath away. She reached up to caress his cheek. "I'm more than all right, Asher."

It terrified her, how right everything could feel when she was with him.

Because sooner or later they would have to leave his bed and face reality.

But not yet.

Not now.

She kissed him, suddenly desperate for him all over again. He groaned against the hard crush of her mouth on his, then let out a hiss when she slid her hand down and wrapped her fingers around his rigid length. "On your back, vampire. It's my turn to torture you."

~ ~ ~

He did as she demanded, despite that he was harder than ever and desperate with the need to be inside her. He had sworn to himself when he escaped Dragos's collar that he would never surrender himself to anyone's whim ever again. But that was before he met Naomi.

This female owned him, and he couldn't deny it.

Especially not when she was staring at him with pleasure-glazed yet still hungry eyes.

His veins throbbed, not only with the need to fuck her, but with another raging urge too.

As he lay back on the bed and watched her straddle him, he bit back a snarl. Blood rushed to his cock and an ache began to pulse in his gums as his fangs extended even further. The razor-sharp points felt like daggers against his tongue.

He reached for her hips, ready to slam her down onto his erect cock, but she batted his hands away. Her smile was sensual, yet determined. "Patience, now. I haven't even started."

He let out a rough breath. "I have no patience when you're naked and within my grasp."

She tilted her head, one of her slender black brows arching over her almond eyes. "Are you suggesting I tie you down, then?"

Holy fuck. Even though there were no restraints in existence that could hold him, the idea of giving himself up to Naomi's pleasure sent lava coursing into every cell in his body. Even though it was torment and a test of his control, he kept his hands on the bed and simply watched as she rained little kisses on his chest and abdomen. Her pink tongue darted out to lick the swirls and arches of his *dermaglyphs*.

"I love to see their colors," she murmured, exploring him slowly with her mouth. She ran her parted lips over the *glyphs* that circled his pectorals, then her small, blunt teeth came together over one of his nipples and he nearly jolted off the mattress.

"Christ, woman. Be careful, unless you want me to bite you back."

It was a mistake to make the threat. Not only because it was an empty one—a breach he would never make. But also because his logical mind was taking a backseat to the hunger—and the thirst—that was racking him with hooked talons the longer Naomi toyed with him.

Now that he'd said the words, the image sprang to vivid life in his head. Naomi spread beneath him, her slender throat bared and arched to him like an offering. His mouth lowering to her, his fangs piercing her vein.

He could almost taste the sweetness of her blood in his mind. It would be delicate like her scent, and bold like the woman herself.

He squeezed his eyes closed and set his jaw, fighting off the ache there that signaled his need to feed. Now more than ever, he was almost desperate for it. That animalistic strike.

The hot, dark taste of blood—Naomi's blood—flooding into his mouth. The sensation of pounding deep inside her as he drank, her tight channel squeezing him as she came.

He growled and shut his eyes, trying in vain to bar the images—and the thirst—from his thoughts. The necessity to find a blood Host was getting urgent the longer he was in Naomi's presence. At least if his physical hunger was slaked he might have the strength to hold one of his needs at bay when it came to her.

Not fucking likely, but he'd be damned if he took anything more from her than he already had.

Cain's reminder last night of what Asher had been—and everything he could never be—had been well-timed. Asher had been getting too comfortable with Naomi. He'd been finding it too easy to imagine what his life might be like with someone to share it with. Someone like Naomi.

No. Not *like* her.

Only her.

He'd told himself that keeping Cain's appearance from her was only to soothe her fears about Slater closing in on her or Michael. But Asher's motives had been selfish too. Naomi didn't know about his past. She didn't know how many lives he'd taken, including too many innocent ones.

His lie burned, but every minute that had passed since his confrontation with the other Hunter only made it harder to find the words he needed to say to her.

She continued to kiss and lick and nip her way down his torso. He lifted his head to watch as she drifted lower, and the look in her eye sent a battering ram of lust slamming into him. His already swollen cock pulsed and leapt, clear fluid weeping onto his stomach in anticipation of what she intended for him.

"You're gorgeous," she murmured, her eyes caressing him as admiringly as her hands. "I could never get tired of looking at every inch of you, Asher."

He wanted to reply. To tell her that he was nothing compared to her. He wanted to shower her with all the words that couldn't possibly do her justice, but all he managed was a strangled groan, lost in her warm grip as she wrapped her fingers around his shaft. Then she began to slide her hand up and down his length.

Her long, unhurried strokes had his pelvis rocking as he strained toward her, into her grasp. "You're killing me, angel. God, I'd do anything as long as you keep touching me like that."

"Anything?" She laughed softly. "Better not make promises you may not want to keep."

She was teasing, unaware of just how apt her warning was. He had a hundred promises he wanted to give her, but had no right to speak a single one.

And then he had no words at all, once he felt the heat of her warm, moist breath on the head of his cock.

"Naomi—" Her name was hardly more than a broken snarl as she closed her lips over him and drew him deep into her mouth. "Ah, God."

He bucked, reflexively driving his fingers into her

dark hair. Her tongue was pure fire and she was burning him alive as she stroked and pulled and sucked. She couldn't fit the full size of him in her mouth but that didn't stop her from trying. He almost had to peel himself off the ceiling as she deep-throated him, those tight muscles gripping him like a warm, wet fist.

All the while, she made sexy little sounds, moans and hums around his girth that told him more than any words could that she was as equally consumed with pleasure as he was.

If he couldn't taste her now, he needed to get inside her at the very least. He quaked with the effort of letting her continue, taking her tongue lashings like a martyr would, suffering this sublime torture in silence.

But then she began sucking in earnest, pulling back until she'd almost expelled him before drawing hard and deep, working the base of his shaft with her fingers, urging him to thrust with her hand around his hips.

The rhythm was like a heartbeat now, relentless, impossible to control. He tightened his grip on her hair.

"Jesus," he ground out, his vision blurring in a haze of red, his fangs extending even further as his climax bore down on him like freight train. "You have to stop before I... ah, fuck... Naomi—"

He broke off as he realized his warning had the exact opposite effect. She only tightened her grip and moved faster, moaning now, desperate, needy sounds that short-circuited his brain.

"Fuck!"

He bellowed her name as every nerve ending fired at once, sending shockwaves through his body. He came harder than he ever had before, hot jets scalding him from inside as she suckled him mercilessly.

A sensation he'd never felt before wrapped around him, squeezing tight in his chest as he stroked Naomi's hair and surrendered to the heat of her mouth. The feeling he had for her went far beyond lust. It was something profound and elemental, something primal and undeniable. Something possessive and permanent.

Mine, he thought, as he pulled her up to lie next to him.

He stroked her beautiful face and the glossy lips that had just given him such intense pleasure.

Mine, he told himself, even though he knew it he had no right to wish it.

He lowered his head and kissed her deeply, until they both were desperate for air. Then he let his fingers trail down her soft cheek and along her graceful jaw line, until he paused on the diminutive scarlet symbol that rode just above the fluttering pulse that hammered in her throat.

"Mine," he said, his fangs bared and aching.

But before he gave in to the one mistake he could never undo, he flipped Naomi over onto her knees, spread her legs wide, then buried himself to the hilt inside her, letting her know she was his in the only way she ever could be.

CHAPTER 16

"Well, what do you think?" Naomi stood in the living room and gestured to the pair of side tables Asher had made. "Didn't I tell you they'd be great in here?"

He shrugged noncommittally, but damn if she hadn't been right about the change being a good one. "It'll do, I guess."

"You guess?" She gaped at him, a broad smile breaking over her pretty face. "This looks a thousand times better and you know it."

To him, the room's biggest improvement was the petite spitfire standing in the center of it. She had her sleek black hair swept back in a ponytail, which only accentuated the beauty of her skin and unusual eyes. Dark jeans and a white T-shirt should have been mundane, but on Naomi it was as enticing as lingerie.

Or maybe that was just Asher's insatiable libido

talking—at least where she was concerned.

He'd finally let her out of bed around noon, primarily because they both needed to shower and she needed to eat. He had opted to keep his distance, best as he could, if only to avoid the temptation of her delicious body . . . and the equally tempting notion of her carotid.

After she had lunch, she had fallen asleep with Sam on the sofa while Asher had holed up in the workshop, alone with his guilt and indecision.

The confrontation with Cain still weighed heavily on his mind. The other Hunter was right about one thing. If Slater were to get wise about Naomi and link the string of suspicious wins to her, he'd be gunning for her with both barrels loaded. And if the bastard should clue in to the fact that she had something to do with Michael's big win the other night?

Asher didn't even want to consider it.

He didn't worry that he couldn't handle Slater or a truckload of his human goons. Hell, he would even take care of Cain if it came to that, or take the male down with him. But, more and more, the very real possibility that Naomi might get hurt in the process—physically or otherwise—was becoming a risk he was loath to take.

And he knew why, too.

That deepening, unquenchable ache behind his sternum was to blame.

He cared about her. Not the way he had in the beginning, as an obligation to shield a female who might one day bear another Breed male's offspring, but as the woman he desired above any other.

As the mate he would never be worthy of, even if his hands weren't stained with countless spent lives.

And caring meant he was liable to make mistakes.

To truly keep her safe, he would need every weapon at his disposal, chief among them his ability to think, act, and react with the emotionless logic of his former life. Allowing Naomi past those walls had changed everything.

She had changed him.

"Come on," she said, grabbing his hand. "Let's go get that armoire for the bedroom. You'll thank me later."

She gave him a little tug, only to draw up short when her phone's text chime went off in her back pocket. "It's Michael."

Asher tensed as she tapped the display and read for a second. "The casino funds couldn't have cleared so soon, could they?"

"No," she said, but when she glanced at him, her face was lit with excitement. "It's not about the money. It's even better news. Penny's back."

"Penny?" Asher shook his head, confused.

"She's one of the kids at the house, a ten-year-old girl who's had a really shitty life so far. She's been gone for nearly two weeks this time, the longest since she first came around. But now she's back."

Asher grunted. "I can see you're relieved."

"Are you kidding me? I'm elated. I've been so worried about her." Naomi put her head down and started texting Michael back. "I have to see her. Even if it's only for a few minutes—"

"Out of the question."

"Do you mind if I borrow the—" She glanced up, frowning. "Excuse me?"

He gave a curt shake of his head. "I don't think it's a good idea. It's too soon. Slater may have eyes on the house—hell, that's practically a given."

Cain's eyes, at the very least, although not until dark. Asher was fairly certain the former Hunter wouldn't harm Naomi now that he knew she was a Breedmate, but it was still his job to look after Slater's money. There were a lot of creative ways to move someone out of the way without hurting them. The thought of a killer like Cain getting anywhere near her was enough to turn Asher's blood cold.

And the idea of letting her leave during the daytime when Asher couldn't even protect her from Slater's human thugs was an option he refused to so much as consider.

"You're not going, Naomi. And definitely not alone."

Her chin hiked up. "And you can't keep me here."

"Yes. I can." He stepped toward her. "But I don't want to do that."

"I want to see Michael and Penny and the rest of the kids."

"It's too soon. If Slater—"

She shook her head. "If Slater had any suspicions about that win the other night, he never would've let Michael out of the casino with the check in the first place. We're having a good time out here together, Asher, but I'm not your property. You don't have the right to keep me from my home."

Her home.

Somehow, he'd actually started to forget that fact. Ironic, considering everything else he was cursed to remember in his life. Naomi belonged somewhere else. Her friend and the troubled kids they were trying to help meant more to her than anything.

Certainly more than him.

He saw her devotion to them in the determined line of her mouth, and in the mutinous sherry-colored eyes that held the power to turn him inside out with a single look. Rather like the one she leveled on him now.

After the intimacy they'd shared the past couple of days and nights, to hear her dismiss it as nothing more than a good time stung more than he thought possible.

Time to recalibrate his thinking. Not to mention his reckless cravings where this female was concerned.

"You're right," he said evenly. "You don't belong to me. If you want to go home, then I won't keep you from it. But I'm going to take you there."

"Fine," she said quietly, her expression softening somewhat. "Thank you."

He stepped away from her without acknowledging her gratitude. "Tell your Michael I'll be coming with you. We'll head out as soon as night falls."

~ ~ ~

The door swung open before he had a chance to knock, and Michael Carson stared up at him from his wheelchair.

"Holy fuck, she wasn't kidding. You're huge." The young man gave Asher a wide grin as he rolled back and made space for him to step inside the house behind Naomi. "I'm Michael."

He held out his hand to Asher and Naomi blanched. "Oh, Michael, wait. Asher doesn't like—"

"It's all right," Asher said, shaking the man's hand in spite of its cost.

He weathered the sudden jolt of ugly memories that hit him on contact, careful to keep his expression neutral in spite of the ugliness—and the agony—of Michael's past suffering. The incident Naomi told him about, the one that ended with an eight-year-old boy's jaw being smashed under his father's fist, rolled over Asher in brutal detail.

He nodded, feeling nothing but respect for the young man who'd suffered so much but survived to make a better life, not only for himself but the kids he welcomed into his home.

"I'm honored to meet you, Michael."

"Likewise. Now I see why Nay was trying to keep you all to herself." His warm, smiling eyes took Asher in again from head to toe, before he slanted a wide-eyed look at Naomi. "Well, come in, you two. We don't want to sit here with the door open all night, do we?"

"How are things?" Naomi asked, code that Michael picked up on instantly.

"Quiet so far." He lowered his voice to almost a whisper. "I can hardly believe how smoothly it's gone. By tomorrow this time, we should be golden."

A sigh gusted out of her. "Thank God." The sound of children's voices carried from other areas of the house and she craned her neck to peer down the hall. "Lot of kids come in for the night?"

"It's early yet so only four, but the rest will be rolling in later."

"And Penny," Naomi prompted, eagerness and relief in her voice. "I'm so glad to hear she's come back."

Michael nodded. "Me too. Apparently, her mom's back in town from Reno. Brought another loser boyfriend with her. Penny wanted to give her a chance, but things got bad again."

Naomi's face pinched in sympathy. "Drugs?"

"Yep, the usual."

"Poor kid."

"Shitty parent," Michael said. "But Penny's got a good head on her shoulders. And she knows she'll always have a place to stay with us." He rolled toward the adjacent kitchen. "You two gonna hang here for a while?"

She glanced at Asher. "Yeah, for a while, I guess."

"Great," Michael said. "We all just had dinner and I sprang for that new superhero movie on cable, so everyone's getting cleaned up before we settle in for that. Meanwhile, I'm on popcorn duty. Now that you're here, you can help."

Asher watched their easy communication, a bitter pang of jealousy welling up inside him. He knew Naomi and Michael were just friends, but their obvious affection toward each other made him feel like an outsider, like the intruder he was.

There was a time, not long ago at all, that his discomfort wouldn't even have registered. Nor now, if the woman in question had been anyone but this one, that is.

While the friends discussed some of the other kids and speculated on who had yet to report in for the night, he glanced around at the comfortable, if modest, house. The large sectional had seen better days, but it was clean and tidy, like the rest of the cozy living room. A flat-screen TV was the obvious focal point of the space, but there were also bookshelves filled with easily hundreds of novels and non-fiction books, along with a small study desk with a computer on it.

Everything in the place had a sense of home and family—things Asher wouldn't have been able to recognize or appreciate if he hadn't met Ned Freeman all those years ago.

Things the kids who came to stay with Naomi and Michael probably wouldn't experience if not for the generosity of both of them.

And the love.

Asher felt it as he listened to the pair talk. And then he saw that care in action a moment later, when the sound of lightly padding feet came up from the hallway.

"Penny!" Naomi's face lit up with unabashed joy as the lanky blonde girl dressed in a long nightgown raced into her open arms.

Penny hugged Naomi close. "Michael said you were away for a while and he wasn't sure when you were gonna be here." The girl glanced at Asher and grew quiet, a wary curiosity stealing into her sky-blue gaze. "Who're you?"

Naomi gave him an awkward glance. "Asher is... a friend of mine."

"Hi," the girl said, her arms still wrapped around Naomi.

Asher nodded briefly, and at the same moment several more kids strayed in from the hallway. Four boys, two of them dark-eyed identical twins, the others a short, chubby kid with a crown of bright red hair and a sullen, round-faced Latino boy. The kids stopped in their tracks and gaped at Asher.

"Who let the giant in?" This from one of the twins.

Michael smiled. "Guys, this is Asher." He shot Asher a wry look. "Allow me to introduce the rest of the welcoming committee this evening. We've already heard from Max, and that's his better-looking brother, Billy." A joke, considering there was virtually no difference between them, but the other boy snickered even as Max playfully cuffed his shoulder. "The strong, silent one here is Juan, and that other little rascal is Tyler."

"Are those tattoos on your arms?" Tyler blurted, pointing at Asher.

The spokesman for the twins, Max, gave the kid an eyeroll. "He's Breed, genius. Those are *dermaglyphs*. A whole lot of them."

Asher nodded at the boy. "I'm Gen One. That's why I have so many *glyphs*."

Juan perked up, a guarded curiosity in the glance that met Asher's gaze. "So, you're, like, an actual vampire?"

Asher smirked. "More or less."

"Cool!" Tyler hooted, his young voice pitched high and squeaky. "Can we see your fangs?"

"When you're hungry, do people look like food to you?" Billy chimed in.

"Guys." Michael waved his hands at the group of kids in a corralling gesture. "We've got a movie to watch, remember? Maybe Asher will let you hooligans interrogate him later."

"Aw, man!" The protests came mainly from Billy and Tyler as Michael shooed them to the sectional.

"Sorry about that," Naomi said, giving Asher a gentle look. "I doubt they've ever seen someone like you before."

"It's all right."

"Hey, Nay," Michael called from next to the sofa, remote in hand. "You mind handling the popcorn while I get things cooking with the movie?"

"Sure." She glanced at Asher. "Want to help?"

He knew about as much about making popcorn as he did anything else when it came to a kitchen, but he nodded and followed her out of the room. As much as he wanted to pretend he could keep his distance from her, she drew him like a magnet. And if her pull was this strong without the tether of a blood bond, how bad would he have it for this female if she truly was his?

He didn't allow the thought to linger. It was pointless imagining, anyway.

This was where she belonged. If he hadn't seen it before, he did now.

He stood back, watching her open the cabinets by rote as she collected a big box of popcorn, napkins, and several large bowls. "You're happy to be home."

"I am." The smile she turned on him was unguarded, filled with pure contentment. "Do you see how special they are? And those five in there are only a few of the ones who'll likely be coming to stay tonight."

He nodded. "They all seem like good kids."

"They're amazing," Naomi said. "They all have so much potential, you know? All they need is one person to give them a break. Just one fucking person to show them they matter, that they're loved."

He stepped closer, barely able to resist touching her. "Then those kids in there are luckier than most. They've got two people offering them a chance. Two people who care."

She bobbed her head tightly, holding his gaze. "Michael and I can't save them all. We won't be able to save them all, and when I think about that it kills me inside."

"You're doing what you can, Naomi. That's more than a lot of other people would do. Including those kids' parents."

"I know. That's the really awful part, isn't it? Parents

who won't, or can't, straighten themselves up even for the sake of their own children. As much as I love my mom, the fact that she chose someone like Leo Slater over me time and again hurts worse sometimes than losing her to death."

She turned away, busying herself with a package of popcorn. Asher moved in close and reached out to stroke the side of her face. "Your mother wasn't as strong as you are. You were stronger, braver than her even when you were that eight-year-old girl begging her to stay."

Naomi swiveled her head toward him, hauntedness in her dark gold eyes. "I hate that you saw me like that." She swallowed hard, then exhaled a soft curse. "I hate that you know how afraid and hurt I was. I've spent my whole life pushing that hurt down, trying to deny that deep inside I'm still that terrified, angry child. And now you… you're the one person I can't ever hide from, Asher. I can't ever be strong around you because you've seen me at my weakest."

"No." He curved his fingers around her bare nape, her satiny black ponytail brushing the back of his hand. "You don't have to hide or pretend to be anything. You can be weak or strong and it's not going to make a difference to me. You're always going to be the most extraordinary woman I've ever known."

She drew in a breath. "Asher, what I said to you today, before we came here—"

"You were right," he said, cutting her off at the pass. "You don't belong to me. You belong here, with these kids. They need you, Naomi. Michael does too."

For a long moment, she only stared at him, her gaze searching. "What about you? Tell me what you need."

"I need to know you're safe. That you're happy." He pulled his hand away from her before he gave in to the urge to hold on any tighter to something he didn't deserve. "I need to know Slater and those who serve him can never hurt you."

"That's all?"

"It's enough." He stepped back from her, putting her out of his reach. "I promised to protect you until we're certain Slater can't hurt you. That's what I intend to do. Then you can resume your life here and I'll go back to mine."

She went utterly still, silent. God help him, her gaze looked so bleak he felt as shamed as if he'd just struck her. For an endless stretch of time, neither one of them spoke or moved or even breathed.

Bare feet slapped the linoleum behind them. Then Tyler's squeaky voice demanded, "Where's the popcorn, you guys? The movie's about to start!"

"It's coming," Naomi said, greeting the boy with a happy smile that didn't quite reach her eyes. "Why don't you give me a hand now that you're here? You can open the packages for me and set out the bowls."

She turned her back to Asher and hastily got to work with Tyler at her side.

Asher faded back into the other room without her notice.

When the corn was popped and brought out from the kitchen, Michael started the movie for the eager group of kids. They were all piled into the living room, each of them gravitating to a certain seat. Max took the recliner, with Naomi on one end of the sectional where Michael had parked his chair. Penny was nestled up close to Naomi's other side.

"Is Asher sleeping here tonight?" Billy asked from his spot at the other side of the sofa.

Michael chuckled. "Not tonight, buddy. Asher's got his own place."

Now Penny turned a curious look on Naomi. "Is that were you've been?"

She nodded. "I'm staying with Asher for a little while, but I'll be back soon."

"Oh." The girl shrugged. "You gonna watch with us or what?"

It took a second for Asher to realize she was talking to him. "Yeah, sure."

She patted the space beside her and offered him a tentative smile which he was certain had everything to do with her trust in Naomi and her taste in friends and nothing to do with him personally. He made his way over and sat, careful not to encroach on the girl's personal space.

Still, she stiffened involuntarily in a way that made him feel queasy as he tried not to think of all the reasons why she might have to fear him, least of all the fact that he was Breed.

The first few minutes as the credits rolled were spent in awkward silence, all of his awareness centered on Naomi's unblinking, stoic face as she stared at the large screen. Soon enough, they all got lost in the movie. Asher never watched TV or movies, but there was something comforting in the shared silence within the room, nothing but rapt faces and the rhythmic crunch of popcorn being stuffed by the handfuls into tiny mouths.

At some point, Penny relaxed, sagging against his shoulder. Her soft snores vibrated through his arm as she nestled against him as innocently as a kitten. He watched her for a moment, and when he glanced up his gaze collided with Naomi's tender regard.

"You should take her," he murmured. Before he realized what he was doing, he reached down to move the child close to Naomi. As soon as his fingers touched Penny's bare arm, he was buffeted with the immense force of her memory—transported from his seat on the big sectional to a dusty floor beneath a small bed as he peered through a torn pink bed skirt. Terror clutched him, sucking all of the breath from his lungs.

No, not his lungs. Penny's.

Her terror seeped through him like acid.

In an instant, her memory imprinted itself on him before he could pull away.

He was here. She could hear him, mouth-breathing. Could smell the stench of whiskey and sour sweat pouring off him. The only question was whether he was too drunk to think of looking under the bed or if he would—

Fear closed around his heart like an icy fist as dark shoes entered her room. The bed skirt fluttered and a pair of watery gray eyes peered through the darkness.

"There you are, Penny-girl. Whassamatter? Come out and give your step-daddy a kiss goodnight."

Asher rolled to his feet, powered by pure, unadulterated rage. Penny stirred, blinking up at him sleepily from her peaceful drowse. Somehow, as he looked into that little girl's eyes, he managed to keep his voice even.

"Sorry. I'm not really into the movie after all. I need to get some air."

He stalked from the house onto the porch and sucked in great gulps of warm Nevada air.

When the door creaked open a few minutes later, he

expected to see Naomi. He had his apology lined up, but he paused when he realized it was Michael.

"You okay?"

"Yeah," Asher replied brusquely. "All good."

Michael nodded, his concerned gaze steady. "It's hard to process sometimes, even for me, and this has been my normal since before my accident. Some nights when a new kid comes through, I lie in bed so full of anger and pain for what they've endured. They don't even need to say the words a lot of the time. When you've known pain, you know how to see it in them." Michael stared out into the night, his hands resting lightly on the wheels of his chair. "Nay's so much better at all of this than me. She never lets them see her anger for what they've gone through—the rage that comes along with this work. I, on the other hand—" He glanced back at Asher with a wry look. "Let's just say there are a lot of times when it gets so heavy I need to walk away for some air too. Or roll, as the case may be."

Asher chuckled. "You do just fine, from what I've seen tonight."

Michael gave a dismissive wave. "Anyway, that wasn't the reason I came out here. I just wanted to thank you. For helping Naomi. She's the most loyal, selfless person I know. Impulsive and hotheaded, too, but I probably don't need to tell you that."

Asher felt a grin tug at his mouth. "Just a few of her finer qualities."

Michael nodded. "My friend is independent as hell, but that doesn't mean she doesn't need someone to lean on now and again."

"She's got you," Asher pointed out.

"Not what I'm talking about. I guess what I'm asking

is, does she have you now too?"

He didn't know how to answer that. Part of him wanted to reassure the man who loved Naomi like a brother that nothing would ever happen to her so long as Asher was breathing. But he didn't know how he could make that promise when he didn't have the right to feel so protective of her, so possessive.

"I will keep her safe," he vowed solemnly.

Even if that meant keeping her away from himself.

CHAPTER 17

They drove for nearly an hour in awkward, strained silence before Asher finally spoke.

"We're going to need some gas before we get back to the ranch."

He gestured to a dimly lit gas station with an attached convenience store, the only sign of civilization they'd seen for countless miles on this stretch of I-15. As they pulled off the deserted road and into the rundown station in the middle of nowhere, Naomi thought back to something Asher had told her.

"Is this the place where you first met Ned?"

He gave a curt nod and killed the engine. Some of her enthusiasm to be sitting in the very spot Asher had been fifteen years ago dimmed at the way he hardly acknowledged her. In fact, he seemed vaguely annoyed by the idea that she knew something about his past. As if after everything they had shared before, now she was trespassing.

He was drawing away from her emotionally, returning to the stony loner she'd met that first night in the desert. She supposed she had no one to blame but herself for the abrupt change in him. After all, she was the one who'd tried to pretend there was nothing between them when it seemed like he had intended to stop her from going to see Michael and the kids. She had felt cornered and her hackles went up. Now, she wasn't sure how to take back what she'd said. If he even cared one way or the other.

"Asher—"

"This won't take long," he said, climbing out of the truck.

She sat back against the old leather seat and waited as he fueled up. A few moments later, the gas cover thumped closed and he rapped on the driver's side window.

"I'm going to pay inside," he said through the glass. "Be right back."

She nodded and watched him walk toward the station. The young woman standing behind the counter was watching him too. Tall and curvy in her low-cut tank top and layers of Vegas showgirl-heavy makeup, the platinum blonde barely concealed her interest in the muscled male prowling with preternatural grace across the empty station lot.

She turned on a big, flirty smile as Asher stepped inside and approached the register. They spoke for a few seconds while he pulled some cash out of his back pocket and handed it to her.

Naomi didn't like the sharp jab of possessiveness she felt to see Asher conversing with another woman when he had hardly uttered a dozen words to her since they'd left Michael's house. Frustrated, she turned the key in the ignition and started scanning for some music on the radio. There wasn't much to choose from, just an old country station that sounded like it was being broadcast from out of a tin can.

"Screw it," she said, turning it off and slumping back to glance out the front of the truck.

Asher was gone.

And so was the pretty cashier.

Naomi's stomach dropped, cold and heavy as a rock. Where were they? She didn't want to think about why they had both disappeared so suddenly, nor did she want to acknowledge the hurt and suspicion that was taking up residence in her breast.

A few moments later, she spied Asher's head and shoulders towering over the top of one of the aisles. While he stalked out of the place and headed for the truck, the cashier went back behind the counter adjusting the strap of her top.

Asher got in without a word of explanation.

Naomi watched him put the truck into gear and turn back onto the road. "Everything all right?"

He nodded. "Good to go. We should be back at the ranch in less than twenty minutes."

As much as it seared Naomi to give in to her jealousy, she couldn't keep a lid on her emotions for long. They had only gone about five miles before she glanced over at him in the light of the dashboard.

"She was pretty. The girl back at the gas station."

He shrugged. "Yeah. I guess so."

"Is that why you went inside?" She tried to seem casual, unconcerned, but to her ears her voice sounded hollow.

He looked at her in question. "I told you, I went inside to pay."

"I know what you told me, Asher."

"Okay." There was an edge of irritation in his level tone. "So, what are you asking?"

"Nothing. Forget it."

She glanced out the window for a long while, knowing she really had no right to ask anything more. He didn't owe her answers or explanations. God knew he didn't owe her any apologies. After all, she'd gone willingly into his bed and he hadn't promised her anything in return.

Still, it hurt to think of him being attracted to another woman. It more than hurt to think he might have taken that attraction even further—especially while she waited in his vehicle outside.

But dammit, she had to know.

When they had finally turned onto the bumpy dirt lane leading to the ranch, she couldn't keep the words from tumbling out of her.

"Did you fuck her?"

He swung a hard look at her. "What? Jesus. Is that what you think?"

"Did you?"

"No." He parked the truck, and took out the key, his jaw held tight.

The tendons in his neck were thick and taut like cables, the angled bones of his cheeks seeming more sharply hewn somehow, unearthly so. Even in the low light of the truck's interior, she could see that the *glyphs* on his arms and neck were dark and pulsating.

"I didn't want sex from that woman, Naomi. I

wanted her blood."

Maybe she should have been relieved. She knew what he was. She understood he had to feed. But even these words carved her out. "That's the real reason you went inside—to drink from her?"

"Yes." A single word. No intonation in his cool, lethal voice.

She gave a stiff nod, then practically lunged for the door handle. She couldn't get out of the vehicle fast enough, couldn't get far enough away from him. She spilled out to the dusty ground and ran, not stopping until she reached the paddock fence where the horses stood.

Asher was right behind her. "What are you doing?"

"Go away, please."

"Why are you so upset?"

She pivoted in the opposite direction of him and stormed another few feet. He seemed to materialize right in front of her. "Tell me, Naomi. Why does the thought of me feeding from another woman piss you off?"

She scoffed brittly. "Because I'm an idiot, apparently."

He gave a tight shake of his head. "You know I'm Breed. You know it's my nature—it's a goddamn necessity—that I take a blood Host."

"Yes, I know all of that," she snapped, glaring up at his carefully schooled face. "I know what you are and what you need."

His eyes flashed with tiny sparks of amber. "Then why are you so hell-bent on condemning me for it now?"

"Because I love you." The admission rushed out of her. Once it was freed, she felt some of the weight lift from her breast. None of the pain ebbed, though. "I love you, Asher. And thinking about you being with another woman—drinking from someone—tears me up inside."

He scowled, a low snarl building. "You shouldn't say such things."

"Why not? Because you don't want to hear it?" She was seething now, all her cards on the table with him. She had never felt so vulnerable in all her life. "I've fallen in love with you, Asher, and that scares the hell out of me."

The sparks that lit his gaze had turned molten as she spoke, his pupils swallowed up by the light. As he reached up to cup her face in his hand, she saw his *glyphs* churning with living color. "Let's go inside now. This is not the place for what needs to be said. And it's not safe for you outside, especially in the dark."

She slowly shook her head. "It's not safe for me in there, either. Because every minute we're together makes me want to pretend the rest of the world—the real world—doesn't exist." She withdrew from his touch, even though it was hard to deny herself his comfort. "I'm just so scared, Asher. I've been through pain before, but I've never given anyone the power to hurt me like you can. I didn't realize what that meant until tonight."

"The last thing I want to do is hurt you." He caught her face in both of his hands and gently brought her to him for a kiss. Tender, unhurried, breath-stealing. "And the only vein I want is yours."

She frowned. "But you and that woman—"

"I went in the station with every intention to feed from her, but I didn't. I couldn't bring myself to put my mouth on someone who isn't you."

"Asher..."

"Don't," he said, shaking his head. "Don't look at me with that kind of relief. Because you're right. Being with me isn't safe for you, either. Because if I ever drink from you like I want to, there's no undoing it. I'll be bonded to you forever, Naomi. I'll always want you, crave you... hunger for you." He drew in a breath and let it out on a dark, strangled curse. "Hell, I'm going to feel all of that whether I have your blood in me or not."

She swallowed, her throat dry. "Then take it, Asher."

His scowl deepened. "You shouldn't say that. You don't really know what kind of man I am. I don't have the honor it takes to turn you down."

"So don't." She reached up, stroking his handsome face. She could see his torment so clearly now. He wanted her, but he was starving in another way too. She could see the anguish of it written all over his face. "As for honor, I've never known a better man."

A faint smile tugged the corner of his lips. "You know at least one. Michael."

"That's not what I mean. I've never known a man I wanted the way I want you."

She tilted her head to the side and pulled out the tie that held her hair in its ponytail. Sweeping the loosened strands around to one shoulder, she bared herself to his fevered gaze. To the razor-sharp fangs that seemed to lengthen even more as his gaze locked on her throbbing artery.

"Ah, fuck," he rasped. "His breath sawed in and out of him as he lowered his face to her neck. His tongue was hot and wet as it brushed tentatively over her carotid. "I can feel your heart racing. I swear, I feel it in my own veins whenever I'm next to you."

He licked her again, more deliberately now, a teasing,

testing stroke of his tongue over her fluttering pulse. Naomi's heartbeat thudded in her breast, hammering in anticipation of his bite.

Asher growled, an animal sound that vibrated all the way into her marrow.

Then he pressed his open mouth to the side of her neck and sank his fangs deep.

"Oh, God." She wasn't prepared—not for the jolting flare of pain, nor the rush of heat that flooded in on its wake. It felt so good, so primal. So powerful.

Arousal bloomed in her core, as sudden as a flashfire, and deep as a volcano. She arched against him, wanton and wild. His body was hard, his erection grinding into her in heavy demand. On a gasp, she tipped her head back and watched the sea of stars overhead blur into a field of diamonds as she lost herself to the pleasure of his heat and his elemental thirst.

Each strong pull of Asher's lips and tongue at her vein was echoed by a sensual and building pressure in the center of her. She was wet and panting, desperate to feel him inside her.

"Asher, I can't bear it... the pleasure is too much. Please . . ."

He groaned sharply against her throat, his tongue sweeping over the punctures. A tingling sensation followed as her wounds healed. He shuddered, and when his gaze lifted to hers it glowed with a devotion that staggered her.

"Now, I'm taking you inside," he rasped, his fangs enormous and glinting in the starlight. He scooped her up into his arms. "My sweet, delectable Narumi. You belong in my bed."

CHAPTER 18

He should have let her go tonight. He should have walked away from Michael's house alone and either left her there or drove her to the Order in Lake Tahoe himself so he could deal with Slater and Cain and anyone else who might pose a threat to Naomi's wellbeing.

Anything would have been better for her than what he'd just done.

But it was too late for second guesses or regrets.

The intoxicating taste of Naomi's blood was still the sweetest fire on his tongue—feeding every cell in his body—and there was no taking that back. Bastard that he was, he didn't want to take it back.

Asher carried her into the house past a befuddled Sam and down the hall to the bedroom. He kicked the door closed behind them and placed her on the bed. "I'm not sharing you with anyone tonight. You're mine."

She smiled up at him, her face slack with desire. "I like the sound of that."

Tonight she did.

Tonight he was still a man she thought she knew, one she believed she could trust. He would rather die than shatter her faith in him, but he'd already done that by withholding the truth about where he'd come from . . . and all the sins he'd committed.

Naomi's dread for a killer like Cain would be tenfold for Asher if she ever knew.

And she would know, if he were ever careless enough to let her drink his blood.

She would see it all and know that she was mated to a monster.

But for now, she loved him.

With her blood roaring through his veins and the bond twined from his soul to hers, he felt her essence alive and shimmering inside him. He knew the goodness and empathy that was Naomi. Her pleasure, her pain . . . it was all his now too.

Her affection wrapped around him like a warm embrace, igniting his blood while kindling an unbearable yearning in his heart.

"You're so beautiful," he murmured as he slowly undressed her, kissing every inch of exposed skin as he lifted away her shirt and unfastened her lacy bra. He stripped off her jeans and panties, pausing to enjoy the sweetness of her sex.

He was ravenous for her, and the power of her blood inside him intensified both his hunger and his need to give her pleasure.

"Please, Asher," she whispered heatedly as he undressed. "Don't make me wait."

He wanted to take his time, savor the gift of her body even though she had already given him more than enough of her. But through the bond he felt her gnawing need in combination with his own and it was too much even for him to endure.

As he came back onto the bed, she trailed her fingers over his shoulder and down his arm to take his hand. She placed it between her legs and moved against him, no inhibitions in her movements or in the fevered look she locked on him as he stroked her and plumbed her tight channel with his fingers.

She sighed and moaned, her slim little body twisting in pleasured agony.

He gazed at her in raw hunger. To think that she was his—even when he knew in the pit of his soul that he would never be worthy of her—made him feel like a king. Like a god, especially when her eyes were locked on his with a yearning that staggered him.

"So beautiful," he uttered, his throat constricted with the depth of his feelings.

Her tight, tawny nipples made his mouth water and he could not resist dropping low and closing his teeth over one of them, his fangs scoring her skin for just another taste of her blood. She gasped his name, her spine bowing into his embrace.

"You taste like heaven," he rasped against her as he licked at the tiny rivulet that flowed over his tongue, the scent of her skin and the sweeter scent of her Breedmate blood driving him to the brink of a need that bordered on madness.

"Asher…"

Her expression was beyond pleasure, beyond desire, as he stroked her sex and tugged at her breast with his teeth and tongue. Her arousal was a tightening coil inside him too. The bond would give him all of her most intense emotions—her deepest joys and ecstasies, her coldest fears and sharpest pains.

As staggering as it was to feel her desire for him, and her uninhibited response to his body and his touch, the thought of experiencing Naomi's distress or discomfort was torture all on its own. If he had anything to do about it, she would never know anything but happiness. And if that meant keeping her in his bed for the rest of their days and nights, he couldn't think of anything he'd enjoy more.

A snarl tore out of him on the heels of that silent pledge. Sealing the small flow of blood that trickled onto his tongue, he rose over her and moved into position between her parted thighs. She was wet and ready for him, her hips rising to meet the full measure of his thrust.

They both moaned at the intensity of their joining. Asher shook as he rocked into her, every cell in his body on fire with the need to claim her, to keep her . . . to love her forever as his mate.

When he was moving inside her, it was easy to deny all the other things he was feeling. The dread of losing her to someone like Slater or his men. The uncertainty of their future even if he were to neutralize that threat, and the pain he would be forced to endure if Naomi were to learn she had given herself to a monster.

He had never thought himself a coward until this moment. But as he coaxed her body to a release that left her clawing at his shoulders and screaming his name in ecstasy, he understood just how weak he truly was. Because this woman owned him with every sharp breath and pleasured sigh, with every powerful beat of her heart.

Asher watched her surrender everything to him. He felt it in his marrow, through the bond he had no right to take from her.

God help him, but it was easy to pretend he was a better man when Naomi was writhing and coming apart in his arms.

It was easy to deny his deep dishonor at having given in to his own selfish needs and desires with her... and the guilt of being unable to regret it.

CHAPTER 19

Naomi stepped out of the shower that next morning, feeling different in so many ways—stronger, more rested, every fiber of her being thrumming with the reminder of Asher's incredible passion last night.

And his bite.

She moaned just thinking about how good it felt to have his mouth on her like that, his fangs piercing the pliant flesh of her neck. Now that she knew what it was to give herself over to his hunger, a deeper craving had begun to take shape within her too.

She wanted to taste him.

She wanted to drink from his vein and feel the same kind of bond to him that he had described after taking his fill from her.

She wanted to feel his bond.

It terrified her how much she wanted that, even knowing there would be no coming back from it. A future with Asher. As his blood-bonded mate.

His Breedmate.

Wrapping a towel around her, she stepped in front of the bathroom mirror and peered at her reflection. She tilted her head, and for the first time in her life she studied the small red symbol under her chin with something other than annoyance or resentment. She'd spent twenty-six years trying to pretend the teardrop-and-crescent-moon stamp on her skin was nothing more than a birthmark, something to be ignored. Now, she couldn't see it without thinking about Asher and the incredible, passionate world that had opened up to her since he came into her life.

She smoothed her fingers over the vein that pulsed just below her ear, unable to contain the broad smile that spread over her face.

She loved him.

He hadn't said the words back to her precisely, but he'd said other things. Tender things. Possessive things. And all the while his molten gaze had scorched her with its intensity, and its raw honesty.

God, she had it bad for him.

More and more since she'd met Asher, she had been allowing herself to imagine shiny places in her future, places that had plenty of room for the kids and Michael, yet always with Asher at the center. It astonished her to realize how deeply she longed for those things, and that the other driving force in her life—vengeance on Leo Slater—had begun to take a backseat to this other one. *Hope.*

"You are a love-struck fool," she told her giddy reflection, but not even that dimmed the happy look on her face.

She shook her head and finished drying off, then hurried to get dressed so she could go find Asher and maybe persuade him to help her out of her clothes again after she made some tea and found something to eat.

She was finger-combing her damp hair when her phone trilled with an incoming call. She retrieved it from the top of the bureau and frowned at the private caller message shown on the display.

There weren't a lot of people who had her number; Michael and the kids, primarily. Instantly her thoughts careened toward Slater, but she couldn't imagine any way he'd know how to reach her. Still, her finger hesitated for a moment over the screen before she decided to answer.

"Hello?"

"Hi," a female voice replied. "Naomi, this is Sheila, from Dr. Davis's office."

"Oh. Sure, of course." Naomi let go of her pent-up breath when she realized it was only the medical assistant at the low-cost clinic where they brought the kids. "Is everything all right?"

"Yes, everything's fine. We, ah, we have Tyler here for his asthma check-up today."

"Okay." Naomi vaguely recalled the appointment, but usually it was Michael who kept track of those things and made sure everyone got where they were supposed to be. "Is there something I can do for you, Sheila?"

"Well, I was just wondering . . . Tyler's been waiting for someone to come pick him up for over an hour, so I didn't know if you—"

"Wait a second," Naomi blurted. "Didn't Michael bring him to the appointment?"

"Yes, he did. But Tyler tells me Michael dropped him

off and was going to take care of some banking and run a couple of errands before he came back to pick him up. Like I said, it's been quite a while since we finished with Tyler and the poor little guy's getting a bit anxious for someone to come and get him."

"I can imagine," Naomi murmured, a niggling sense of unease creeping over her. "Have you tried to reach Michael?"

"Yes. We've called him several times, but his phone goes straight to voice mail."

"Okay." Naomi pinched the bridge of her nose. "Okay, I'll try him too. I'm not in the city right now, but I can get there in about an hour. Can Tyler wait there for a while longer?"

"He's welcome to stay as long as needed," the assistant said. "I'm sure he'll be relieved to hear that we were able to get a hold of someone."

"Of course. Please, tell him not to worry."

As she ended the call, Asher appeared in the open doorway of the bedroom. "What's wrong?"

"I'm not sure. Maybe nothing."

He shook his head. "It doesn't feel like nothing to me."

She knew what he was referring to—the blood bond that had evidently alerted him to the concern that was forming into a cold ball in her stomach. "One of the boys, Tyler, is waiting at the medical clinic in the city for Michael to pick him up. He's been sitting there for more than an hour."

Asher frowned. "It doesn't seem like Michael to leave a kid stranded like that."

"No. It doesn't. He told Tyler he had some banking to take care of and run some errands." She tapped

Michael's number on her phone and shook her head when the call went directly to messages. "Asher, I need to use the truck."

A dark look came over his features. "Not a good idea, Naomi. Not when I can't be there with you. I don't like it."

She strode up to him and pressed her palm to the side of his tense jaw. "I know you don't, but I can't leave that little boy waiting all alone. He's been abandoned by people he's trusted all of his short life. I'm not going to be one of them."

She didn't need the benefit of a blood bond to know that Asher was two seconds from refusing. Not that he had much choice. The truck was his, but she knew he couldn't deny her the use of it when it came to one of the kids.

"There's nothing to worry about," she promised him. "Michael gets distracted sometimes. He's probably trying to do ten things at once and will fly into the clinic parking lot around the same time I get there. Anyway, it's not like it's the middle of the night—"

"No," Asher muttered. "It's the middle of the morning, when I can't spend more than ten minutes outside these four walls without incinerating."

"I'll be fine." She went up on her toes and kissed him, holding his dubious gaze. "I'll call you along the way, and as soon as I hear from Michael and make sure Tyler's home safe I'll come right back home."

The light in his eyes changed as she said that word, home. His stern face softened, if only marginally. He speared his fingers into her hair and brought her back to his mouth and kissed her, unrushed and deep. "You call as soon as you reach the city."

"I will."

She gathered her phone and the keys to the old Chevy and raced out the door.

Several times on the hour-long drive up to Vegas she called Michael's phone but only got his voice mail. Each unanswered call made her concern grow colder, edging toward real worry that something had gone wrong with the payment from Moda.

Or, worse, that Michael ran into trouble.

There was no sign of his van in the clinic parking lot when she pulled in. Once inside, she was greeted by a distressed Tyler, slumped into one of the waiting room chairs with tears streaking down his freckled cheeks.

"Hey, buddy," she said, hurrying over to him and hunkering down in front of him to ruffle his shock of red hair. "I'm sorry you had to wait so long. You okay?"

His sweet little face was pinched, nose swollen from crying. "Where's Michael?"

"He probably got stuck somewhere running errands. I'm not sure, but we'll find him."

Tyler frowned. "I thought you guys forgot about me."

"Never," she assured him earnestly, shaking her head. "Never, ever. You hear me?"

He nodded stiffly and she took his hand as he got to his feet. With a wave to Sheila behind the glass reception window, she collected her sniffling charge and escorted him out to the nearly empty parking lot.

"Isn't this Asher's truck?" Tyler asked as she helped him into the passenger side.

"Yes, it is."

"Where is he?"

"Back at the ranch, sweetie. He wanted to come with

me to get you, but he had to stay inside."

"Because he's Breed, right?"

She nodded, struck by how easily the boy had accepted Asher as a part of their makeshift tribe. Seeing everyone together at Michael's house had given her a glimpse of what a true family felt like. Her family—the one she hadn't been born into, but wanted desperately to have for the rest of her life.

She stroked her hand over the little boy's head. "Buckle in, okay? Let's get you home now."

As discreetly as she could, she tried Michael's number again as she got settled behind the wheel. No luck.

Dammit, where was he?

She took another second to check in with Asher, careful to keep the concern out of her voice so that Tyler didn't detect the panic that was beginning to slither through her veins. But Asher knew. His voice was gentle and reassuring, telling her he'd checked the news for reports of accidents and traffic problems, but found no cause for worry.

"Thanks," she murmured. "I'll call you when I get to the house."

For the duration of the drive to the other side of town, she kept Tyler occupied with questions about school and homework and what he might want for dinner. They fell into a familiar, easy chatter until they rounded the corner onto the street leading to Michael's house.

And then Naomi's heart clenched behind her sternum.

Michael's van was parked in the driveway. Which on any other day might seem normal, but at this moment felt very, very wrong.

"What the heck?" Tyler blurted, sending her a confused look. "You mean he's been home the whole time?"

"I don't know, honey." Naomi parked beside the vehicle, unable to shake the bone-deep chill that was spreading over her. "Why don't you stay out here and let me go talk to him first, okay?"

To her relief, the boy didn't argue. Naomi climbed out of the truck and let the rusted door close behind her with a groan.

As she entered through the unlocked front door, she dimly remembered that she had promised to call Asher when she arrived. But her feet were moving of their own accord, carrying her inside the quiet house. God, it was too quiet by far.

"Hello? Michael? Anyone home?"

It wasn't unusual for the kids to be scattered and off doing their own thing during the day. There was school for some, while others were either too young or too rebellious to attend with the kind of regularity they needed. Part of the deal with the kids who filtered in and out of their house was that they stayed only because they wanted to. To most that meant having someplace to go when night fell or when the desert got too cold, or too hot, to survive long outside. Letting them have their freedom was part of that equation, no matter how hard it was for Michael and her to adhere to the agreement sometimes.

Right now, Naomi couldn't think of anything she wanted more than to hear a herd of young teens and other kids come tearing through the house, preferably with Michael rolling right behind them, or summoning them all into the kitchen for a meal.

Anything but the tomblike quiet that surrounded her as she stepped farther inside.

"Michael?"

She drifted toward the bedroom at the end of the hallway. The door was partially open—only wide enough for her to see his empty wheelchair just inside.

"Michael…"

Her steps slowed as she approached, her mind reluctant to process what every instinct in her body was trying to tell her. Something bad had happened. Something horrific.

She entered the room and glanced toward the floor next to his bed. His legs were sticking out at an odd angle as if he'd fallen out of his chair and into the open closet. Then she saw his blue, lifeless face… and the taut leather belt fastened tightly around his neck.

Her heart plummeted.

No. Oh God, no.

She stumbled back a step.

And she screamed.

CHAPTER 20

The idle waiting and wondering had been driving him insane, so in a fit of activity Asher had installed his new headboard in the master bedroom. It wasn't ever going to be finished to his liking, and since he needed something to do with his hands, he'd impulsively decided to put the damned thing to use.

He had just stepped back to look at the hand-carved piece when an invisible blade plunged into his chest. He staggered back on his heels, bewildered for a moment, uncertain where the attack had come from.

And then he knew.

With a shredding certainty, he realized the pain he was feeling was hers.

Naomi.

"No." A jagged cry rose up to strangle him. "No!"

The shock and grief she was experiencing tore through him like serrated steel, so agonizing it nearly took him down to his knees. But she was alive. Thank God for that, she was still living and breathing.

He could feel her energy in his veins, telling him their connection hadn't been severed by anything as unthinkable as her death. But she was hurting deeply. Not because of physical wounds but with a loss she could hardly bear.

She should have called by now. She should have been at Michael's house several minutes ago by Asher's estimate.

His body still gripped in her anguish, he fumbled for his phone and called her.

"Asher." Her voice was wooden, barely a whisper. A sob choked out of her. "Oh, my God... Asher, he's dead. Michael's dead."

"Ah, Christ." He swallowed hard, hating that he wasn't there with her. "Are you all right? Tell me what happened."

She explained how she found him a few moments ago, dead of an apparent suicide. She told him that she was outside the house waiting for the police, whom she'd just hung up with in the second before he called.

"He didn't kill himself, Asher. Slater's behind this."

"Yes." He glanced at the time on his phone and wanted to roar his fury.

It would be several hours before sundown. The woman he adored was eighty miles away and he could do nothing to help her. Nothing to save her, if the danger that found Michael were to lock its sights on her next.

At least he could be assured it wasn't Cain who harmed her friend. That lethal bastard would be as hampered by the UV light as Asher was.

But without Asher to level the odds, even a human coming after Naomi was a risk he couldn't take.

"You have to get out of there, sweetheart. Right now. Come home, Naomi."

"I-I will as soon as I can," she said, her voice nearly drowned out by the rising wail of sirens. "I told Tyler what happened and he's afraid the police are going to take him and the other kids away to an orphanage."

"Jesus," Asher hissed. "Let him know we'll never let that happen."

He heard the small catch in her voice. "I will. I'll tell him that, Asher. Okay, that's the police coming now. They're pulling up to the driveway, and Tyler's waiting in the—" Her voice cut short on a gasp. "Oh, no. Tyler just saw the cops and ran off. Tyler!"

"Naomi, tell me what's going on there."

He heard her breath change as she began walking briskly to meet law enforcement. "I have to go. I'll call you as soon as I can."

He heard the thump of car doors closing and officers speaking to her in the second before she ended the call.

He drew the phone away from his ear and stared at it with blazing eyes. Fear clawed at him, but this time it wasn't Naomi's emotion—it was his own.

He'd never felt so powerless, he the unstoppable killer who had feared nothing, lost nothing—loved nothing—for the entire beginning of his brutal existence.

Now he could do nothing but wait.

And worry.

And pray that the woman he loved wasn't ripped away from him before he had the chance to tell her how much she meant to him.

He gripped his phone in a crushing grasp, but knew he couldn't sever the only line of communication he had with Naomi.

So, on a bellow that shook the four walls of his daytime prison, Asher brought his fist back and drove it into the center of the headboard he'd made, splintering the wood into a thousand jagged shards.

~ ~ ~

Naomi leaned against Asher's truck and answered all of the questions the police and first responders asked her.

No, she wasn't in the house when the deceased took his life.

No, she had no knowledge of drug abuse, financial problems, or any other cause that might have driven her best friend and roommate to tighten a belt around his neck and slowly strangle himself with it.

No, she didn't know of any other family members who should be contacted about Michael's death.

There was only her. And the group of parentless kids who were going to be as destroyed as she was to learn that one of the kindest, most compassionate people on Earth was suddenly, inconceivably, gone.

"How many children came and went from Mr. Carson's home on a regular basis, Ms. Fallon, and what would you estimate their ages to be?"

"Excuse me?"

The female officer from JUSTIS, the law enforcement department comprised of both human and Breed officers, gave her an apologetic look. "I know some of these questions are difficult, but I'm just trying to establish the possible mental state of Mr. Carson in his final hours. Could he have been harboring any secrets or possible guilt pertaining to any of the kids he invited to stay in his house?"

"You can't be serious." Naomi gaped, fuming. "No. Of course, not. Michael was the one good thing to happen in any of these kids' shitty lives."

The officer lifted her shoulder. "Just trying to cover the bases."

"Well, consider them covered," Naomi snapped. "We're done here."

Her gaze drifted to the curb where the black zippered bag holding her friend's body was being loaded off a gurney and into a waiting ambulance.

"Here's my number," the JUSTIS officer said, handing her a card with her name on it. "If you think of anything else we should know, just give me a call."

Naomi stuffed Officer Rachel Reynolds' card into her pocket without looking at it. She was never going to use it.

She hadn't told the officer that she already knew what happened to her friend. That Slater or his henchmen had gone after Michael and staged his murder to look like a suicide. She didn't know the how of it, but she knew the why.

If anyone was harboring unbearable guilt or secrets, it was her.

And now, because of her, her best friend was dead.

Why had she let Michael convince her to let him be part of that last job? He'd been so adamant, but she could have refused him. Dammit, she should have.

As for sharing what she knew about his death with law enforcement, while it might spark an investigation into Slater's criminal activities, she had zero confidence he would be made to pay for what he'd done to Michael.

Just like he'd never paid for what he did to her mother, either.

Men like Slater were untouchable.

Why she hadn't come to terms with that fact before it cost Michael his life was a burden she would never be able to put down.

Naomi got in the truck and started the engine. As she backed out of the driveway and onto the street, grief swamped her. It was too deep for tears, the shock wrapping her in a cocoon that seemed to numb her from the inside out. All she wanted to do was curl up in a ball and cry for a week, but she had things she needed to do. Priority One was locating Tyler and the other kids before they scattered to the wind in fear of being taken away somewhere by strangers.

And then she needed to get back to the ranch.

Back home with Asher.

He would know what to do. He would be able to help her find the kids. They could come back to the city tonight as soon as it was dark and start searching until they found them all.

She hadn't driven two blocks before her phone chimed with a familiar ringtone.

Michael's ringtone.

For an instant, as she hurried to retrieve the device from her back pocket and saw his number on the screen, she thought she had imagined this whole horrific day. But the icy reality settled in just as quickly when she brought the phone to her ear and heard an airless, menacing voice on the other end of the line.

One she'd heard only in her nightmares since the time she was eight years old.

"Hello, Naomi. Or should I say Narumi?" She felt the blood drain from her face the way he spoke her given name, full of dark amusement. "Pity about your friend. Suicide is such an ugly thing."

"You did this." No need to pretend she wasn't aware of Leo Slater's evilness. "You sadistic bastard, you killed him."

A low chuckle sent a shudder through her bones. "No, my dear. You did."

She could hardly deny her part in all of this. The guilt washed over her in a black tide, and it was all she could do to keep her sob from choking her. "Keep talking, Slater. I'm going to take everything I know about you straight to the police. Including what you did to my mother."

"No, Narumi, you won't." He sounded so confident, she wanted to scream. "You won't, because if you intended to do that, you'd still be talking to those officers parked in your crippled friend's driveway right now."

She sucked in a shallow gasp. He'd been close enough to see her? Was he still lurking somewhere on the road with her? Her gaze darted to the rearview and side mirrors, taking note of the scores of vehicles that surrounded her. He could be anywhere, following her by himself or accompanied by any number of his gangster lackeys.

"What do you want?" she demanded, knowing there was nothing he could take from her now that meant more than what she'd already lost.

"I'm sure you know what I want. My money. All of it."

She swallowed, shaking her head as she stared out at the sunlit road and the garish signs that flanked the Strip.

"If that's what you wanted, then you shouldn't have killed Michael. The money's in his bank account. I can't get to it."

"Find a way, Narumi. And I want the rest of it too. By my accounting, you owe me another two-hundred-and-thirty-seven-thousand dollars in addition to what you and your friend stole from me the other night."

She scoffed, but her heart was racing with fear. "I have no idea what you're talking about."

He exhaled a tight, impatient sound. "You may have cheated me right under my fucking nose, but do not take me for a fool. I've seen the video footage from my casinos over the past many months. I don't know how you did it and I don't care. I want my money back. Every. Fucking. Cent."

He was asking the impossible—more than the impossible—and she didn't think for a minute that he didn't know that. She'd spent more than half of his money on the kids and helping Michael run the shelter. That money went to food, clothing, countless other necessities. As for the little bit she'd made waiting tables here and there or doing any number of other odd jobs, it wouldn't make even the smallest dent in what she owed him and besides, her menial wages were gone practically before she even brought them home. "I don't have all of your money to give it back to you."

"Then find a way to get it. All of it," he said again, menace in the calmness of his viper's voice. "Or you'll be forcing me to take something else from you if you fail."

The line went dead. Naomi's breath gusted out of her, part in relief, part in paralyzed dread. She hardly cared what Slater might do to her personally, but she didn't want to imagine how far he'd stoop to hurt anyone else she loved.

Her hands were shaking so hard she had to pull over. She sat in a loading zone for several minutes, until a truck blasted its horn at her and nearly made her jump out of her skin.

God, what had she done?

For the last eighteen years of her life she'd lived with the sole purpose of getting even with Leo Slater. Making him pay for hurting her mother, for taking her away and destroying everything Naomi had.

For nearly two years now, she'd been chipping away at the monster of her past. Cutting him where he would hurt, in the only place a man like Slater would bleed. But even as she was taking his money, each of those little victories felt hollow. That's why she kept going, kept hitting him for more and more and more.

Now, she was the only one who'd lost.

And even if she had the chance to take every last nickel of Slater's fortunes—even if she could be assured that one day she could destroy him completely before stabbing him in his black heart—she knew that would be an empty triumph too.

Simply put, Leo Slater didn't matter.

The cost of her vengeance was already too high.

She just wanted it to be over.

If she could, she'd surrender all of his damned money right now, just as he'd demanded. But she didn't have access to Michael's personal bank account, nor did she have the more than two-hundred grand she'd taken from Slater's casinos over time.

But she had some.

And she could never spend it anyway, knowing every

penny she took from Slater was now stained with Michael's blood.

Numb and wracked with tears she refused to let spill, she glanced at her phone and tapped one of the numbers stored on the device.

A perky voice answered. "Anytime Private Vaults, can I help you?"

"Yes," Naomi said. "I need to empty my safe deposit box."

CHAPTER 21

Less than an hour later, Naomi walked into Casino Moda carrying a Las Vegas souvenir tote bag filled with eighty-seven-thousand dollars cash in large bills. Everything she had left from all of her repeated hits on Leo Slater's casinos.

Asher had been calling her repeatedly since she left Michael's house, but she had yet to speak to him. She felt awful for silencing her phone, but she knew what he would say if she told him she was heading in to give Slater what he demanded. Or, part of it, at any rate. She hoped the money she had to give him would appease him enough to back off and not hurt anyone else close to her.

If she had to work the rest of days to earn back the remainder of what she owed him, she was fully prepared do it. She just wanted him out of her life now and forever.

She just wanted to be able to grieve for Michael and bring home Tyler and Penny and the rest of the kids and never let them go.

Those plans bolstered her as she marched through the casino toward the glass central elevator that would take her to the executive offices on the top floor. Her finger only trembled a little as she pushed the button on the panel and waited for the car.

Someone was on the way down.

As the lift descended smoothly to the lobby level, she found herself staring into the face of a man she'd never seen before. A dark-haired man with arresting silver eyes who she would never mistake for human.

The massive Breed male who stepped out of the car stood easily as tall as Asher, and was built just as solidly beneath the crisp white button-down shirt and graphite-colored dress slacks that strained over his muscled physique. In the open V of his shirt collar an elaborate tangle of *dermaglyphs* curled and twisted onto his neck.

Every instinct in her body told her this was not only a Breed male, but the trained assassin Asher had warned her was on Slater's payroll.

Cain.

Those shrewd silver predator's eyes glanced down at the bag in her hands then back up at her in glowering suspicion. "Where the fuck do you think you're going?"

"I need to see Slater." She tried to step around him, but he was too enormous. His body blocked the elevator doors, which had slid closed on a whisper behind him.

"Like hell you do. What's in the bag?"

She knew the only thing she should be feeling under this menacing male's gaze was fear for her life, but she was still too numb and in shock from Michael's death to feel anything but fury now that she was staring up at one of the men likely responsible for taking his life.

"I'm sure you know why I'm here. To deliver your boss what he's demanded. His blood money."

Cain shook his head, his scowl deepening. "I can't let you do that."

"What are you going to do?" She scoffed. "Kill me right here in the lobby of the casino? Or take me somewhere and string me up to make it look like I killed myself the way you and the other thugs working for Slater did to my friend?"

The vampire's lips pressed flat on a low snarl. "I had nothing to do with that. In fact, I just heard about it from some of the men on the security team."

She glared at him, bitterness in her voice. "Like I'm going to believe you? I'm sure Slater and the rest of you thugs have been up there patting yourselves on the backs for killing a man who had little chance of defending himself."

A tendon jumped in Cain's tense, beard-shadowed cheek. "You couldn't be more wrong, at least as far as I'm concerned. And on the occasions that I have killed someone, I've never needed an excuse or a reason to make it look like something else."

She swallowed, seeing a glimpse of the coldness that lived inside him. "I'm sure you must sleep like a baby knowing you have such high standards. Now, get out of my way and let me pass."

"Naomi." His hand clamped around her wrist like a band of iron. His face darkened, even while his irises lit with amber flecks of irritation. "If you go up there, Slater will never let you leave. At least, not while you're still breathing."

She tried to wrench loose, but there was no breaking his hold. From his expression, that kind of strength came easily, without even a thought.

"Cut your losses and leave town as soon as possible," he told her. "There are plenty of places you can go. As a Breedmate, you'll find safe shelter in any of the Breed communities around this country or any other. Go there. Stay away from Las Vegas."

Strange how different this advice sounded coming from someone other than Asher. In the beginning, he'd insisted on nothing less than her getting the hell out of town and staying gone. As much as she'd balked at the idea then, the thought of being driven away from her city and her life here was something she'd never consider now.

Especially if Cain were suggesting she should leave Asher behind too.

She glanced down, realizing only now that Cain had a black leather duffel bag at his feet. "Where are you going?"

He grunted. "I don't know. Anywhere but here. I've spent too much time working for slime like Slater. I'm done."

She frowned, shocked and not quite sure she could believe him. But as he held her stare, she saw deep shadows in his cold silver eyes. She saw the same haunted, bleak abyss that she still glimpsed in Asher's deep blue eyes sometimes.

"I'll help you get somewhere safe," he said, his tone too solemn to be a lie, even for a killer like him. "You can come with me right now, Naomi. I promise, you can trust me on this."

Maybe she could, but she didn't want what Cain was

offering her. Her life was here, and if she needed a safe haven she had Asher.

She shook her head and stood her ground. "I'm not going anywhere. I'm already right where I belong."

Cain studied her, then exhaled a slow breath. "You're making a mistake."

"I don't run for anyone, not even Slater. Especially not him."

"No," he said. "I'm not talking about Slater. I'm talking about Asher."

That took her aback. Suspicious of this killer now, she hiked up her chin. "You're going to warn me about him? That doesn't mean much coming from someone like you."

"Like me?" Those sharp eyes narrowed on her in question.

"I know what you are. Asher told me. You're a cold-blooded killer. A trained assassin."

Cain said nothing, not for a long moment. "I am all of those things, Naomi. I was born a Hunter. But so was he."

"What?" A frisson of uncertainty crept along her spine now. She knew the term Hunter, if only in broad terms. There had been a madman among the Breed twenty years ago who'd been raising a homegrown army of killers in his hidden labs for decades. All boys, all bred off the same monstrous father using dozens of imprisoned Breedmates. The babies born inside the lab were enslaved from the moment they took their first breath and raised to be killing machines by Dragos until he was finally destroyed by the Order.

Was Cain saying he and Asher had been part of that awful program? If so, why wouldn't Asher have mentioned it?

"You didn't know." He chuckled, but it was a sympathetic sound, one that said he might even pity her. "I'm not surprised that you don't, considering the fact that he actually seems to care for you. Never would've thought a bastard like Asher to be capable of the emotion."

The bag of money in her arms had been heavy before, but now it was beginning to feel like a lead weight. "Tell me what you know."

He gave a gruff shake of his head and started to walk past her. "Never mind. It's not my place."

"It is now," she said, taking hold of his shirt sleeve. "Dammit, tell me what you know about Asher."

"You already know the worst of it just by saying his name."

"What are you talking about?"

"One of the tenets of the Hunter program was obedience to our master, Dragos. But there were always some who resisted, headstrong boys, cocky teens . . . adult males who refused to be broken. Dragos believed in discipline. He believed in making examples for others to follow or to learn from. And to help him maintain his control he had mind slave servants to monitor us, but he also had enforcers—other Hunters who'd excelled in their training and who could be called on to mete out justice as he deemed fit."

"What does any of this have to do with Asher?"

After the wracking pain of what she'd already been through today, she was surprised she still had the capacity for more fear or dread. But she did. They were carving a chasm in her as she waited for Cain to tell her the rest of what he knew.

"All of us in the Hunter program wore ultraviolet collars that would detonate if we tried to run or if we fought back against our training. Or if we gave Dragos any reason to want us gone. There was one enforcer he relied on the most. One Hunter within the program who had no qualms about pushing the detonator that would ignite the ring of UV light around a Hunter's neck—his brother's neck—and reduce him to smoldering dust."

Naomi closed her eyes as a wave of understanding swamped her. *"Asher."*

Cain grunted. "There were rumors that he enjoyed his role so much he would touch the condemned in the seconds before he killed them. Just to savor their pain. To feel their terror while some of them begged for mercy in the seconds before he ashed them."

Naomi felt sick thinking about Asher's gift to recall—to relive—the worst of someone's memories with his touch. God, if this were true it would make him an animal. Worse than an animal, a sadistic monster. She didn't want to think it. Part of her refused to. She'd only known Asher a handful of days, but she could hardly reconcile the man she loved with the cold killer Cain was describing.

"I can't believe he's using that name after all this time. He could've chosen to call himself anything once he was freed—we all had that choice." He shrugged. "Hell, maybe it's a badge of pride for him."

"Stop." Naomi shook her head, overwhelmed with everything she'd heard. She had wanted to know, but she couldn't take any more. Not now. Not after today.

"He hasn't told you any of this." It wasn't a question, because the look of shock on her face must have been enough to remove any of Cain's doubt. But then he seemed to clue in on something more. "Ah, Jesus. You're in love with him?"

Part of her wanted to deny it, but she couldn't force the words out of her arid mouth. Not even when Cain's steely gaze was looking at her as though she were the biggest fool on Earth.

"Walk away, Naomi. From Slater. From Asher. From all of this shit. Do it for yourself . . . before you end up regretting it any more than I think you already are."

CHAPTER 22

More than a dozen calls and twice as many texts and she still hadn't responded.

Asher paced the house like an animal in a cage, his *glyphs* writhing all over his skin and his eyes burning like hot coals in his skull. His fangs filling his mouth, he snarled and cursed as he wore a hard track in the living room rug while Sam stared anxiously from his position nearby.

Asher wasn't angry at Naomi. All of his self-hatred and futile rage was directed entirely at himself.

He never should have let her go today. They could have found another solution for the boy stranded at the doctor's office—anything but the one that had sent Naomi back to Las Vegas without him. But even as he thought it, he knew she'd never stand for shirking her responsibility to a child who was counting on her. Hell, even Asher wouldn't have suggested it.

And none of that would have changed the fact that Michael Carson was dead.

Murdered in cold blood.

He could hardly believe the kind, smiling young man was gone now.

Asher blamed himself for that too.

He should have known Slater wouldn't take such a big loss at his casino in stride. He would have been scrutinizing Michael with laser focus, sniffing around for any cause he could find to renege on the payment or snatch it back before it was fully out of his grasp.

Killing the winner was certainly not the smartest way to go about that, but if Slater thought he had another way to get his hands on the money…

Fuck. Where the hell was she?

He took out his phone again and started to hit her number when he heard the crunch of gravel in the distance. Finally.

It was just after noon with the sun shining high overhead, but he didn't give a damn. As Ned's old truck bounced on the narrow dirt lane out front, Asher practically yanked the latch off the screen in his haste to meet Naomi as she pulled to a stop at the house.

The light seared his vision and the rising cloud of yellow dust gathered in his throat like cinders as he raced to the driver's side of the vehicle and tore open the door.

"Thank God you're okay. I've been going fucking crazy here."

She didn't answer. She hardly looked at him as she stepped down from the seat and onto the ground. He gathered her close, ignoring the sharp sting of the sun's deadly rays on his exposed skin. Relief rocketed through him to be holding her again and seeing for himself that she was still in one piece and not a mark on her.

"Naomi." He didn't want to let go, but she was wooden in his embrace. Her breath was shallow, her expression blank. "Baby, are you all right?"

He could feel that she was—his bond to her blood told him she hadn't been injured. But she was awash with a shell-shocked quiet that shredded him inside. He knew that look. He had seen this kind of numbness before, in other Hunters back when he was a boy. He'd felt it himself after he'd completed his first kill order from Dragos.

A shock and horror so deep it hollowed you out.

Touching her now gave him a jolt as a new and awful memory flowed out of her to take root in his mind and senses. Naomi's grief and horror as she discovered her friend slumped in his bedroom, his face almost unrecognizable for the awful color and swelling the leather garrote around his neck had caused.

He ran his hands over her face, smoothing her slack ebony hair out of her eyes. "What happened after you left Michael's? I've been calling and texting all this time. Why didn't you respond? Have you been out there looking for Tyler or the other kids?"

She swallowed and shook her head, her gaze still vacant. How she managed to make it home in her state of shock, he had no idea and he didn't want to consider.

He glanced past her and saw something odd on the floor of the truck's cab.

A tourist-style tote bag emblazoned with a glittery Las Vegas slogan. The bag was filled with cash. Lots of it.

What the fuck?

He searched her face, dread snaking up the back of

his skull. "Naomi, no. Tell me you didn't go to see Slater…"

But no, he rationalized. If she'd done that, she wouldn't be alive and standing in front of him now.

She blinked dazedly, and a frown pinched her brow. "You're burning, Asher. You can't be out here."

He didn't even feel the pain of the angry red patches sizzling on his bare forearms and face. All of his focus, all of his concern, was on her. "Let's go inside."

Grabbing the tote in one hand and her in the other, he shut the truck's door and brought Naomi into the house. Sam immediately trotted over, showering her with affection she barely seemed to notice.

"Come on," Asher said, leading her into the living room and sitting her down on the sofa.

He put the tote bag on the floor then sat beside her. When her eyes met his again, he felt a withdrawal from her that had nothing to do with Michael or her ordeal today.

Something else was wrong here. If her wounded eyes hadn't told him so, the stab of anguish that pierced him through the bond left no doubt.

"Talk to me, Naomi. Tell me where you've been." He looked back at the tote full of large denomination bills and cursed under his breath. There had to be tens of thousands of dollars stuffed into that bag. "What are you doing with all of that money?"

"I was leaving Michael's house after I talked with the police," she murmured, her voice sounding rusty and unused. "I got a call. Michael's number. Only it wasn't Michael."

"Slater." Asher practically spat the name.

"He told me he wants all of his money back. Not just

the money Michael and I took the other night. All of it. Everything I've ever stolen from him."

Asher recalled the steep figure Cain had tossed around. "You don't have that kind of money in that bag," he said, dread coiling inside him when he realized where this conversation was going. "Tell me you didn't plan on doing what Slater asked. You aren't planning to go bring him that money, are you?"

"I'm not planning to," she murmured. "I already did. Tried to, that is."

He vaulted to his feet on a savage curse. "Holy fuck. What do you mean, you tried?"

She gazed up at him, a bleakness in her expression. "I ran into someone you know. I was on my way to find Slater at Moda and Cain was on his way out. Quitting and leaving town, according to him."

Asher would consider that surprising newsflash later. Right now, the only important detail was the fact that Naomi had evidently come face to face with the former Hunter.

"What else did he have to say?"

"A lot of things, Asher. Mainly what he said was that I needed to be wary of you." She stared at him, her soft sherry-colored eyes leaving him nowhere to hide. "He told me about your past. About the fact that you were part of the Hunter program, all of it. He warned me that I should leave Las Vegas and you and never look back."

His chest felt as though it were being cracked open from the inside. He didn't need to know the specifics of whatever else Cain had told her. The details didn't matter. Everything between them had changed because of her conversation with the other Hunter.

"Why didn't you tell me? Why did I have to learn it

from someone else, Asher?"

He took a step away from her, unable to hold her accusing expression. "I didn't want you to know."

She exhaled sharply. "I guess that's understandable. Hard to sell me on the fact that only you can protect me from a man like Slater, or even Cain, when it turns out you're more dangerous than either one of them. Is that it? Don't you think I deserved to know?"

"In the beginning, I saw no reason to tell you. And then... it wasn't long before I hoped you'd never find out."

She stood up on slightly shaky legs, then turned to head out of the room. Asher told himself he should let her go. She was right. He was worse than Slater and Cain combined. The things he'd done. The deaths he'd dealt at Dragos's command. Scores of them, each one seared into his memory in total, vivid detail.

If Naomi left after learning all of that, he could blame no one but himself.

But he wasn't ready to let her go.

God, he would never be ready for that.

Moving faster than her eyes could track him, he blocked her path. "You do deserve to know. As much as I wish you'd never find out all the things I've done, I owe you the truth. Even if it does make you leave me and never look back."

"Is it true? Were you not only part of that awful program, but its executioner too? Did you really kill little boys and men—your brothers—for Dragos?" Her questions came rapid fire and hitching, a barrage of ugly truths. "Asher, my God." Her breath caught sharply as her stark gaze studied him. "Did you really enjoy it so much that you used your gift to revel in their pain?"

So, Cain hadn't spared a detail about his past. That came as no surprise. His Hunter brethren had plenty of reason to despise him, but Cain had one thing wrong.

"No. I didn't revel in my duty. I hated every second of it. But I did it because I wanted to survive... and because if I didn't carry out Dragos's orders, someone else would. Or he would do it himself, and I wouldn't wish that on anyone, least of all my brothers."

He saw her struggling to accept what she was hearing from him. He felt her recoil emotionally through their bond. But she didn't turn away from him. She wasn't trying to leave and never look back. Not yet, anyway.

"Cain said you made a point of touching the ones you—" She broke off, briefly closing her eyes. "He said that before you executed another Hunter, you used your Breed ability to feel their fear as they begged you for their lives. He said you wanted to feel their agony before you killed them."

Asher slowly nodded. "That much is true, yes."

"Oh, my God." Revulsion seeped through their connection, oily and bitter. "Oh, shit. I didn't want to believe him..."

She was repulsed by his admission, he could see it in her stricken expression as much as he felt it in her blood. She drew back from him, but Asher caught her around her nape.

"It's true that I laid my hand on every Hunter I had to execute. I did want to feel their terror and their anguish." He spoke over her strangled moan, forcing her to hold his gaze as he bared the blackest pieces of his soul. "I did it, Naomi, because I never wanted to forget them. I wanted to remember every face, every pair of fearful or defiant eyes that fixed on me as the last thing they saw. I never wanted to let myself forget the brothers I killed in order that I could keep living. That was my penance, to never forget."

She relaxed in his loose grasp, only the slightest bit. Her body sagged with the weight of her heavy exhalation. When she spoke, her voice was almost too soft to be heard, her eyes turning tender on him, even pitying. "How many, Asher?"

He shook his head. "Too many. I was selfish, even then. And without honor. If I hadn't carried out Dragos's edicts I would've been the one to die. I made certain that when I delivered death it was swift, even when Dragos called for suffering."

"I can't imagine how terrible your life was," she murmured. "All of the Hunters' lives."

No, she couldn't. He wished no one could be able to imagine that kind of brutal, bleak existence. But he and Cain weren't the only Hunters walking the Earth with memories of those years, and sins to be reconciled.

There were others. Scythe in Italy now, along with Trygg, another former Hunter serving the Order over there.

Countless more scattered to each corner of the globe in the two decades since the program, and Dragos, were destroyed.

Asher smoothed the pad of his thumb over Naomi's slackened lips. "As awful as my life was back then, I didn't want to die. For a long time, I didn't know why it was important to me to keep going, to keep living." He stroked her cheek. "Now I know what I waiting for."

She wept softly, but kept her arms down at her sides, refusing to touch him.

"It was unfair of me to drink from you before you

knew who I was… what I've done. I don't deserve your bond, and I know I won't ever be worthy of it. I'll never be worthy of your love, if I haven't already lost that." He held her face tenderly in his palms and searched her bereft, hurting gaze. "I love you, Naomi. All I want is a future with you at my side, but I don't know if you can ever look at me the same way as you did before."

"No, I can't," she admitted softly. "But I can't blame you, either. I won't blame you for doing what you'd been born and trained to do, Asher. What hurts the most is that you didn't give me the chance. You didn't trust me enough to be honest about your past and how it shamed you. Instead I had to learn it from someone else. I've never felt like a bigger fool."

"I know," he muttered, his own self-loathing like acid in his throat. "I'm sorry for that. I'm sorry for so much where you're concerned."

She eased out of his reach, her voice constricted. "It doesn't matter right now. Michael's dead, Asher. Because of me, my best friend is dead. And Tyler and the other kids could be anywhere in the city now with no place to go."

"We'll figure that out," he vowed. "And as soon as the sun goes down, I'll take care of Leo Slater."

"No." She shook her head, wearier than he'd ever seen her. "He's taken everything he can from me now. I'm finished fighting him. He won. He doesn't matter anymore, only those kids do."

She stepped away from him, bringing her arms across herself. Then she turned and headed down the hall to the master bedroom and closed the door, quietly shutting Asher out.

He stood there, knowing she wouldn't want him to

follow. Not this time.

He felt her sorrow in his veins as she broke down in private behind the closed door and mourned her friend alone.

CHAPTER 23

A quiet knock sounded on the door. Naomi had dozed off on the bed at some point, exhaustion and grief finally dragging her down into a deep sleep. She roused now, feeling both rested and yet utterly drained.

"Come in."

Ironic to be granting Asher permission to enter when it was his bedroom, his house—his life—that she had intruded upon with all of her problems.

She sat up on the bed as the door swung open and he stepped inside accompanied by Sam, whose entire body wiggled in excitement as he trotted up to her looking as though he hadn't seen her for a week.

"Hey, sweet boy," she said, unable to resist ruffling his neck and stroking his floppy ears. Tongue lolling, he danced and whined in front of her, his blissful ignorance of the day's many traumas somehow comforting to her now.

"How are you doing?" Asher asked, watching her pet and scratch the happy hound. "I hope I didn't wake you."

"No." She shook her head. "I was awake when you knocked. What time is it?"

"Just after five."

She blinked, stunned. "You let me sleep all afternoon?"

Asher's smile was hesitant. "You needed the rest."

She had needed it, if only to escape the grief that was still clawing at her over losing Michael. But sleep was only temporary relief. Sooner or later, she had to wake up.

Just like sooner or later, she would have to deal with all of the arrangements and adjustments that would now need to be considered not only for her friend but for the kids who'd just lost their only port in a storm.

And then there was Asher and her.

Eventually, they would have to decide what things might look like for them moving forward from today too. Whether that meant together or on their own, she wasn't ready to contemplate.

His brow was knit as he looked at her from where he stood, just inside the room. "I thought you might be hungry, so I made you something to eat."

She didn't know if she was hungry or not, but the fact that he had thought to take care of her warmed her when all she'd felt before was aching cold. "Thank you."

She couldn't look at him now the same way she had before. Cain's revelation, and Asher's own confession afterward, had cast him in a different light. As a man Asher was now less of a mystery than when she first met him, but even more complicated than she ever could have imagined.

Her feelings for him were complicated too.

Her love hadn't dimmed, not even after Cain had given her more than enough reason to doubt Asher. To despise him, even. But she couldn't stop loving him, not even before she knew the full truth from Asher himself.

Asher, she thought, her heart aching for everything he had endured.

As for his name, the epithet he'd kept all this time, she understood now that it wasn't a badge of pride as Cain had assumed. Asher had kept his derogatory name for the same reason he kept the memories of all the Hunters he'd been forced to execute—as yet another reminder of his remorse, his penance.

Cain had totally misunderstood Asher.

So had Naomi, until today.

She glanced at the pile of splintered wood that lay on the floor of the bedroom. "What happened to your beautiful headboard?"

He shrugged, his mouth pressed in a flat line. "After you found Michael... feeling your pain and fear through your blood... knowing I was miles away and couldn't do anything to help you if you needed me?" He abruptly stopped speaking and let out a low curse. "It tore me up, not being able to be there with you."

"Oh, Asher."

The hand-carved piece she'd seen him labor over for days and which had obviously been a project that he'd been perfecting for far longer than she knew was completely destroyed. The center of it looked as if it had been smashed with a sledgehammer.

Or a Breed male's driving fist.

"It's just a slab of wood," he said. "Maybe I'll make

another one someday."

Naomi got off the bed and walked up to him, laying her palm against his cheek. It astonished her, how much this man meant to her after only a few short days and nights together. How deeply would she tumble if they had forever?

She went up on her toes and pressed a kiss to his lips. She intended it to be only a small kiss, but she didn't realize how much she'd been missing his contact until his strong arms wrapped around her, holding her close to him.

They kissed for a long moment, tenderly, apologetically. When Asher finally released her, his irises were glittering with flecks of amber light. He wanted her, but he was holding that need in check, if only barely. Naomi felt it too, the yearning to lose herself in something good after all of the bad they'd been through today.

But she couldn't indulge in her own needs or desires.

Not when there were still things to be done back in the city.

"Come on," he said, taking her hand. "Once you get something in your stomach it'll be dark outside. We can head in to Vegas and start looking for Tyler and Penny and the rest of the kids."

"Thank you." She twined her fingers through his as they walked, grateful beyond words for the fact that he understood without her even saying so. "What did you make me to eat? It smells delicious."

She stared in surprise—and amusement—when she saw the feast he'd prepared. Waiting for her on the table was a large bowl of canned chicken soup, cooked chicken breast on a plate of salad, a bowl of cereal and a cup of fresh fruit, plus the entire loaf of French bread they'd brought home from the grocery store the other night.

"I didn't know how hungry you'd be," he murmured. "So I made all of the things I know you like."

She laughed in spite of the anguish that had ridden her all day. "It's perfect. I think I know who to call the next time I need to feed an army of starving kids."

She sat down and ate, amazed to find she did have an appetite after all.

Once she'd had her fill, she and Asher headed out from the ranch and made the drive in to Las Vegas to begin searching for the kids.

They started with the parks and shelters in and around the Strip. They'd found plenty of kids and young teens hanging around, but none of the group they were hoping to locate.

They had even driven past some of the seedy areas of the city, through industrial lots and freight depots, some of the places desperate kids tended to look for shelter when they had no better options.

As the night wore on, Naomi couldn't hide her frustration. Or her fear.

"I hate knowing they're out here somewhere and don't know I'm looking for them. What if they run, Asher? What if we never find them?"

"We will," he assured her, his deep voice determined. "We'll search the whole damned state and more if we have to."

She nodded and sat back, looking out the truck's window at the flashing casino lights and soaring high-rise hotels. Casino Moda stood out like a tower made of diamonds, all the way up to the winking beacon lights on its rooftop helipad. Sleek, inviting. No hint at all of the monster who dwelled inside.

Asher cleared his throat. "Maybe we should drive past Michael's house."

She had deliberately avoided asking him to go there, not at all ready to revisit the place that would always be the source of her worst nightmares now. But Asher was right. They had to try everything.

At her nod, he turned on to the street that would take them into the residential area off the Strip. She reached over and grasped his hand as they turned on to Michael's street. She didn't realize she was holding her breath until the truck approached the darkened house and Michael's van still parked in the driveway. The air in her lungs leaked out of her on a ragged sob.

"It hurts so bad, Asher."

"I know, sweetheart." He brought her fingers up to his lips and kissed them.

"I can't ever come back here again. Neither can any of the kids who lived here."

He nodded, turning a solemn look on her. "You don't have to. None of you do. There's plenty of room for everyone out at the ranch."

"Are you serious?"

"Yeah. We'll find a way to make it work."

Her heart leapt inside her rib cage. She tried to reach him for a hug, but her seatbelt restrained her. "Shit." Laughing in spite of her tears, she popped the buckle and threw her arms around him, peppering his face with grateful kisses.

He bent his head to hers, a smile playing at the edges of his sensual mouth. "Maybe I should pull over if you're going to do that."

She was so swept up in the moment that the sudden ringing of her phone in her back pocket took a second to register.

Michael's ringtone again, only this time it hit her senses like a hammer on glass.

"Oh, my God."

Asher's face darkened even as his eyes lit up with fire. He veered over to the curb and put the truck in park. "If it's Slater, let me handle it."

But she already had the phone at her ear. "Hello."

"You disappoint me, Narumi." Slater's voice sliced through her. "I would've thought my message today was clear enough. And yet you still haven't brought my money."

"I told you, I don't have it. I have some, but—"

"All of it," he cut in sharply. "That was my demand."

Asher's eyes blazed as he listened next to Naomi. If Slater were in arm's reach, Naomi had no doubt that Asher would already have torn the man's throat out with his bare hands.

"Why do you insist on making me hurt you, Narumi? Do you remember what I said? If you don't give me back the money, I'll be forced to take something else you care about."

She didn't want to guess what that might be. He'd already ripped out her heart today. What more could he do?

"I can give you what I have. Eighty-seven-thousand dollars. The rest of it—"

"Every. Fucking. Penny," Slater said. Then he started to laugh. A maniacal sound that chilled her veins. "Every penny of mine in exchange for yours, Narumi."

Her breath caught. "What?"

In the background, she heard commotion followed by a young girl sobbing hysterically.

"Bring her here," Slater ordered.

The cries got louder as the girl came closer to the phone. She sniffled and choked on her tears. "N-Naomi?"

"Oh, my God." Penny's jagged, fear-filled sobs shredded her. "Penny, don't worry. We're not going to let anything happ—"

The sound of a hand striking a tender cheek split the air on the other end of the line. Penny shrieked, then started bawling, begging Naomi to help her.

"Bring the money. All of it," Slater snarled. "Or sweet little Penny here is going to have a terrible accident too. Unless I decide to take my debt out of her flesh."

CHAPTER 24

"Holy shit! I just won a thousand dollars!"
"Jackpot! Oh, my God!"
"Twenty-five-hundred bucks! I can't believe it!"

Asher strolled about twenty paces behind Naomi as she made her way through the large pit of slot machines at Casino Moda. As she walked, she casually traced her fingers over every machine she passed, lingering just long enough to finesse the mechanism inside into hitting a payout on every spin of the wheel.

The din of excited voices in the casino grew like a swelling tsunami in her wake, along with the nearly deafening sounds of the whirring, chiming, dinging machines as they vomited out thousands upon thousands of Leo Slater's profits.

It didn't take long for the shouts and cheers of the twenty, thirty, fifty and more winners to incite a stampede of new players to elbow their way in for a chance at the money that seemed to be flowing nonstop from the slot pits. People on the street began pouring into Moda now, too, as word got out that something unusual was happening inside.

"Cash grab!" someone shouted. "Cash grab in the slots!"

Asher couldn't help marveling at Naomi's steely resolve as she set off pandemonium right under Slater's nose.

The plan to go on the offense had been hers. Instead of dissolving into paralyzed hopelessness at the threat he'd issued a few minutes ago, the news that he was holding Penny hostage had galvanized Naomi.

"No amount of money's ever going to satisfy him," she'd told Asher in the truck as they considered their few options. "Even if I had the one-point-three million plus the two-hundred grand I owe him, he's not going to let me walk away. Now, he won't let Penny walk away, either. This isn't going to end unless I end it."

She was right, Asher had no doubt.

So, she'd returned to Slater's domain like a warrior on the march. Utterly courageous, armed with her spine made of iron and the power of her unique Breedmate gift.

And him.

Asher stayed out of the line of sight of the casino's various eyes in the sky. His best means of helping her at the moment was the element of surprise. For now, this was her show, and he'd never been prouder of anyone in his life.

As the uproar grew, the pit bosses all convened in the middle of the casino, five guys in black vests and white dress shirts standing around with their dicks in their hands and shrugging in useless confusion.

When the chaos had reached a fever pitch, Naomi glanced at Asher. He gave her a nod and moved in close enough to listen as she took out her phone and dialed Michael's number.

It took Slater a moment to answer, and when he did, it was in the midst of apoplectic distraction.

"—And tell Thompson to get his ass up here with some answers and I mean now! What the fuck do I pay you people for? Narumi," he snarled. "You'd better be calling to tell me you have my fucking money."

"Yeah, I've got your money. I've got my hands on every last dime in your casino, Slater. And unless you let Penny go in the next two seconds, I'm going to drain every slot machine and roulette wheel in the place."

"What the fuck are you talking about?"

"This." She held the phone out for a moment and let him hear the feeding frenzy under way on his casino floor. "Let Penny go, or this is only the beginning."

"I'll kill the bitch first," he hissed. "Then I'll come for you."

"Wrong answer." Naomi's voice was steady, cool control.

Asher smiled as he watched his incredible woman stroll along another row of machines in the pit, touching each one, setting off jackpot chimes and sirens while Slater listened. The crowd of people scrambling to get to the money closed in like a hive full of bees, swarming the machines and shrieking with greedy excitement.

Naomi glanced at Asher, nothing but steel in her gaze. "I want Penny," she demanded of Slater. "Send her down. Right now."

"You're gonna pay for this, you fucking little cunt."

"You first," she said, emptying the half-dozen machines beside her as she spoke. "Let Penny go."

"Somebody, go get that damn kid!" he shouted, his voice shrill over the receiver. When Slater came back to talk to Naomi, he was panting with rage. "Nobody threatens me. Nobody steals from me. You understand? You're dead, bitch. You're fucking dead!"

Naomi barely blinked at the threat. She hung up on him and turned to Asher. "Do you think this is going to work?"

He reached out and palmed her cheek. "You just did the hardest part. You're fucking amazing, you know that?"

She gave him an anxious look, the first he'd seen her falter tonight. "I just want Penny safe."

"We're not leaving without her." He glanced up, his head and shoulders towering over most of the buzzing crowd. "We've got company on the way."

The group of pit bosses finally clued in on the source of the disruption. A couple of them touched their wireless earpieces and blanched, no doubt on the receiving end of Slater's tirade. All five men started jogging toward them.

"Go," he told Naomi. "Stay low. I'll handle these dumbfucks."

The men split up, three sprinting toward Asher while two others fanned out to cover the perimeter of the clot of shouting, screaming, shoving casino patrons. Naomi disappeared into the throng, her petite size and sleek agility aiding her in hiding in plain sight.

Asher swiveled his head in the direction of the oncoming casino managers. A simple flash of his fangs convinced one of the men to turn tail and run in the opposite direction, but the other pair kept barreling toward him.

He charged at them too, grabbing their lowered heads in his hands and skull-smashing them unconscious. He had more trouble on the way. Slater's security detail had decided to join the party now.

Half a dozen men moved in from other parts of the casino to look for him. One cowboy already had his service pistol in hand, brandishing it as he charged for Asher. Bad move. Asher was in motion before the human even knew what hit him, tossing the guard halfway across the floor.

Another trigger-happy rent-a-cop fired his weapon over the teeming swarm of casino patrons and suddenly the excited squeals and cheers turned into a panicked stampede.

As the crowd screamed and dove for cover, the other security men opened fire. Shots rang out from multiple directions, a few of them hitting their mark. Asher didn't feel the bite of the multiple rounds that slammed into him. His attention was focused completely on something else.

Across the large casino, the glass elevator descended to the lobby. Inside stood Slater, short and stocky, with graying dark hair and a jowly face currently pinched with anger. His hands gripped Penny's thin shoulders in front of him, as if he were prepared to use the lanky girl as a shield. Surrounding the pair were Slater's team of heavily armed bodyguards.

Fuck. Where was Naomi?

Asher scanned the area for her as the floor security closing in on him tightened ranks with guns blazing. He dodged the fire and the relentless stream of terrified civilians bolting from all directions for the exits.

"Naomi!"

Another shot hit him, square in the chest. Asher's fury was on full boil now. Bellowing, he mowed down the team of humans, his hands a blur as he crushed bones and twisted spinal columns, working to clear a path toward Slater and the child.

As the elevator doors opened, the new team of armed men spilled out.

And then he saw Naomi.

Slater took his hands off Penny as he stepped out of the car and gaped at the chaos going on inside his prized casino. The momentary inattention was apparently all the opportunity Naomi needed. She raced forward, making a desperate lunge for the elevator.

"No," Asher growled. "Naomi, no!"

Too far away to warn her and hit with a new barrage of gunfire, he couldn't reach her before Slater realized she was there.

Asher roared. "Naomi!"

She was in the open elevator car and had the sobbing girl under her arm as Slater pivoted around and saw them. Without a second's warning, he slammed his fist into Naomi's jaw. She went down like a stone, crashing into the back wall of the glass compartment.

Asher tore forward on a leap and a thundering war cry.

He was only a second too late. His bloodied body collided with the closed doors as the car began a swift upward climb with Slater looming over Naomi's unmoving body and Penny slumped in the corner dissolved in terrified screams.

CHAPTER 25

Naomi opened her eyes on a groan. Her face was pressed against the cold marble floor of the elevator as it rose swiftly through the center of Casino Moda.

Penny's thin arms were wrapped around Naomi's shoulders, the girl sobbing over her slumped body. Naomi's jaw hurt like hell, but she was alive. Penny was alive.

Oh, God. Asher.

She'd seen him under heavy gunfire from casino security and Slater's personal bodyguards. He was Breed, so she knew it would take a lot to slow him down, but that didn't ease the terror that was sitting like ice in her stomach.

"Barnes, get up to the helipad and start the chopper." Slater was talking to someone on his phone a couple feet from where Naomi had dropped after he struck her. "Just me. I'm on my way up now."

Naomi pushed herself up onto her hands, her vision swimming. A heavy foot slammed into the center of her spine, knocking the wind from her lungs as she was pinned to the marble tile once more.

"Leave her alone!" Penny wailed. "Stop hurting her, you asshole!"

Like a viper, Slater struck hard and without warning. The savage blow sent the girl flying backward into the wall of the elevator car. The instant her blonde head hit the sharp chrome hand rail, she slumped bonelessly, leaving a trail of blood on the glass behind her.

"You son of a bitch!" Naomi vaulted to her feet, adrenaline and fury surging into her bloodstream. She would have jumped on Slater in attack, but when she wheeled around to face him, she found herself staring into the business end of a big black pistol.

His expression darkened with menace. "Let's go, Narumi."

The elevator car stopped and the doors slid open soundlessly on to a private floor of the building. Naomi managed a furtive glance at Penny and was relieved—if only marginally—to see her chest rising and falling even though she hadn't moved.

"Start walking." Slater fisted his hand in the hair at the back of Naomi's head and marched her at gunpoint toward a steel door marked *Roof Access - Personnel Only*.

"You always were a pain in my ass," he complained. "You and your mother both. More trouble than either of you were worth. Doesn't surprise me that you turned out just as uppity as she was."

Naomi didn't miss the past-tense reference he used. "Is that why you killed her?"

He chuckled. "I didn't want her dead, but what choice did she leave me? That last night she came to my place with her fucking ultimatum—get help for my anger issues or she was going to press charges on me? Stupid bitch had a camera full of photos, all the bruises I gave her, the broken bones. I mean, who the fuck did she think she was?"

Naomi's bile rose to hear these facts now. After years of wanting the answers, thinking her mother hadn't been strong enough to walk away from a deadly relationship, the truth hurt even worse. "So, she stood up to you and you had some of your thugs get rid of her? Or did you have Cain put his special skills to use for you?"

"Cain." Slater scoffed. "That Breed bastard turned out to be a goddamn traitor. I paid the asshole a million a year to look out for my interests—inside and out of the casinos—and what did he do? Stab me in the back. He must've known for months about your thieving, but I had to learn it from one of the pencil pushers in accounting over at the Gold Mine."

Naomi drew in a breath, more than surprised at that information. But Slater still hadn't totally answered her question about her mother. "What happened to my mom? It doesn't matter if you tell me. I'm sure you have no intention of letting me live."

And as terrified as she was at the idea, she took small comfort in the fact that Penny was alive back in the elevator, and if Asher was at all able to reach her, he would make sure the girl was safe.

She didn't want to consider all of rounds Slater's men had fired at Asher.

She'd seen him in action. He was unstoppable. But he wasn't immortal; even one of the Breed could be killed if the wounds were catastrophic enough.

She refused to let the thought take root. She couldn't let herself imagine that he might be suffering... or worse.

"Tell me, you cowardly piece of shit," Naomi pressed. "Did you have your men kill my mom?"

He yanked her hair, wrenching her head back until she was staring up into his cold reptile eyes. "No, Narumi, I didn't have anyone kill her. I kept that pleasure all for myself. I took her far out to the Mojave and bashed her head in with a tire iron. Then I left her for the vultures and the other garbage eaters to fight over."

Naomi's gag choked out of her. Even though she had suspected something close to this all along, hearing him say it—hearing the satisfaction in his voice as he described how he'd brutalized a woman who had truly, foolishly, loved him—made the bile surge up her throat.

"You sick fuck. You monster!"

"It's been great reminiscing, Narumi, but I've got to fly." The fist that was wound tight in her hair twisted even harder now. And that pistol jabbed cold and hard against her temple. He nudged her once they were standing in front of the roof access door. "Open it."

She did as he ordered, wishing for the chance to reach up and touch the gun that was cocked and loaded at her head. She'd never tried to finesse a weapon before, but dammit if there was any hope at all, she was going to try.

A warm breeze gusted at them from atop the fifty-two story casino. Overhead the sky was inky black, the stars out-glittered by the lights of the surrounding Strip. The moon cast a milky glow onto the roof's concrete surface, and glinted off the black helicopter that sat on the large bullseye circle of the helipad. The rotors were unmoving, no sign of anyone in the cockpit.

At her back, Slater let out a curse. "Where the hell is my pilot? Barnes!" he shouted. "Why the fuck isn't this bird ready to fly?"

"Barnes had another commitment."

Asher's deep voice was an unearthly growl coming from somewhere behind them.

With his hand still grasping Naomi's hair, Slater whirled around, holding her in front of him like a shield. "What the fuck?"

Standing atop a large air conditioning unit, Asher looked like something out of a horror movie. Immense, seething, otherworldly with his *glyphs* churning everywhere they were visible on his body. His eyes were molten coals, throwing off heat like a furnace. His lips were peeled back in a murderous snarl, baring his teeth and the enormous dagger-sharp lengths of his fangs.

He'd never looked more formidable than he did in that moment, but Naomi saw the way his chest labored with each breath.

And he was dripping blood from more wounds than she could count.

"Your boyfriend's Breed?" Slater gave a dry chortle. "I might've guessed your taste in men would be as questionable as your taste in roommates."

God help her, she wanted to see Slater suffer. He deserved nothing less than a slow and protracted death—things she could only dream of delivering on him.

If Asher's narrowed glower were anything to go by, he wanted Slater's pain too.

He leapt into the air, a swift arc of motion that carried him over Naomi and Slater in less than a second. Slater looked up, gasping as he watched Asher vanish into the darkness.

"Holy shit! Where'd he go?"

The hold on Naomi's hair fell away as Slater pivoted wildly with his weapon. And then Asher was in his face, grasping him by the throat.

Slater bellowed like a man possessed, squeezing the trigger over and over and over again. Sharp staccato clicks that didn't release a single round.

"W-what the fuck?" he sputtered, disbelief in his wild eyes. "What'd you do to my gun?"

Asher raised a questioning brow at Naomi. She shrugged and smiled.

Slater's grasp on his weapon went slack as Asher lifted him onto the toes of his polished loafers with the strength of one arm. Then he walked Slater backward across the rooftop, not stopping until they were very near the edge of the more than six-hundred-foot drop.

Slater clawed at Asher's grip, but it was no use. "P-please," he sputtered. "L-let me go. Oh, fuck. Oh, shit!"

Asher pushed him even closer to the ledge, lifting him until his feet barely skimmed the concrete of the rooftop. Slater's face was a mask of horror, bleached white and slack. His cruel eyes rolled in his skull, as if his brain were torn between looking down at the Strip all that distance below him or into the emotionless face of the Breed male who literally held his fate in his hands.

"You can't do this," Slater gasped. "What do you want? I'll give you anything!"

"Beg," Asher said, inching him farther. Slater's heels hung off the building now, his toes dancing on the very edge. "Beg for your life, and maybe I'll let you live."

"Please!" Slater wailed. "Yes, I'll beg you! I'm pleading with you, please! Don't do this to me!"

Asher shook his head. "Don't beg me. Beg her."

Slater swallowed, a strangled croak under the pressure of Asher's fingers clenched around his windpipe. "P-please… Narumi, I am begging you! Forgive me. I loved your mother, I swear it. I never meant to hurt her. If I could take it back, I… I would take it all back, you have to believe me."

"No. I don't have to believe you."

He choked on a blubbering sob. "Then let me make it up to you. Keep the money—all of it. You can keep it… I'll give you more if that's what you want."

"It's not what I want," she replied tonelessly, feeling nothing for the man now. Not even hatred. He was nothing to her. Less than nothing. "I thought I wanted slow revenge on you after what you did to my mom. But then what you did to Michael—"

"I'll confess to it all," he blurted, desperation climbing as Asher continued to hold him aloft over the lights and noise of the Vegas Strip. He started sobbing in earnest now, his pride completely deserting him. "Please! For the love of God, tell me what you want from me!"

"Nothing."

She shook her head and walked up closer to him, so he could see her face through the darkness—a face that looked so much like her mother's—and know that Aiko Sato would live on in her, Narumi, long after Leo Slater and his empire were dust.

"I want nothing from you," she told him. "And you'll get nothing from me, either. Least of all, forgiveness."

A low whine began to build inside him as he stared at her, fury rolling to a swift, hard boil. Spittle flew from his slack lips as he railed at her. "You cunt! You fucking little thief! I should've crushed your skull the same night I killed your whore of a mother. Goddamn it, let me go!"

Asher didn't look to her for permission to see it done. His judgment on Slater was already passed; now all that remained was the sentencing. He tightened his hold and closed his eyes for a long moment.

Naomi realized what that was—that focused moment of hesitation.

He was savoring Slater's final moments of fright, absorbing every facet of his terror and desperation so he would remember it forever.

Slater struggled frantically, spewing threats and curses. "You fucking bloodsucker. Let me go!"

Asher exhaled calmly and opened his eyes. "Okay."

Then he dropped Leo Slater over the edge.

"Asher." Naomi rushed to him, burying herself in his arms. The scent of his blood overwhelmed her. Everywhere she touched him, her fingers came away wet and sticky. "Oh, my God. What have they done to you?"

He pressed a kiss to the top of her head. "I'm all right. I'll live. Let's get Penny and get out of here."

Penny was just coming to inside the elevator when they returned from the roof. She threw herself into Naomi's arms, shaking uncontrollably and weeping in relief that the ordeal was over.

It looked like a bomb had gone off in Moda's lobby. The place was all but cleared out, except for a few shell-shocked stragglers, and numerous dead security personnel who lay in bloody pools where Asher had taken them down. Money and personal effects were strewn all over the floor, dropped by the hundreds of people who'd fled once the gunfire began.

And inside the nearly empty ruined casino, the musical chiming and racket of the slot machines competed with the blare of sirens from the arriving JUSTIS vehicles outside.

With Penny clinging to her, Naomi took her own comfort from the warmth of Asher's arm draped around her shoulders as the three of them exited the casino.

"Excuse me, sir. Ma'am." A female officer approached as soon as they stepped outside.

It was the same woman who'd responded to the call at Michael's house earlier that day, Officer Reynolds. Naomi bristled at the sight of the woman, even though she couldn't fault her for doing her job.

"Oh, hello. Ms. Fallon, isn't it?"

At Naomi's nod, the officer studied her with more than passing curiosity, then she turned her suspicious gaze on Asher. With his fangs extended and his eyes lit like coals, there was no mistaking him for anything other than Breed, but the law enforcement official didn't even flinch.

"Can either of you tell me what happened in there tonight? From what we understand the machines malfunctioned and it sounds like casino management got a little... overzealous in their response to the situation."

Asher grunted. "More or less."

The officer looked him up and down. "You don't look so good. We've got an ambulance out here, if you need medical attention. Or an emergency blood Host."

He shook his head. "I don't need any of those things."

"What about you, Ms. Fallon?"

Naomi hugged Asher closer. "I just need to be home."

They started to walk away and the JUSTIS officer cleared her throat. "Just one more thing, if you will." When they paused, she gestured to the street several yards from the casino entrance. "You wouldn't happen to know anything about the body that landed on the pavement a few minutes ago, would you? Hard to tell for sure, but we think it's Moda's owner, Leo Slater."

Asher glanced at Naomi before meeting the officer's narrowed stare. "After the amount of money he lost tonight, odds are good Slater probably jumped."

The female snorted. "Suicide, then?"

"Stranger things have happened," Asher replied.

The cop nodded. "All right, then. JUSTIS will be taking a look into this whole thing... but maybe not that closely," she added, low under her breath.

And as she waved them off, Naomi glimpsed a peculiar mark on the officer's wrist. The same teardrop-and-crescent-moon symbol she had under her chin.

"You all take care now," the officer called from behind them.

CHAPTER 26

Naomi stuck like glue to his side the whole drive back to the ranch. Asher knew his wounds were as severe as they were numerous, but they would have been much worse if he didn't have some of her Breedmate blood inside him.

As bad as his condition was, that thought kept him grounded as he pushed Ned's old truck to its limit in order to get Naomi and Penny home and safe as quickly as he could. His own needs could wait.

After the night they'd just had—and having come too damned close to losing either one of them—he wasn't taking any chances.

"Is he gonna be okay?" Penny whispered to Naomi as they arrived at the house. "Can vampires die?"

"Asher's not going to die." Naomi cupped the girl's worried face, but turned a solemn look on him in the low lights of the dashboard. "Not as long as I have something to say about it."

They headed toward the house, Naomi tucking herself under his arm. He didn't mistake the concern in her careful steps, nor in the steady pound of her heartbeat.

Her love for him buoyed him, as much as her petite body wedged tightly against him propped him up as he hobbled onto the porch.

"You have a dog?" Penny's eyes lit up the instant she spied Sam waiting to greet them. She had a decent-sized knot on the back of her head from Slater's assault in the elevator, but all of the day's traumas seemed fleeting for the girl in the face of the old hound's eager reception. She raced to the screen door ahead of Asher and Naomi. "Look at him, he's so cute!"

Even Asher had to admit, if begrudgingly, that the dog was a welcome sight after the hellish past few hours. They stepped inside, Asher leaning heavily on Naomi. His blood dripped in multiple puddles on the floor, making Sam whine and tilt his big head at him in wary curiosity.

Naomi gently cupped the girl's head with her free hand. "Penny, will you do me a favor? Take Sam into the kitchen over there and see if he needs some food or water while I help Asher clean up."

"Sure. C'mon, Sam!" She headed off, led by the enthusiastic dog who had never met a stranger.

Asher grunted. "She's resilient."

"Most kids are," Naomi said. "That's the only way they can survive a lot of the time. Right now, I'm most concerned about you."

She marshalled him into the bathroom and sat him down on the closed toilet. "Sit still," she commanded him, turning to search the cabinet for a clean washcloth and towels and a pair of scissors, which she used to cut away his blood-soaked, grime-stained T-shirt.

He let her work, telling himself it was simply for the pleasure of watching her tend him, but the truth was he'd taken a lot of hits. The gunshot wounds hadn't killed him, but they sure as hell would have slowed him down or dropped him if it hadn't been for her blood, feeding his body the way no amount of human blood ever could.

"You saved me, Naomi."

She slanted him a glance and shook her head. "Not yet, I haven't."

"Yes, you have. When I stopped on that desert road a few nights ago, I thought I was saving you. But I was wrong. It was you who saved me."

He couldn't resist reaching out to stroke her black hair, hooking some of the ebony strands behind her ear so he could see her face and watch those tender, almond eyes gaze at him in such focused attention.

And love.

It humbled him to see that emotion directed at him, to feel it pulsing and alive within his bond to her.

"You need blood, Asher."

"Yes," he admitted. "But more than that, I just need you."

He curved his fingers around her nape and drew her close for his kiss. He could have gone on for hours without letting her go, but the worst of his wounds were still bleeding and the arousal making his heart pound even harder wasn't helping.

"Drink from me," she urged him, drawing back and gathering her hair away from her neck. "Take all you need."

God help him, he didn't have the will to refuse.

He sank his fangs into the soft column of her throat and drank, then drank some more. Her blood rejuvenated him instantly, mending torn flesh and muscle, repairing bullet-shattered bone. The rounds embedded in him were pushed out one by one. They clinked against the bathroom tiles as they fell.

On a shivery sigh, Naomi stroked her fingers in his hair and held him close as he gave himself over to the power of her healing, intoxicating red cells. As his body knit back together, desire roared through him.

He wanted her, but not here. Not like this.

When he made love to her next, he wanted to do it slowly, reverently. He wanted to make love to her as his mate.

He groaned and swept his tongue over the twin punctures, sealing them closed.

"I need you," he whispered against her skin, his voice rough with emotion. "Not just in my blood, Naomi. But in my life forever."

He pulled back and took her face in his palms, his transformed eyes bathing her milky skin in a warm amber glow. "I love you so much. For a few minutes tonight, I didn't know if I was ever going to be able to tell you that again. When I saw Slater take you up in that elevator and I wasn't able to reach you in time . . . fuck. I was so afraid I was going to lose you."

She shook her head, leaning forward to kiss him. "I love you too, Asher. I never want anything to separate us."

"Nothing will," he assured her, then blew out a harsh breath. "I was so damn proud of you tonight. Even though it scared me shitless to see you take Slater on the way you did, I was in awe of you, the fact that you don't run from any challenge. No matter how much I might wish you would."

She laughed softly, pressing her forehead to his. "I guess I'm a lot like my mom. It's strange how much I realize that now. I thought she was weak, but Slater's confession proved just the opposite. She stood up to him. In the end, she took him on too. And he killed her for it."

Asher cursed, fury flaring in his gut. "I wanted to make him suffer in his final moments."

"I know," she whispered. "I saw what you did . . . with your gift."

He couldn't deny it. "That was the first time I ever savored a death. Now, every time I think about what he did to you and to Michael, even to your mother, I'll remember his horror. I'll remember his hopelessness and I'll like it."

"Asher." She caressed his cheek, her gaze tender. Then she bent her head and began to kiss the patches of his chest and torso that weren't riddled with mending wounds.

"You've healed me, Naomi. In places you can't see too. But you've also ruined me. I never want to know what it's like to live a day without you in my life."

She looked up at him. "I'm not going anywhere. This is home. Right here," she said, lifting her head to kiss his mouth. "And right here." She placed a kiss to the base of his throat, then another to the center of his chest, where his heart banged strongly behind his sternum. "And right here."

Asher smirked. "Keep going. I'm all yours."

She laughed and stood up, taking his hand as she

reached into the shower and turned on the water.

"Let's work on the rest of you first. But I definitely want to come back to that idea."

CHAPTER 27

Naomi stepped out of the master bedroom wearing Asher's T-shirt, her hair still damp from the shower. As much as she wanted to lose herself in the comfort and passion of his arms, her thoughts were also on the little girl inside the house with them.

She crept up the hallway and smiled to find Penny sound asleep on the sofa, Sam's big body wedged tight against her on the thin cushions. The child slept as if she hadn't had a good rest for weeks, and maybe she hadn't. As quietly as she could, Naomi walked over and retrieved a crocheted afghan and placed it over both the snoring dog and the girl.

She stepped back, simply gazing at the peaceful scene, her heart clenched with contentment.

"Hey." Asher's low whisper caressed her senses as he came to stand beside her in nothing but a loose-fitting pair of gym pants. His wounds were all but vanished now, the worst of them nothing but raised pink marks on his golden skin. "Sam's in his glory."

Naomi nodded. "I can't stop thinking about the rest of them. The other kids back in the city."

He placed a soft kiss to her shoulder. "We'll go back tomorrow night, as soon as the sun's down."

"What if we don't find them all, Asher?"

"Then we'll go back again the next night, and the one after that. Until we bring them all home."

"Home," she murmured, turning to look at him. "I like the sound of that."

"Me too." He lifted her chin and brushed his lips over hers. "Come with me, Naomi. The girl will be asleep until morning."

He brought her back to the bedroom and closed the door silently behind them.

His kisses were passionate, yet tender. Reverent. Worshipful.

As weary as she was from their ordeal, his mouth on hers awakened a feverish desire. She wanted him. Each touch left her on fire. Each kiss left her desperate for more.

And he wanted her too.

Naomi slid her hand beneath the slack waistband of his pants and took his length in her grasp. He was pure steel as she stroked him, yet velvet and hot against her palm. When he reached under her T-shirt to caress her breasts, she sagged against him. Then he moved his hand to the drenched and aching juncture of her thighs and she was lost, whimpering softly with longing.

There was no hesitation once he brought her to their bed. He entered her with a long, slow stroke that nearly made her come on the spot. They made love quietly, chasing a swift, shared release that left both of them shuddering with the intensity of their need for each other.

It was some time before either of them moved or spoke. Naomi had never felt more joy in all her life. Nor more fulfillment. But her thoughts kept coming back to Slater and the unforgivable price Michael had paid for participating in her pointless quest for vengeance.

The souvenir tote bag full of Slater's money sat in the corner of the bedroom. She stared at it, hating the sight of it now.

"I can't keep any of his money," she murmured. "I meant it when I said I didn't want anything from Slater, not even the money."

Asher rose up on his elbow and gave her a sober nod. "We don't need it."

"We don't, right? We'll figure it all out. I can get work somewhere." She smirked at him. "Work that doesn't require wigs or a dozen fake IDs. I'm going to go totally legit from this point on."

He smiled. "You don't have to worry about that."

"Yes, I do. Taking care of half a dozen kids doesn't come cheap, Asher."

"I realize that," he admitted. "And correct me if I'm wrong, but aren't we going to make room for more than that? I was thinking we've got room here at the ranch for at least eight to start. More, once I outfit the spare rooms with some of Ned's furniture and make a few more bunkbeds. At some point, we could even add an addition to the house."

"Are you serious?" Naomi stared at him. "I love that idea. But, Asher, unless you've discovered gold out here or you're sitting on some oil rights, I don't think we're going to be able to do any of that."

"I don't have either of those things."

"Then what?"

"When Ned died, he left me this house and the land that came with it. He left me that beat-up truck and that old yellow dog out there too. But he also left me something else."

He rolled off the mattress and strode gloriously naked over to the bureau and took something out of the top drawer. In his hand was an envelope bearing the return address of a bank in Las Vegas. He handed it to Naomi.

"Open it."

She tore it open and pulled out the folded sheet of paper inside. "It's a bank statement from last month with your name on it." Her gaze drifted to the account total. "Holy shit. That's a lot of digits."

He chuckled. "We'll get by. We'll more than get by."

"But where did—"

"One of Ned's passions was making furniture. Another was playing the lottery every week without fail. Two years after Ruth died, he hit big. A million and a half, plus change."

"Oh, my God." Naomi sat back against the pillows, her fingers trembling as she stared at the total again, which had compounded with interest into a figure teetering near twice that amount.

"He didn't spend a penny of it," Asher said. "He told me that without Ruth around to enjoy it with him, what did he need it for? I don't think anything would please the old man more than to know his windfall was going to help give a bunch of kids a new start in life."

She couldn't believe what she was seeing, what she

was hearing. "Asher, I don't know what to say."

He sat down on the edge of the bed, his gaze intense. "Say you'll let me share it with you—and those kids. However many you want."

An image flashed through her thoughts—through her heart and soul. She saw Asher and her some years into the future, a house full of chattering, wild kids and a ranch full of animals. She saw herself holding a tiny baby in her arms, one with beautiful *glyphs* like his father and her own black hair and tilted almond eyes.

Asher nodded. "I want it too. I want the whole thing... with you, my amazing Narumi... as my woman and partner, the only friend I'll ever need. As my blood-bonded mate."

Her throat clogged with joy. "I can't think of anything I want more."

A low groan vibrated in Asher's chest as he moved closer to her and brought his wrist up to his mouth. With eyes flashing bright and hot, his pupils as thin as razors, he sank his fangs into the corded muscles and tendons and opened his vein for her.

"Drink," he said tenderly. "Be mine forever."

"Asher," she whispered, lowering her head to accept his gift—and his bond. "I have been yours all along."

He dropped his head back on a hissed curse as she took the first sip. His blood rushed hot and tingling across her tongue.

Each swallow was a revelation, sending heat and power roaring into her with the force of a tidal wave.

She moaned and took some more, her thirst uncoiling, awakening something inside her that she never even knew existed.

It was *him*... Asher.

She felt him in her senses, in her marrow, in every shimmering, unfurling particle of her being.

She felt his love braiding together with hers as their bond took hold.

Asher eased her back down onto the bed beneath him and entered her while she fed, her hungry mouth still latched on to his wrist.

She couldn't get enough of him, this incredible Breed male.

Her man.

Her love.

Her eternal mate.

CHAPTER 28

Four weeks later

Asher hammered the last nail into place and stood back with a grunt of satisfaction.

"What do you think, guys?"

Five young boys stood in a semicircle in the wood shop, assessing the newly finished bunkbed they'd all worked on together. Max, the oldest of the dark-haired twins, mirrored Asher's stance, with his hands cocked on his hips and his hammer dangling from the loop on his belt.

"Looks good and strong to me."

His brother Billy nodded in enthusiastic agreement. "I like it."

Another nod from Juan, who stood between Tyler and the newest kid to move out to the ranch, a shy twelve-year-old named Kevin.

Asher met the kid's uncertain gaze. "You think this'll work for you, Kev?"

"Yeah," he murmured, trying to hide his smile.

Rather than run the ranch as a shelter, he and Naomi had decided to make it a true home. Guardianship papers were in process with the state for Penny and the four boys, and if Kevin decided to stick around, they would soon be adding him to the official family roster too.

While it could normally take months, if not years, for adoption cases to clear the courts, Asher and Naomi had a little help on their side in the form of a certain JUSTIS officer who'd since become a friend. Rachel Reynolds had not only swept the investigation of Slater's death under the rug, but had also made sure none of the surveillance footage taken at Moda that night survived.

As for Slater's money, Naomi had donated it to a family shelter in the city—including the million-plus casino prize she inherited from Michael as the only beneficiary listed in his will. His house was razed and the lot would soon be repurposed into a neighborhood park.

Asher smiled at the boys and clapped Max on the shoulder. "Think we should go get Naomi and Penny so they can check out our work?"

"Sure," Max said. "Then will you show me how to carve detail work like you're doing with that piece over there?"

Asher nodded, glancing at the new project he'd been working on solo for the past couple weeks. It was covered with a sheet to keep Naomi from getting nosy about the gift he was making for her, but he'd already shared the secret with the boys.

"Yeah, buddy. I'll be glad to teach you what I know."

Max gave him a rare grin. "Awesome."

With the new bunk finished and three others in place in the spare bedrooms, they had ample space for everyone—plus a few more. Asher had a feeling it wouldn't take long to fill these new beds and the extra room in the house. If he had his way, within a year he and Naomi would also be filling the crib he planned to surprise her with as soon as it was finished.

"Let's go, guys."

He led the group of boys out to the porch, where Naomi had gone with Penny and Sam earlier to watch the sunset. But they must have ventured out onto the property at some point between then and now. Asher didn't worry; he could feel his Breedmate in each beat of his contented heart.

Dusk had settled over the desert, casting everything in a cool blue hue that was neither day nor night. His favorite hour. He smiled as he spotted the girls and the dog coming in from a small patch of ground on the western side of the property, where Naomi had spent the past week or so transplanting flowering cacti and succulents.

Last night, Asher had helped her place two small headstones next to the sun-beaten pair that had stood there for years longer. Now Naomi's mother and Michael had a place with them, too, along with Ned and Ruth, who would be considered family for as long as Asher lived.

Naomi's smile as she approached sent warmth into every cell and bone in his body. As well as a few other places.

"It's such a beautiful evening," she said, greeting him with a brief kiss. "Penny and I decided to take a walk and pick some wildflowers for my mom and Ruth. How's the furniture-making coming along?"

Billy was first to answer. "We finished the bunkbed and it looks awesome!"

Naomi rewarded all five boys with a bright smile. "That's great news. I can't wait to see it."

Typical of kids, they were already distracted by Sam, who'd found a stick and was now begging someone to play with him. Within moments, the group took off together along with Penny, taking turns tossing Sam's new favorite toy in the front yard.

Asher glanced at Naomi, watching her delight as she observed the giggling pack of rambunctious children.

"Look how happy they are, Asher."

He grunted and drew her close. "I like looking at how happy you are."

"I am," she said, glancing up at him. "I never knew I could be this happy. I didn't realize how good it could feel to finally be home."

He kissed her, ignoring the groans and shouts of, "Eww, gross!" from Tyler and Billy out in the yard.

"I love you," he told his mate. "The home that makes me happiest is the one I see in your eyes."

Naomi's gaze held his in the soothing calm of the rising darkness. "Come sit with me for a while," she said.

Then she took his hand and led him back toward their house, where Ned's pair of hand-carved rockers waited for them on the porch.

~ * ~

The Hunters are here!

Presenting the second novel in the-new Midnight
Breed spinoff series

Hunter Legacy ~ Book 2

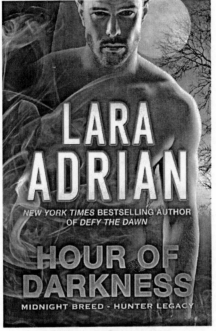

Hour of Darkness
Coming Summer 2018

Thrilling standalone vampire romances from Lara Adrian
set in the Midnight Breed story universe.

For information on this series and more, visit:

www.LaraAdrian.com

Discover the Midnight Breed
with a FREE eBook

Get the series prequel novella
A Touch of Midnight
FREE in eBook at most major retailers

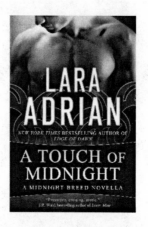

After you enjoy your free read, look for Book 1

Watch for the next book in the bestselling
Midnight Breed Series from Lara Adrian!

Break the Day

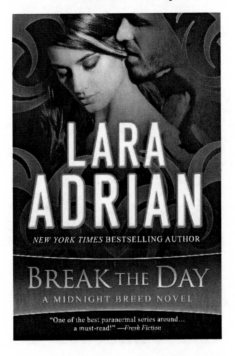

Available Fall 2018

eBook * Paperback * Unabridged audiobook

**For more information on the series and upcoming
releases, visit:**

www.LaraAdrian.com

Pick up the latest book in the bestselling
Midnight Breed Series from Lara Adrian!

Claimed in Shadows

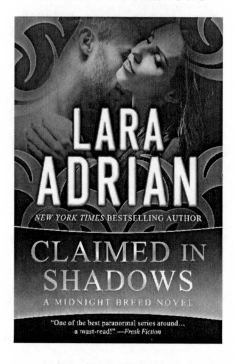

Available Now!

eBook * Paperback * Unabridged audiobook

**For more information on the series and upcoming
releases, visit:**

www.LaraAdrian.com

Never miss a new book from Lara Adrian!

Sign up for the email newsletter at
www.LaraAdrian.com

Or type this URL into your web browser:
http://bit.ly/LaraAdrianNews

Be the first to get notified of Lara's new releases, plus be eligible for special subscribers-only exclusive content and giveaways that you won't find anywhere else.

Bonus!
When you confirm your subscription, you'll get an email with instructions for requesting free bookmarks and other fun goodies, while supplies last.

Sign up today!

Turn the page for an excerpt from former Hunter Scythe's story in the Midnight Breed vampire romance series

Midnight Unbound

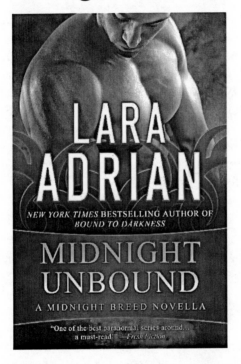

Available now in ebook, trade paperback and unabridged audiobook

For more information on the series and upcoming releases, visit:

www.LaraAdrian.com

A lethal Breed warrior is called upon by his brethren in the Order to bodyguard a beautiful young widow he's craved from afar in this new novella in the "steamy and intense" (Publishers Weekly) Midnight Breed vampire romance series from New York Times and #1 international bestselling author Lara Adrian.

As a former Hunter bred to be a killing machine in the hell of Dragos's lab, Scythe is a dangerous loner whose heart has been steeled by decades of torment and violence. He has no room in his world for love or desire--especially when it comes in the form of a vulnerable, yet courageous, Breedmate in need of protection. Scythe has loved--and lost--once before, and paid a hefty price for the weakness of his emotions. He's not about to put himself in those chains again, no matter how deeply he hungers for lovely Chiara.

For Chiara Genova, a widow and mother with a young Breed son, the last thing she needs is to put her fate and that of her child in the hands of a lethal male like Scythe. But when she's targeted by a hidden enemy, the obsidian-eyed assassin is her best hope for survival . . . even at the risk of her heart.

~ ~ ~

"It was such an AMAZING feeling to be diving back into the dangerous and sensual world of the Midnight Breed... If you are looking for a fast-paced, paranormal romantic suspense, full of passion and heart, look no further than MIDNIGHT UNBOUND."
—Shayna Renee's Spicy Reads

Chapter 1

Scythe had been in the dance club for nearly an hour and he still hadn't decided which of the herd of intoxicated, gyrating humans would be the one to slake his thirst tonight. Music blared all around him, the beat throbbing and pulsing, compounding the headache that had been building in his temples for days.

His stomach ached, too, sharp with the reminder that it had been almost a week since he'd fed. Too long for most of his kind. For him—a Breed male whose Gen One blood put him at the very top of the food chain—a week without nourishment was not only dangerous for his own wellbeing, but for that of everyone near him as well.

From within the cloak of shadows that clung around the end of the bar, he watched the throng of young men and women illuminated by colored strobe lights that flashed and spun over the dance floor as the DJ rolled seamlessly from the track of one sugary pop hit to another.

This tourist dive in Bari, a seaside resort town located at the top of Italy's boot heel, wasn't his usual hunting ground. He preferred the larger cities where blood Hosts could be hired for their services and dismissed immediately afterward, but his need to feed was too urgent for a long trek to Naples.

And besides, that journey would take him past the vineyard region of Potenza—an area he made a habit of avoiding for the past few weeks for reasons he refused to consider, even now.

Hell, especially now, when blood thirst wrenched his gut and his fangs pulsed with the urge to sink into warm, tender flesh.

A snarl slid off his tongue as he let his gaze drift over the crowd again. Against his will, he locked on to a petite brunette swaying to the music on the far side of the packed club. She had her back to him, silky dark brown hair cascading over her shoulders, her small body poured into skinny jeans and cropped top that bared a wedge of pale skin at her midsection. She laughed at something her companions said, and the shrill giggle scraped over Scythe's heightened sense of hearing.

He glanced away, instantly disinterested, but the sight of her had called to mind another waifish female— one he'd been trying his damnedest to forget.

He knew he'd never find Chiara Genova in a place like this, yet there was a twisted part of him that ran with the idea, teasing him with a fantasy he had no right to entertain. Sweet, lovely Chiara, naked in his arms. Her mouth fevered on his, hungered. Her slender throat bared for his bite—

"Fuck."

The growl erupted out of him, harsh with fury. It drew the attention of a tall blonde who had parked her skinny ass on the barstool next to him fifteen minutes ago and had been trying, unsuccessfully, to make him notice her.

Now she leaned toward him, reeking of too much wine and perfume as she licked her lips and offered him a friendly grin. "You don't look like you're having much fun tonight."

He grunted and glanced her way, taking stock of her in an instant.

Human. Probably closer to forty than the short leather skirt and lacy bustier she wore seemed to suggest. And definitely not a local. Her accent was pure American. Midwest, if he had to guess.

"Wanna hear a confession?" She didn't wait for him to answer, not that he planned to. "I'm not having much fun tonight, either." She heaved a sigh and traced one red-lacquered fingernail around the rim of her empty glass. "You thirsty, big guy? Why don't you let me buy you a drink—"

"I don't drink."

Her smile widened and she shrugged, undeterred. "Okay, then let's dance."

She slid off her stool and grabbed for his hand.

When she didn't find it—when her fingers brushed against the blunt stump where his right hand used to be, a long time ago—she recoiled.

"Oh, my God. I, um... Shit." Then her intoxicated gaze softened with pity. "You poor thing! What happened to you? Are you a combat vet or something?"

"Or something." Irritation made his deep voice crackle with menace, but she was too drunk to notice.

She stepped in close and his predator's senses lit up, his nostrils tingling at the trace coppery scent of human red cells rushing beneath her skin. The rawness in his stomach spread to his veins, which now began to throb with the rising intensity of his blood thirst.

His body felt heavy and slow. The stump at the end of his wrist ached with phantom pain. His normally razor-sharp vision was blurred and unfocused.

Usually, in some dark, bizarre way, he relished the sensation of physical discomfort. It reminded him that as dead inside as he might feel—as disconnected as he had been ruthlessly trained to be as a Hunter in the hell of Dragos's laboratory—there were some things that could still penetrate the numbness. Make him feel like he was among the living.

This particular kind of pain, though, bordered on unbearable, and it was all he could do not to grab the woman and take her vein right there in the middle of the club.

"Come on. Let's get out of here."

"Sure!" She practically leaped at him. "I thought you'd never ask."

He steered her away from the bar and out the club's exit without another word. Although the Breed had been outed to their human neighbors for more than twenty years, there were few among Scythe's kind—even a stone-cold killer like him—who made a habit of feeding in public places.

His companion wobbled a bit as they stepped out into the crisp night air. "Where do you wanna go? I'm staying at a hotel just up the street. It's a shithole, but we can go there if you want to hang out for a while."

"No. My vehicle will do."

Desire lit her features as she stared up at him. "Impatient, are you?" She giggled, smacking her palm against his chest. "Don't worry, I like it."

She trailed after him across the small parking lot to his gleaming black SUV.

In some dim corner of his conscience, he felt sorry for a woman who valued herself so little that she would traipse off with a stranger who offered her nothing in return for the use of her body.

Or, in this case, her blood.

Scythe had been born nothing better than a slave. Had nearly died one. The concept of taking from someone simply because he had the physical prowess to do it pricked him with self-loathing. The least he could do was make sure that when he took he left something behind as well. The woman would be weak with an unexplainable satisfaction once he was finished with her. Since he was feeling an uncustomary twinge of pity for her, she'd also walk away with a purse fat enough to rent a room for a month in the best hotel in Bari.

"This way," he muttered, his voice nothing more than a rasp.

She took his proffered arm and grinned, but it wasn't the coy smile that had his blood heating. It was the pulse fluttering wildly in her neck beneath that creamy flesh that had his fangs elongating. They punched through his gums and he went lightheaded with the need to feed, denied for too long.

They got into his vehicle and he wasted no time. Pivoting in the seat, he reached for her with his left hand, his fingers curling around her forearm. She uttered a small, confused noise as he drew her toward him and brought her wrist to his mouth.

Her confusion faded away the second he sank his fangs into her delicate flesh.

"Oh, my God," she gasped, her cheeks flushing as her whole body listed forward.

She speared the fingers of her free hand into his long black hair, and he had to resist the urge to jerk away as blood filled his mouth. He didn't like to be touched. All he wanted to do was fill the gaping hole in his gut until the next time he was forced to feed.

She moaned, her breath coming in quick pants as he drank. He took his fill, drawing on her wrist until he could feel the energy coursing through his body, replenishing his strength, fortifying his cells.

When he was done, he closed the tiny bite marks on her skin with a dispassionate swipe of his tongue as she twitched against him breathlessly.

"Good Lord, what is this magic and where do I sign up for more?" she murmured, her chest still heaving.

He leaned back against the cushioned leather, feeling the calm begin to move over him as his body absorbed the temporary nourishment. When the woman started to shift toward him with drugged need in her eyes, Scythe reached out and placed his palm against her forehead.

The trance took hold of her immediately. He erased her memory of his bite and the desire it stirred in her. When she slumped back against her seat, he dug into the pocket of his black jeans for his money and peeled off several large bills. He tossed them in her lap, then opened the passenger door with a silent, mental command.

"Go," he instructed her through her trance. "Take the money and go back to your hotel. Stay away from this club. Find something better to do with your time."

She obeyed at once. Stuffing the bills into her purse, she climbed out of the SUV and headed across the parking lot.

Scythe tipped his head back against the seat and released a heavy sigh as his fangs began to recede. Already, the human's blood was smoothing the edge from his whole-body pain. The malaise that had been worsening for the past twenty-four hours was finally gone and this feeding would hold him for another week if he was lucky.

He started up his vehicle, eager to be back on the road to his lair in Matera. He hadn't even pulled out of the lot when his cell phone chirped from inside his coat pocket. He yanked it out with a frown and scowled down at the screen. Only three people had his number and he wanted to hear from exactly none of them right now.

The restricted call message glowed up at him and he grimaced.

Shit. No need to guess who it might be.

And as much as he might want to shut out the rest of the world, Scythe would never refuse the call of one of his former Hunter brethren.

On a curse, he jabbed the answer button. "Yeah."

"We need to talk." Trygg's voice was always a shade away from a growl, but right now the Breed warrior's tone held a note of urgency too. Scythe had heard that same note in his half-brother's voice the last time he called from the Order's command center in Rome, and he could only imagine what it meant now.

"So, talk," he prompted, certain he didn't want the answer. "What's going on?"

"The Order's got a problem that could use your specialized skills, brother."

"Fuck." Scythe's breath rushed out of him on a groan. "Where have I heard that before?"

Six weeks ago, he'd allowed Trygg to drag him into the Order's troubles and Scythe was still trying to put the whole thing behind him. As a former assassin, he didn't exactly play well with others. He damned sure wasn't interested in getting tangled up in Order business again.

But there were only a handful of people in the world who knew exactly what Scythe had endured in the hell of Dragos's Hunter program, and Trygg was one of them. They had suffered it together for years as boys, and had dealt with the aftermath as men.

Even if they and the dozens of other escaped Hunters didn't share half their DNA, their experience in the labs couldn't make for truer brothers than that. If Trygg needed something, Scythe would be there. Hell, he'd give up his other hand for any one of his Hunter brethren if they asked it of him.

Scythe's preternatural ability to sniff out trouble told him that Trygg was about to ask for something far more painful than that.

"Tell me what you need," he muttered, steeling himself for the request.

"You remember Chiara Genova?"

Scythe had to bite back a harsh laugh.

Did he remember her? Fuck, yeah, he remembered. The beautiful, widowed Breedmate with the soulful, sad eyes and broken angel's face had been the star of too many of his overheated dreams since the night he first saw her. Even now, the mere mention of her name fired a longing in his blood that he had no right to feel.

He remembered her three-year-old son Pietro, too. The kid's laugh had made Scythe's temples throb with memories he'd thought he left dead and buried behind him more than a decade ago.

"Are she and the boy all right?" There was dread in his throat as he asked it, but his flat tone gave none of it away.

"Yes. For now." Trygg paused. "She's in danger. It's serious as hell this time."

Scythe's grip on his phone tightened. The woman had been through enough troubles already, starting with the unfit Breed male she'd taken as her mate several years ago. Chiara's bastard of a mate, Sal, had turned out to be a gambler and a first-class asshole.

Unable to pay his debts, he'd wound up on the bad side of a criminal kingpin named Vito Massioni. To square up when Massioni came to collect, Sal traded his own sister, Arabella, in exchange for his life. If not for the Order in Rome—more specifically, one of their warriors, Ettore "Savage" Selvaggio—Bella might still be imprisoned as Massioni's personal pet.

As for Chiara, she was essentially made a captive of Massioni's as well. Sal's treachery hadn't saved him in the end. After his death, Chiara and her son lived at the family vineyard under the constant threat of Massioni's danger.

Six weeks ago, it had all come to a head. The Order had moved in on Massioni, taking out him and his operation... or so they'd thought. Massioni had survived the explosion that obliterated his mansion and all of his lieutenants, and he was out for blood.

Chiara and her son had ended up in the crosshairs along with Bella and Savage, putting all of them on the run. Trygg sent them to Scythe for shelter, knowing damned well that Scythe wasn't in the habit of playing protector to anyone. Least of all a woman and child.

And he still wasn't in that habit now.

Nevertheless, the question rolled off his tongue too easily. "Tell me what happened."

"According to Bella, Chiara's had the sensation she was being watched for the past week or so. Stalked from afar. Last night, things took a turn for the worst. A Breed male broke into the villa. If she hadn't heard him outside her window and had time to prepare, she'd likely have been raped, murdered, or both."

"Motherfu—" Scythe bit off the curse and took a steadying breath. His rage was on full boil, but he rallied his thoughts around gathering facts. "Did the son of a bitch touch her? How did she manage to get away?"

"Sal kept a sword hidden beneath the bed in case Massioni ever sent some muscle there to work him over for the money he owed. After he died, Chiara left the weapon in place. By some miracle of adrenaline or determination, she was able to fight the bastard off, but barely."

Holy hell. As he thought of the tiny slip of a woman trying to fight off a healthy Breed male he shook his head slowly in disbelief. The fact that she survived was beyond lucky or even miraculous, but Trygg was right. The odds of her doing it again were slim to none.

Which was, apparently, where Scythe and his specific set of skills came in. Not that it would take a request from Trygg or the Order to convince him to hunt down Chiara's attacker and make the Breed male pay in blood and anguish.

The very idea of her cowering as some animal attempted to harm her made Scythe's whole body quake with fiery rage.

"So, the Order needs me to find this bastard and tear his head off, then?"

"Just killing him isn't going to get to the root of the problem. We don't think this attack is random. The Order needs you to protect Chiara and Pietro while we work to figure out who's after her and why."

Scythe could not hold back the snarl that built in his throat. "You know I don't do bodyguard duty. Damn it, you know why too."

"Yeah," Trygg said. "And I'm still asking you to do it. You're the only one we can trust with this, brother. The Order's got all hands on deck with Opus Nostrum, Rogue outbreaks, and ninety-nine other problems at the moment. We need you."

Scythe groaned. "You ask too fucking much this time."

Protecting the woman would cost him. He knew that from both instinct and experience. For almost a score, he'd kept his feedings down to once a week. His body's other needs were kept on an even tighter leash.

He'd only spent a few hours with Chiara Genova six weeks ago, yet it was long enough to know that being under the same roof with her was going to test both his patience and his self-discipline.

But the kid? That was a no-go. There were things he just couldn't do, not even for his brother.

He mulled over Trygg's request in miserable silence.

"What's it gonna be, Scythe?"

The refusal sat on the tip of his tongue, but damned if he could spit it out. "If I do this, we do it my way. I don't answer to the Order or to anyone else. Agreed?"

"Sure, you got it. Just get your ass to Rome as soon as you can so we can go over your plan and coordinate efforts."

"What about her?" Scythe demanded. "Does Chiara know you've contacted me to help her?"

The stretch of silence on the other end of the line told him all he needed to know and he grimaced.

"Savage and Bella are bringing Chiara and Pietro in as we speak," Trygg said. "They should all be here within the hour."

Scythe cursed again, more vividly this time. "I'm on my way."

He ended the call, then threw the SUV into gear and gunned it out to the street.

MIDNIGHT UNBOUND

is available now at all major retailers in eBook, trade paperback, and unabridged audiobook.

Although this extended novella can be read as a standalone story within the series, it also connects the Midnight Breed Series with the exciting new Hunter Legacy spinoff launching Spring 2018!

Thirsty for more Midnight Breed?

Read the complete series!

. . . and more to come!

If you enjoy sizzling contemporary romance, don't miss this hot series from Lara Adrian!

For 100 Days

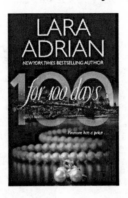

The 100 Series: Book 1

"I wish I could give this more than 5 stars! Lara Adrian not only dips her toe into this genre with flare, she will take it over . . . I have found my new addiction, this series." --The Sub Club Books

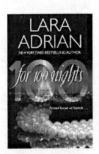 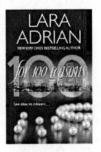

All available now in ebook, trade paperback and unabridged audiobook.

More romance and adventure from Lara Adrian!

Phoenix Code Series
(Paranormal Romantic Suspense)

"A fast-paced thrill ride." –Fresh Fiction

Masters of Seduction Series
(Paranormal Romance)

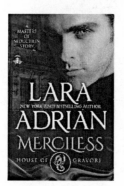
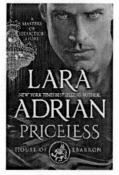

"Thrilling, action-packed and super sexy." –Literal Addiction

Award-winning medieval romances from Lara Adrian!

Dragon Chalice Series
(Paranormal Medieval Romance)

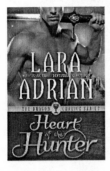

"Brilliant . . . bewitching medieval paranormal series." –Booklist

Warrior Trilogy
(Medieval Romance)

"The romance is pure gold." –All About Romance

ABOUT THE AUTHOR

LARA ADRIAN is a New York Times and #1 international best-selling author, with nearly 4 million books in print and digital worldwide and translations licensed to more than 20 countries. Her books regularly appear in the top spots of all the major bestseller lists including the New York Times, USA Today, Publishers Weekly, Amazon.com, Barnes & Noble, etc. Reviewers have called Lara's books "addictively readable" (Chicago Tribune), "extraordinary" (Fresh Fiction), and "one of the consistently best" (Romance Novel News).

Writing as **TINA ST. JOHN,** her historical romances have won numerous awards including the National Readers Choice; Romantic Times Magazine Reviewer's Choice; Booksellers Best; and many others. She was twice named a Finalist in Romance Writers of America's RITA Awards, for Best Historical Romance (White Lion's Lady) and Best Paranormal Romance (Heart of the Hunter). More recently, the German translation of Heart of the Hunter debuted on Der Spiegel bestseller list.

Visit the author's website and sign up for new release announcements at www.LaraAdrian.com.

Find Lara on Facebook at
www.facebook.com/LaraAdrianBooks

Connect with Lara online at:

www.LaraAdrian.com

www.facebook.com/LaraAdrianBooks

www.goodreads.com/lara_adrian

www.twitter.com/lara_adrian

www.instagram.com/laraadrianbooks

www.pinterest.com/LaraAdrian

CPSIA information can be obtained
at www.ICGtesting.com
Printed in the USA
LVOW11s0831190418
574072LV00004B/91/P